KINSHIP COVE: BOOKS & BAES

THE COMPLETE COLLECTION

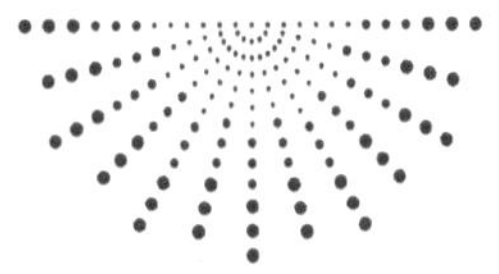

ELLIS LEIGH

BIBLIOPHILE AND THE BEAST

KINSHIP COVE: BOOKS & BAES

Kinship Cove loves a good story—especially a fairy tale retelling—which is why their library is a popular place to be. Welcome to the Kinship Cove library where the local librarian is about to find a happily ever after in the stacks.

As the local house cat shifter, I have three things I adore about my little Kinship Cove life—working at the town library, listening to podcasts about true crime, and dipping into a little catnip on a Friday night. So, imagine my dismay when a man with predator energy and hair the color of a sky on fire comes strolling into my research section and comments on my Dewey decimal system. But when his eyes meet mine and the string of destiny tugs us together, I know this is my fated mate.

There are just a couple of problems.

He's far too big and dangerous for a little house cat like me. Too predatory for my level of prey. He's also completely obsessed with me.

What's it going to take for an introvert like me to tame such a beast?

And what will I do if I find out that taming him isn't a possibility?

BRITTANI

You ever just have one of those days when you remember why you really don't like most people? If you've ever worked retail or in food service, I know you have. I was right there with all my brethren slinging fries and refolding shirts, except I worked at the public library.

"Excuse me." A woman—short, round, tiny hands, beady eyes—came barging into my office and rapped her fist against my desk. "I need to talk to you."

I tugged out an earbud, paused the podcast I'd been listening to, and pasted on my most professional smile. "Yes, ma'am. How can I help you?"

"You shouldn't be allowed to wear those things in here. You can't hear your customers."

"I'm not in a customer-facing position, ma'am." I nodded toward the circulation desk across the room. "The man at the desk over there—the one under the Information sign—is here to help customers find what they need."

"But you're closer." She rolled her eyes and coughed one of those angry huffs, as if I'd somehow insulted her by letting her know customers could retrieve information at the information desk. "I need to find a book."

I sat back, eyebrows raised. "You're in the right place for that."

Because—again—library.

"It's a particular book. One of the ones that romance writer who writes a lot wrote. The real famous one."

Danielle Steele, Nora Roberts, Beverly Jenkins, Jackie Collins, Brenda Jackson…names began to fill up my brain, the mystery of whom this woman was talking about piquing my interest.

"Well, romance is up on the—"

"It's not a romance novel."

My mind screeched to a stop. "It's not a romance novel, but it's written by a famous romance novelist."

"Yes. It's a mystery. There's a couple of cops in the city. New York. Or maybe Chicago. I can't remember."

That was about as unhelpful as *it's by that one romance author.* "Okay, so mysteries—"

"They're married, you see. The detectives. Married detectives are the main characters in—"

"The In Death series by Nora Roberts writing as J.D. Robb." I picked up my earbud, ready to get back to work and listening to murdery words. "The first book is *Naked in Death* and can be found in the paperback area of the mystery section."

"I don't want paperback."

Of course she didn't. "Well, you can borrow an electronic version. The library—"

"Eh, that's not reading." She huffed again. She was a major huffer. "Kids today, reading on their phones. That's not real reading."

I would beg to differ, but arguing was not my goal. Getting her away from me was my goal. "What format are you looking for?"

"Hardcover, of course. Large print, too. Size matters in font, you know? I like them big."

There were so many things to say to that. I chose the high road—waking up my computer so I could see if we even had a large print, hardcover version of the book and ignoring the innuendo. I tapped a few keys and hit enter, searching both our own collection and the regional database.

"Jackpot."

"You have it?"

"No. But it's in the region." I printed off a sheet of paper with the information Ms. Size-Matters would need and handed it to her. "Take this to the man at the information desk. He can order the book for you."

"You can't do that for me here?"

"No, ma'am. I don't have access to the borrowing system back here."

Another huff, though this time as she turned to walk away. "I don't know why you're in a customer service office if you can't actually help the customers."

I didn't have the heart to tell her nowhere on my office plaque did the words Customer Service reside, so I let her believe Library Director and Head of Collection Development somehow meant what she thought it did. She rolled on out the door, heading for the information desk where poor Matthew—children's librarian and the head of our IT —sat. I sent the man a quick text.

Incoming. She's a huffer.

I watched him look down then immediately back up, his eyes coming my way. They picked up on Ms. Size-Matters right away, and he shot me a nasty glare before refocusing on her and her huffing needs. I would have watched, but I was already over it. Plus, I still had work, a lot of work, to do. Collection development and curation—selecting the books we'd house and what formats to buy them in—was my job. Matthew and I worked closely together on the children's book offerings, but the rest was placed solely in my lap. I had a budget, a need for new product, and unfettered access to almost every book ever written.

I shopped for books for a living, which truly was as amazing as it sounded.

Earbuds in, podcast picked up where I'd left off, and catalog of upcoming releases before me, I got back to work. Women's fiction, mystery, horror, literary, crafts…the books racked up dollars in my cart. I preferred nonfiction myself—leaning far into the world of true crime —but my customers preferred lighter fare. Still, I spent a good thirty minutes looking over the upcoming true crime releases and plotting my buying strategy. Some would be needed at the library, but most I'd be purchasing on my own for my personal collection.

I was halfway through the nonfiction catalogs when Matthew popped his head in.

"I'm heading down to close the computer lab. You'll be all alone up here."

Up here, as in the second floor. And all alone in Kinship Cove was not nearly as dangerous as he made it sound. "Thanks. I'll meet you downstairs at closing."

He gave the doorframe two pats then turned and left. If he was shutting down the lab, that meant the library was likely empty. A quick glance at my phone confirmed that it *was* awfully close to closing time, but that was really more for customers than employees. I had stuff to do.

I dove back into work, determined to finish the single catalog I had left while listening to a true crime podcast about my favorite serial killer. Not favorite because he murdered people—that was horrific and awful. Favorite because of the story behind him, the way he killed, what happened after he was caught. Those were the details that kept me coming back to true crime. That and the absolutely amazing tales of survival often woven into the depravity. Mary Vincent, you know?

A good twenty minutes of focused work, and I was finished. I was just about to close up—and reaching the pinnacle of the Night Stalker case where Richard Ramirez was about to be found out—when a shadow passed in front of my door. I looked up, prepared to see Matthew again, but found myself watching a man who was definitely not Matthew walk into the stacks across the room. I checked my computer for the time—two minutes until closing—and rose to my feet. My stomach clenched and my body had gone a little cold, the knowledge of being alone on the floor with a strange man late at night bringing out my fear response.

It's Kinship Cove. Nothing bad happens here.

Which is likely what a lot of victims said of their own small towns.

It was time to investigate. I snuck out of my office, slipping between the bookshelves and slowly working my way across the floor. Being a cat shifter—domestic, not big—meant I had decent hunting skills. I could hear a mouse scurry from across the room and could knock threats off countertops like a boss. Stalking an actual human being? Much harder. Especially in Kinship Cove, a town filled with shifters of all varieties. The man could have the senses of whatever animal he shifted into, which could be bad for me. But I couldn't stop following him. My hunter mode had been activated, and nothing but a confirmed sign of danger would dissuade me from following him.

Totally ignoring a thing or obsessed to the point of distraction—there was no in-between for me.

The man made it halfway across the library before I caught up with him. I was just sneaking around the corner of the aisle he was in—Section 301, Social Sciences—when he suddenly appeared. He'd tricked me, that wily man. I had assumed he'd exit toward the stairs at the other end, but he'd turned around and scuttled toward the back of the room instead. My cover was blown, my investigation over, my...

Balance. It no longer worked.

When the man rounded the corner, he startled me. I jumped and lost my balance, landing on my feet but still falling forward. The man caught me, his big hand grasping my arm and holding me up. I was humiliated to have been caught and to have nearly fallen, so I coughed and pulled away, moving to straighten the skirt I was wearing.

"So sorry about that," I said, finally ready to have him be mad about my following him or laugh at me. I looked up his tall body, my eyes landing on his chin. "I was coming to tell you that the library is—"

I made it to *is* before I actually looked all the way up to his face. First, the man was handsome. Like, really, really handsome. Reddish hair with enough gray in it to speak of experience in the world, a chiseled jaw that could have sold cologne in any country, and big, dark eyes with laser-like focus. All of that was a bit of a shocker. Second, and much more surprising, was the fact that I felt the tug of fate the second his eyes met mine. That was unexpected, to say the least.

"Oh." Yes, I was a brilliant conversationalist. I was also reduced to a puddle by those dark eyes and the way his lips had turned up into a half smile. "I...uh..."

"Are you all right?"

I shivered. Totally shivered from head to toe. Unfortunately, the man was still holding on to my arm, which meant he felt my tremble. How embarrassing.

I pulled out of his hold and took a step back, needing a little space. A little air. "I'm fine, of course. As I was saying, the library is about to close. I'd be happy to help you acquire the books you're hunting for if you're having trouble."

He held up a tome, that smile firmly in place. "Found it. God bless the Dewey decimal system."

"Indeed." So…that was it. All I had. My brain refused to offer me any assistance in the small-talk category, which meant I was fully stuck in librarian mode. "Well, if you'll come with me, I can get you checked out."

"Of course." He held out an arm, indicating I should lead the way. I slipped past him, my steps quick and long. I'd just met my mate, but he was acting as if nothing had happened. So was I, apparently. Was this some sort of trick? A game the fates were playing on me? Tease the silly kitty with exactly what everyone wants but make it impossible to seize? First, they put me in the body of a house cat with the instincts of a tiger or something, making me more snuggly than feared. It infuriated me to no end to have people pick me up and try to rub my belly when I was in full hunt mode. Second, they throw this man—who was so handsome it hurt, who had a voice that felt like silk against my skin, and who smelled amazing—right at me like some sort of carcass to gnaw on, before yanking him away. How could they be so cruel? How could they—

He grabbed my hand.

I nearly fell forward, the momentum dragging my body out of balance once again as he…held my hand. Just held it, standing there between two bookshelves with no one else around. Pretty sure my heart was about to beat right out of my chest.

"Sir, I—"

"My name is Griff." He lifted my hand to his lips, turning it so he was presented with the back. "I'm doing this entire thing wrong, but you surprised me. So, I want you to know that my name is Griff, and I felt that connection, too."

Oh. So, he… Okay. He wasn't being yanked away. Got it. Good. Now I just needed to—

He kissed the back of my hand, and my entire body shivered again. By the smug little smile he shot me, he felt that one too. My nervous system was fully betraying me tonight.

"It's nice to meet you, Griff. I'm Brittani."

"That's a beautiful name." He tugged me a little closer, almost leaning over me. "So, tell me, Brittani. May I take you out? I'd love to have dinner tonight or even just drinks so we can get to know each other. Whatever works for you."

It was so hot in the library all of a sudden. Blazingly so. My face and neck were on fire from the excessive heat. I opened my mouth to accept, had fully intended to say yes to dinner with this handsome man, when Matthew appeared at the end of the row.

"You okay back here, Britt?"

Griff spun, practically shoving me against the shelf and placing his body firmly in front of mine. I would have been thrilled with that move —let's be real, the daring Prince Charming protecting his woman was an intriguing trope—but then he growled. Long and loud and way too aggressively for the situation. The rumble coming from his chest, the way the sound filled the room, it screamed predator. And if the way Matthew—a massive wolf shifter with instincts much sharper than mine—reacted, if the look of pure rage and hostility that crossed over his face and the returning growl he released were any indication, Griff wasn't just a predator. He was an apex predator. A threat to even Matthew.

And I was nothing but a tame little kitty cat.

"Stop!" I pushed past Griff, jumping between the two men. "Both of you, just stop."

The growls ceased, the library once again going silent. Still, I was filled with the weight of something close to dread. Maybe disappointment. Or maybe just the realization that the fates really were being cruel to me. A domesticated kitty and an apex predator were an absolutely ridiculous match. It was as if the fates were playing a wicked joke on me, with my heart being the punch line.

"Check him out, then lock up," I said, directing my statement to Matthew. I noticed Griff's head whip in my direction, felt his stare on my body. I refused to look up into those eyes, though. I knew better. One look, and I'd fold. One glance, and I'd follow him to a dinner that would lead to sex that would lead to mating that would lead to... nothing. Death. Murder at the hands of a hunter whose instincts would eventually dictate his actions.

I wasn't about to become some sort of case study on my true crime podcast. *She thought she'd found love, but there was no controlling the simmering rage of her predator mate.* No thanks.

Griff tried, though. He stepped closer, reaching for me. "Brittani, I—"

But there was only one thing left to say. "We're closed."

2

BRITTANI

You are an idiot.

That was the thought that played on repeat through my mind as I walked home from the library. It was dark outside, and the streets were pretty well empty. Good thing, considering a tear or two fell when I couldn't control them. I really was an idiot—the fates had thrown that man, Griff, my fated mate, right in front of me, and I'd kicked him out and told him I wouldn't go on a date with him. Why? *Why?*

Okay, fine—I knew why. But I was allowed a little pity party after all that.

I made it home without incident—not surprising—and unlocked the door to my cottage around the corner from the best bakery in the history of the world. Seriously, their Breton butter cakes were to die for. I would need one or twelve in the morning to get over the fact that I had tossed my mate aside without so much as a chance to get to know him.

I released the resin stabber I kept on my key ring from between my fingers and recapped my pepper spray, turned off the app that would alert the police if I didn't follow the exact route I had set up, and laid all my work stuff on the foyer table. Next came the locks and alarm— engaging one and switching the other from away to home once I entered my code. A quick sweep of the rooms and a double-checking of the locks and windows was all it took to finally relax. I was home—no serial killers or apex predators around to try to kidnap me. I then sent one text for the evening to my friend Margaret, who was also single and lived alone.

I'm safe.

Her response came two seconds later.

Everything locked up?

As if I would forget.

Of course.

I was in the kitchen warming up some milk for a before-bed snack when she responded again.

Good. A new episode of MFM just released, and there's a discussion on the Discord about a current serial killer in Tampa. Fascinating stuff. Chat later.

And so, my night ended the same way they usually did—me alone, drinking warm milk to relax, being entertained by true crime, and chatting online with other people who found serial killers as fascinating as I did. Not fascinating in a good way—it was still a disgusting act that broke my heart and often left me in tears. Fascinating in an educational way. I was a domesticated hunter without the instincts or abilities to fight off a threat. Heck, even the armadillo shifters could roll up in a ball and pretend to be dead if provoked. I had nothing but speed and smarts.

True crime podcasts, discussions, books, and documentaries were educational resources for me.

But even as I listened and tried my best to relax, my mind spun back to the incident with Griff. To the disappointment that had gutted me when he'd growled. I had never given much thought to having a mate and what they would be like, but my first assumption was that they wouldn't want to kill me. Apex predators had instincts to kill everyone, and I had no strong defense against them.

"Okay," I said to myself when it was simply too much to keep wondering and worrying and replaying those moments with Griff. "This is over. We need to sleep."

I hopped up and began my nightly bedtime routine—washing my dishes, putting my blankets and pillows back where they belonged, tucking away the little furry mice I chased for exercise, and doing one final sweep of all the doors and windows in my house to make sure I was secure. I then headed into my bedroom, shut and locked the door, and engaged the alarm with motion detectors.

"Time to sleep."

But sleep didn't come easily. I was lying in bed, staring at the wall with images of Griff in all his moppy-haired glory dancing through my head and wondering exactly how old he was, when a shadow that shouldn't have been there appeared. I was wide awake in an instant, staring at the dark spot and trying really hard to make sense of it.

"Maybe a car drove by," I whispered, needing my voice to stay calm. "Or parked. Yeah, it's not moving. A car pulled up and parked. That has to be it. It would move if it were a person. No one stands still—"

The shadow moved.

I leaped to my feet, bounding halfway across the room without even thinking of moving. My eyesight sharpened, and a low rumble formed in my chest. Not like Griff's—no way. I was only a house cat, but I could growl and hiss with the best of them. I could also grab my nightstand pepper spray and my phone so I was prepared to both call the police and fight back.

But first...I had to know. I dropped to the floor and crept closer to the window, wanting to peek outside so badly. I was on my knees with the curtain in my hand when the shadow moved again. This time, I got a good glimpse of the shape—definitely humanoid.

I rolled away from the window and dialed 9-1-1, tapping the screen to connect the call.

Two rings in and a friendly female voice answered the line. "9-1-1. What's your emergency?"

I'm a simple house cat shifter living alone, and there's a scary predator outside my bedroom window.

But I couldn't really say all that. "There's a person outside my bedroom window."

"Yes, ma'am. Can you please confirm your address for me?"

I gave the woman my address as I kept my eyes locked on the shadow of the person outside. There was more movement, a back-and-forth almost. Were they...pacing?

"Okay, ma'am," the dispatcher said after just a few seconds. "I have an officer en route. I need you to stay on the line with me. Are your doors locked?"

"Definitely."

"Good. How about your windows?"

"All secure. I also have an alarm system with entry and motion detectors. I don't own a gun, but I have pepper spray and a few other personal protection devices in case they get inside."

"That's good. I'll let you know when the officer is there, so you don't pepper spray them."

"Yeah. Okay. That would be bad."

"Yes, ma'am. It would." She typed something, the clicking coming through over the call. "Do you have any idea who could be out there? Any trouble with neighbors or a previous relationship partner?"

I laughed. Whether from the absolute ridiculousness of the question or the stress of the moment, I couldn't be sure. "No. No trouble. I'm a librarian."

As if that meant I was some sort of quiet, demure woman. I wasn't—not really—but that three-word sentence seemed to help the dispatcher understand me a little better.

"Okay, ma'am. The officer is almost there. I don't want you to worry. We're coming to help."

And they did. Just seconds later, headlights lit up my bedroom, and I could hear the rumble of engines and yelling.

"I think they're here," I whispered into the phone.

"Yes, ma'am. The officer is on scene. Let's give her a minute to evaluate the situation before we make any moves, okay?"

I settled deeper into my spot beside my dresser. "Okay. I'm sitting still."

"Good. Good. Hold on for me." There was a pause, more clicking, and then she came back through. "Ma'am, the officer has the suspect in custody. She'd like you to come outside to your front porch so she can talk to you."

I took a deep breath, still shaky. Still really worried. Refusing to let that stop me from anything. "Okay. I'll be out in a minute."

I ended the call and stood up, feeling unbalanced and almost as if I were underwater. Someone had been outside. They really had been there. The officer had someone *in custody*. That was absolutely terrifying —that someone had invaded my property. I ended up wrapping a fuzzy bathrobe around myself and pocketing my pepper spray—just in case.

After turning off the alarm and disengaging all the locks to my front door, I took a deep breath and stepped outside. A woman in a thick, brown uniform jacket with a ski cap on her head greeted me from across the porch.

"Are you okay, ma'am?"

I nodded, pulling the robe tighter, my eyes darting around the area. "Where are they?"

She nodded toward her car, where a man stood. An unsecured man. As I watched, he took a step forward, an expression of chagrin on his stupid, handsome face.

"Griff?"

"I'm really sorry. I never meant to scare you, Brittani."

The officer held up a hand. "Stay over there, or you get the cuffs."

Griff put his hands up and stopped moving. Obviously following directions.

The officer turned back to me. "This man says he's your mate. Is that true?"

Oh. Oh no. "Well, yes. But...we only just met, and he's really dangerous—"

"Dangerous how? Does he have a history of abuse?"

I shook my head, bouncing my gaze from her to him. "No. I only just met him. I don't even know him." I leaned closer and lowered my voice. "He's some sort of predator—I heard him growl."

She blinked at me, not saying a word. As if that didn't register the same way with her as it did with me. Likely because she was also a predator. Wonderful.

Time to expose my soft underbelly to the world. "I'm a cat shifter." When she still didn't respond, I sighed. "House cat. Domesticated cat. I'm—"

"Ah." The officer nodded, making a note in the little pad of paper in her hand. "I understand. You feel vulnerable around larger predators."

"Yes." And they were all bigger than me. I didn't feel the need to remind her of that, though. "I met him and he growled at someone and I ran. That's all. I barely even talked—"

My heart jumped, and my blood turned cold as realization washed over me. We had hardly spoken, which meant he shouldn't have known where I lived. My fear turned hotter, meaner, and I raised my voice as I hollered, "How did you know where I live?"

Griff glanced from the officer to me and back again, flinching. "I sort of...followed you. After you left the library."

The officer raised her eyebrows. "You stalked her?"

"No." Griff moved as if to take a step forward, but the officer responded by reaching for her belt. He put his hands up and backed away again. "I wasn't stalking her in a bad way. It was late, and she walked home alone. I was worried, so I followed her to make sure she was safe."

The officer's frown didn't lessen a bit. "And why were you on her porch?"

"Yeah. Why were you on my porch?" I shrugged when the officer shot me an annoyed look. "Sorry."

Griff sighed. "It really was simply because I was worried. I've waited a long time to find my mate—knowing you were all alone in this house was too much for my instincts. I swear, I never meant to scare or hurt you. I was just guarding you."

The officer nodded in his direction, looking my way. "You believe him?"

I gave that a thought, letting what little I knew about fated matings percolate for a minute. Finally, I nodded. "Yeah. It fits a mating scenario."

"I agree." The officer slipped her notebook into her pocket and tugged her hat a little lower. "Would you like me to remove him from the property?"

Griff glanced at her, obviously unhappy with that. "Please, Brittani. I won't hurt you. If you make me leave, though, I'm going to go a little stir-crazy. The idea of you being in danger..."

He growled, coughing at the end as if to hide it. Sending ice shooting up my spine.

And warmth shooting…somewhere else.

"You don't need to hang around," I said to the officer, still feeling a bit unbalanced. "I'm safe here."

Griff shook his head. "There's no such thing as safe if I'm not there to defend you."

The officer bit back a smile, leaning closer and dropping her voice to a whisper. "He seems really sincere."

He did. But still… "He's a predator."

"I get it. If you're not comfortable, then I'm not leaving until he does. But I have a feeling a conversation would be a good tension-breaker for the evening."

She made a lot of sense, which really just irritated me even more. Still, I nodded and wrapped my arms around myself, accepting her sensible recommendation. "Okay. Fine."

"Good." She stepped back, raising her voice as she directed her words to Griff. "You've got ten minutes to talk to the lady, then I want you off her property. I'm not leaving until the lady tells me I can too."

Griff dipped his chin in acceptance, glancing up at me. "May I come up on your porch, please?"

I nodded, still tucked into my doorway. Not moving an inch closer to him. Paying attention to his approach and the officer slipping back inside her car. As promised, she didn't leave. That gave me a little more confidence in the situation.

Not a lot, though.

Griff stepped onto my porch and stopped moving, staying a good distance from me. Looking awfully contrite. "I truly am so sorry about this. I swear to you, I was only worried about your safety."

The sound of his voice so close to me made me shiver, sent a tremble throughout my body. One he obviously noticed. "Are you cold? Maybe we should—"

It was his step forward that had me pulling the pepper spray from my pocket and aiming it at him. "You are not coming inside my house."

3

GRIFF

By the fates, the woman was feisty. Standing there in nothing but a robe with that spray bottle of something I had a feeling would sting if she pressed the lever pointed right at me—she was a beautiful, brave warrior. I was not at all worthy of her.

"Of course not." I inched back once more, giving her the space she needed to relax. "As I said, I was only worried about your safety."

My brave queen raised her chin, a frown on her beautiful face. "Kinship Cove is safe."

I glanced meaningfully at the spray bottle still in her hand. "Not safe enough, apparently."

She tucked the bottle back into her pocket and recrossed her arms over her chest. "I've never had an issue. Before tonight."

I inched forward. Unable not to. Wanting so badly to touch her, scent her, feel her body against mine. To have her in my arms so I would know she was truly okay. Slow. I needed to be slow with her.

"Kinship Cove is not safe enough…for my mate."

Her expression softened a bit, and her shoulders relaxed. That was apparently what she needed—reassurance and reminders of our connection. It was in that moment, when the harshness of her fear slipped away, that I got another look at her in her natural state. She was

19

so damned beautiful. Simple in an elegant sort of way, with a healthy glow that pushed back the night. Long, straight hair and wide-set eyes accenting a petite nose and defiantly sharp chin. A pixie warrior, ready for battle. I was obsessed.

Growing up as a lion shifter in a pride filled primarily with women, I had gotten used to the flashiness of our breed. Don't get me wrong—there was beauty there as well. The jewelry, the makeup, the complex hairstyles...a female lion loved to put on a show. But I had never been more gobsmacked by someone's natural beauty the way I was with Brittani. Whether that was because she was my mate or not, I had no idea. But I would forever remember her just as she was right then—radiant in nothing but her bathrobe. No jewelry, no makeup, no garish clothing, no excess. Just her.

I couldn't take my eyes off her.

"What?" she asked, her brow slipping down in a display of confusion. "Why are you staring at me like that?"

I shook my head, unable to say anything except the truth. "You are stunningly gorgeous, and I am feeling very much like an inexperienced youth trying to impress a queen."

She ducked her head, but not before I caught her biting back a grin. I inched forward again, needing to be near her. Wanting so much to skip all the necessities and get right to the part where she loved me and was mine.

Slow, Griff. Must take it slow.

"Can I ask you a question?"

She darted her eyes my way, no longer smiling but not nearly as stiff as before. "What sort of question?"

"Will you join me for a date? Perhaps dinner."

"I told you—I'm not inviting you inside."

I put my hands up. "No, no. Dinner at the hotel where I'm staying. They have a lovely wine list, and the food really is delicious. I would bring you to the restaurant—a public place. No funny business."

She stared me down, my fiery queen. "If I agree to go out with you, will you leave my property?"

My head was shaking a no before I could stop it. "I told you. I'm here for your safety."

Those eyes—so bright and colorful, swirling with greens and yellows—rolled. "And I told you. I'm safe."

I couldn't help myself. I growled low and deep, moving closer. Practically pinning her against the doorframe while still not touching her. Just...crowding.

If I touched her at all, I'd lose total control.

"You are my mate, Brittani. My only true love connected by the fates. If you think for one second that I'm going to risk you in any way, you don't know the type of man I am."

She took a deep breath, staring up at me with wide eyes. "I don't... I only just met you."

"So, get to know me. Over dinner." I dared to tempt my control, running a single finger down her cheek. Nearly vibrating in my need for more. My inner lion roared in my mind, but I held strong, not letting him out. Not allowing his voice to scare our queen again. Not until I was certain I had him under lock and key did I continue my request. "I promise I will make it worth your time."

Brittani stared up at me, not speaking. Not demanding or pushing or treating me the way the lionesses in my pride did. So quiet and calm, so fierce without the need to scream it. I had never been more impressed with a woman in my life, and she would destroy me if she refused my offer.

Finally, she gave me a single head nod. "Fine."

A growl slipped out—one of happiness and pride. I gave Brittani her space, moving backward across the porch so the sound of my lion wouldn't cause her to withdraw again. "Really?"

Another nod. "Yes, but only if you get off my property so I can sleep."

I hopped down, throwing my arms wide. Unable to stop my grin. "Step one—I am off the porch, my queen."

Off the porch and not nearly close enough to keep her safe, my lion whispered in my brain, causing that irrational need to protect to come roaring back.

"You need to lock up," I said, my voice tight with the sudden urge I had to grab her and tuck her into my arms. To secure her in my den so no one could get close to her. All things I needed to resist for fear of scaring her. "I will get off your property if you go inside and lock up."

"I always lock my doors."

"I need to hear the latch engage to be sure."

She rolled her eyes again, raising her arm to wave to the officer still seated in her car. "I'm good. He's leaving. You can go."

The officer flashed her lights before slowly backing up, leaving Brittani and me alone in the darkness.

"Good night, Griff," Brittani said, stepping inside her house. "Off my property."

"The second I hear the click of the lock."

She shut the door—a little harder than necessary, in my opinion— and engaged the lock. The click practically exploded through the quiet night. It wasn't enough in my mind, though. Still, I did as I had promised. I left her property. In fact, I left her property and settled on to mine.

Brittani reopened the door within a minute.

"Sitting on your car is not much better than being on my porch."

"You told me to leave your property." I waved my arm, indicating my car, which was parked on the street in front of her house. "I am not on your property."

"You are ridiculous."

"And you are supposed to be inside that locked house and resting. You need your sleep if you're going to join me for breakfast."

She took a single step outside once more, mouth open and eyebrows furrowed. "Breakfast? You asked me out for dinner."

I leaned back, supporting my weight on a single hand behind me. "Yes. We're doing that, too."

"I didn't agree to—"

"Trust me," I said, shooting her a grin. "I'll make it worth your while."

My radiant queen stood stock-still, staring at me for a long moment before she asked, "What sort of shifter are you?"

"Lion, my love. King of the jungle."

"Huh. With all your trickery, I would have guessed a hyena."

That was…well, insulting. "A hyena? With this mane?" I ran a hand through my messy hair. "I'd say I'm insulted, but I almost think that was the point."

Brittani didn't answer me. Instead, she stepped back inside her house and slammed the door, engaging the lock. I spotted her shadow through the sheer curtains of what must have been her bedroom, but then nothing. No noises, no lights, no movement. My queen had indeed taken to her bed.

A place I hoped to join her in. Soon. Once I made sure she understood the power of her lion mate.

Hyena. As if.

Instead of sitting on my car being useless, I pulled out my phone and typed a message to the concierge at the hotel, making sure to notify him that I would be bringing a guest for breakfast and requesting a secluded table. After that, I lay back and let my lion take over more of my senses. Let his sense of smell and hearing grow within me. I hadn't been joking when I'd said I wanted to keep her safe. Finding my mate had left me downright giddy, and I would do anything—kill anyone—whom I saw as a threat to that happiness. I had waited a long time for my queen.

No one would be taking her away from me.

Especially not before I had convinced the gentle creature to love me back.

Remembering the fire in her eyes, the weapon in her hand, and the way she had bickered with me only secured my conviction that we were meant to be together.

I simply had my work cut out for me in getting her to admit that.

4

BRITTANI

If I were chatting with my true crime friends, they'd have said walking into a hotel to meet a man I barely knew for a meal was likely asking for trouble. Thankfully, I hadn't found the time to chat with them that morning. I did, of course, find time to text Margaret with my location.

At the Seaside Hotel. I will definitely not be going up to his room.

Her response was, as usual, almost immediate. *You say that now. If you disappear for more than 20 minutes at a time, I'm driving over there.*

Seemed reasonable.

I tucked my phone away and slipped out of the car, licking my lips before taking those first few steps toward the front door. Anxiety roiled in my belly and made my body feel too hot and almost itchy. I wanted to shift, to fall into my cat form and let her run the show for a bit. Let her instincts take over. I always felt safer with her in charge—more comfortable. Alas, that wasn't a possibility. I had a feeling Griff wasn't interested in having breakfast with a house cat.

Speaking—or rather, thinking—of Griff, the man himself appeared at the front doors as I approached. He rushed toward me, smiling broadly. Looking so damn handsome with his wild hair and gray temples and...yeah. All of it.

"Good morning, Brittani." He stopped before he reached me, a slight frown pulling down his smile. "I have no idea how to greet you. A hug seems too forward but a handshake too formal."

I bit back a smile, appreciative of his need for direction. "Side hug?"

"Perfect." He slipped an arm around me, bringing me into his side with just enough pressure to make it noticeable. He didn't hold the position too long or make me feel uncomfortable, which was nice. "I hope you're hungry. I reserved us a table."

"You have to reserve a table for breakfast?"

"Their brunch is quite popular. Besides, I wanted to make sure we were in a location where we could talk. The main dining area tends to get a little too loud for me."

Oh. Okay. That sounded...like more than I had been prepared for. And as we walked inside, the feeling of being out of my element only grew. The sundress I'd worn—one of my absolute favorites that always made me feel pretty—suddenly seemed too casual and cheap. The wedge heels on my feet too clunky and unrefined. The entire space outshone me with its crystal chandeliers and white tablecloths.

I dropped my hand to the hem of my dress, fingering the edge of it and wishing I'd thought to wear something fancier. For breakfast. Which made no sense.

I was twisting the hem when Griff reached down and grabbed my hand. I released my dress and looked up at him, watching as he raised my hand to his mouth. As he held my gaze while flipping my hand so he could press his lips to the back.

"Excuse my brashness," he said, smiling down at me. "You're just so beautiful standing here. I couldn't help myself."

Okay, yeah. The dress was fine. "Thank you."

"No, thank you." He gave me a look over, one that normally would have made me uncomfortable but that instead made me feel sexy and pretty. "That dress is the stuff of fantasies."

I rolled my eyes and took my hand away. "Now you're just being silly."

"Men like sundresses. You can google it." With a wink and a smile, he led me into the open restaurant area overlooking the bay. A waiter in what looked like a tuxedo greeted him by name then had us follow him to the very back of the restaurant. To a quiet, secluded corner with a phenomenal view.

"This is…" I shook my head, a grin pulling at the corners of my mouth. "Thank you, Griff."

"You're very welcome." He nodded toward the waiter who had not yet left us alone. "Would you care for some coffee or a juice? Perhaps a mimosa to start your day?"

"Can I have some hot tea instead?"

The waiter nodded. "Of course, my lady. I'll have my assistant bring 'round a tea box."

I returned my gaze to the water outside, basking in the sunlight that streamed through the windows. Feeling the need to stretch and roll around in the rays. Resisting, but wanting it.

I needed to find a house with a sun-room or something. "This is gorgeous."

Griff came up behind me, his arm just barely touching mine as he kept his eyes on me and not the window. "Yes, it is."

I couldn't resist a chuckle. "You already have me on a date—you don't need to try so hard."

He shook his head and directed me to the table as a man approached with a trolley. "I will never stop trying to make you smile, my queen. Now, I do believe your tea service is here."

"Madam," the waiter said, giving me a head nod as Griff pulled out my chair for me. The man held up a wooden box filled with neatly organized rows of tea bags, his white gloves practically glowing against the dark lacquer. "We offer a full selection of teas from some of the best blenders in the world. Do you have a preference?"

I took a glance at the teas, a bit overwhelmed. "I like a green tea usually."

"Perfect." The waiter set the box down and selected three different bags. "We have a royal jasmine green with hints of citrus at the front. Our newest collection includes a green tea with honeysuckle and vanilla, which is quite delicious. But my favorite is the ginger green tea with just the slightest note of lime at the end. It's very refreshing."

"I'll take the ginger green. Thank you."

"My pleasure." He tore open the bag, directing his attention to Griff. "Any for you, sir?"

But the man across from me wasn't paying the waiter a bit of attention. Instead, he had his eyes locked on me and wore a sexy, distracted sort of smile. I cocked my head as he stared, suddenly very interested in what was happening inside his mind.

"Griff?" I finally said, smiling as he quite literally shook himself to attention. "Were you having tea?"

"No," he said, glancing up at the waiter. "No, thank you. I'd prefer a coffee."

The waiter nodded. "Of course, sir. I'll retrieve that while this steeps."

He disappeared back into the regular dining area, leaving me alone with Griff once more.

I couldn't resist. "What happened there?"

"Where?"

"When the waiter first asked you if you wanted tea. You seemed to be in another world."

"I was enjoying the show."

"What show?"

"You. Picking out tea. You were very interested in what he was saying."

I shrugged, sitting a little deeper in my chair. "I like tea."

"That much is obvious." He picked up his menu, pulling a pair of dark glasses from the pocket of his jacket. "Now, let's see how excited you get about food."

And that was how we spent the next hour or so—casual discussions about food, the weather, the birds that passed by our window. We kept the topics very surface-level, the basic getting-to-know-you stuff that I assumed all people in the dating world dealt with. He didn't ask why I grabbed my phone every now and again and sent a text, or with whom I might be messaging. I apologized each time, but he would wave me off as if my apology weren't necessary. I still felt bad, though.

Finally, after another check-in text, I sighed. "I really am sorry about that. My friend is worried about me, so I have to text her every twenty minutes."

"Why is she worried?"

I shrugged, grabbing my teacup for another sip of the delicious green tea. That waiter who recommended it needed a huge tip.

"We keep an eye on each other since we're both single and living alone."

"That's actually quite smart."

"It is. We text each other every twenty minutes or so and share our locations when we're out. That way, someone knows where to find us should we go missing."

"Last night, you were adamant that Kinship Cove was safe."

"Oh, it is." I lifted a shoulder in a sort of half shrug. "But safety isn't a passive thing—you have to work for it. Besides, you could be a serial killer."

He choked on his coffee, grabbing a napkin and covering his mouth. "I'm sorry. Did you just call me a serial killer?"

"Yes. I mean, not call you, really. I said you *could be*. Not that you are."

He set his napkin down with a laugh. "I can assure you, I am not a serial killer."

"Then, what are you? What do you do for a living? You already know I'm a librarian."

"I do," he said with a nod and a look that set my skin on fire. "Another male fantasy, by the way. Well done there."

If my eyes had rolled any harder, they likely would have gotten stuck. "Yeah, yeah. That one I know about. Quit dodging the question. I'm a librarian, and you are?"

He set down his coffee and leaned an elbow on the table. "I'm a homicide detective."

I blinked. Again. Three times. "You...but the officer..."

"I'm not on the local force. I work for the FBI's shifter crimes division."

My heart raced, and I leaned forward. Completely focused on the man before me. "What are you doing here?"

"I'm on vacation, actually. I was in the area investigating the disappearance of a woman farther up the coast. The area seemed lovely and I'd never been to this region before, so after we closed the case, I decided to take a little time to explore." He shot me a wink, looking sexier than any man had a right to be. "Apparently my need to stick around was more of the influence of the fates than anything else. I should send them a present."

I sat back, absolutely stunned. This man…my fated mate…was a detective with the FBI. A dream job. Handsome, smart, kind, charming, and a detective. I was smitten.

And really, really wishing I could ask him questions about every case he'd ever worked on.

Thank the fates I knew better than that, but maybe later…

We finished breakfast at a leisurely pace, neither of us delving much deeper than the most mundane conversational topics. It was a nice, relaxing meal—much easier than I had expected. It was on the way out that I finally gave up trying to control my interest.

"So, with you being a detective, I have to imagine you have opinions about some of the more famous unsolved mysteries of our era."

He hummed, placing a hand on my back to lead me through the doors out onto the balcony overlooking the bay. "You imagine correctly. Are you a true crime buff?"

"I have an interest."

His returning grin told me my casual answer was not enough to convince him. Without thought, I grabbed his hand, bumping into his side.

"Fine. I'm a bit of a true crime aficionado."

"*My Favorite Murder* or *Last Podcast on the Left*?"

"Murderino. Totally."

"Me too."

I nearly stumbled. "You listen to true crime podcasts?"

"I do. I like hearing the theories and knowing that the job I do brings meaning to people. That when a case goes cold, I won't be the only one left wondering about it."

We stopped at the railing, the breeze coming in off the water keeping us cool in the sunlight. Our shoulders and arms touching as we stood closer than before.

"It's so pretty out here," I said, distracted by the view once more. Griff hummed in agreement, running his fingers over the back of my hand. Both of us quiet for a moment.

But then he got my full attention. "So, tell me, my queen—which recent cases do you want to learn more about?"

That was easy. "JonBenét, of course."

"The brother did it."

"Agreed. Caylee Anthony."

"Good one—and the mother is guilty as sin."

"Totally." I found myself turning toward him, and he mimicked my body language. Both of us inching closer as the conversation continued. "What's the unsolved case you always want to know more about?"

He didn't even need to give that one any thought. "The Black Dahlia."

"And you think—"

"George Hodel. That's my guess."

My breaths came faster, and I reached for his arm, needing that touch to stay grounded. He upped my gesture, wrapping an arm around my waist and pulling me closer.

"What about you?" he asked, his voice deep and husky. "What's your favorite unsolved case?"

I licked my lips, staring into those intense, dark eyes. Barely able to pull my thoughts together enough to make a complete sentence. "The disappearance of Madeleine McCann."

"Solid choice." He pressed his body against mine, a low rumble coming from his chest. Not a scary one, though. This was…enticing. "On the count of three, name your favorite serial killer."

I nodded, definitely into this game. He counted down, keeping his eyes on me the entire time.

"One, two, three."

"Green River Killer."

There was no confusion, no words tangled together. We both said the exact same thing at the exact same time. I couldn't tell what happened next—who moved first or how the shift happened. One second, I was standing in front of Griff talking true crime, and the next, my lips were on his and I was trying to climb him like a tree.

Best breakfast date ever.

5

BRITTANI

You ever have one of those moments where time stands still then seems to almost jump? That was kissing Griff. Somehow I went from having my arms and legs wrapped around him on a balcony overlooking the harbor to me being pinned against the wall in the elevator on the way to his room with no recollection of how that change had happened.

The fates truly knew what they were doing.

"Are you okay with this?" Griff asked as he rocked his body into mine. I felt every inch of him, from his chest to his knees. He was so big and strong, so long and hard in the right places. There was no resisting him. No worrying about predator versus prey. There was just a man and a woman who wanted to connect physically.

"I'm sure." I returned my mouth to his, needing more of his taste. Of the feel of him kissing me. The man was neither gentle nor rough—he took what he wanted but in a smooth, calm sort of way. I never felt overpowered by his lips, never thought the motion of his tongue against mine was in any way sloppy. 5.He kissed like a man who both truly enjoyed kissing and who knew how to do it well.. I could have kissed him for days.

Thankfully, when the elevator came to a stop, Griff kept kissing me.

33

He also picked me right up off the floor and carried me down the hallway, keeping his hands on the backs of my thighs to hold me up. Hands that kneaded my flesh as he walked. I couldn't hold still, needing more than a kiss and some massage. Wanting so badly to get naked and rub my body all over his.

"Fuck, Brittani," he said as he came to a stop outside of a door. "Give me a second to get us into the room."

I couldn't help myself—I bit his lip and rolled my hips again, purring my pleasure. "I hate waiting."

He practically fell into the door, landing with his body pressed hard into mine. Growling through a deep, sensuous kiss that had me clawing at his shoulders.

"Bad girl," he said as he let go of my thigh to smack my ass. I jumped and mewled, angling my hips to rub myself over his hard length again. Griff could only chuckle. "You are a lot naughtier than I expected."

I grinned as he finally let me go enough to reach into his pocket and retrieve his keycard. "Is that a bad thing?"

The door flew open behind me, Griff rushing inside and kicking it closed behind us. "Not in the fucking least, but I don't want to share that fact with others." He kissed me again, slowing down a little. Letting his hands wander more now that we were alone in the room. Lifting the hem of my skirt so he could rub all over my thighs, my ass, my waist. "Tell me this is okay."

I loved a man who was adamant about consent. "This is okay. More than okay. I need you naked."

His responding growl left me wet and shaky, desperate for him.

"Your wish is my command, my queen." He set me on the bed and kissed me again, his hands slipping between us. Within seconds, he was tugging his pants down his legs, then he pulled back to yank his jacket off and lift his shirt. As I lay on the bed fully dressed, he stood naked before me, looking like a model out of a magazine. Muscles and bronzed skin and a thick, smooth cock jutting out from his hips greeted my gaze.

Mine. All mine.

"My turn," I said. I slipped my hands under my dress and dragged my panties down my legs, letting my knees fall open so he could see me. All of me. Or rather, most of me. I still had my sundress on.

Griff didn't seem to care about the dress, though. He dropped to his knees and spread my legs wider, dragging me to the very edge of the bed. He looked like a man about to dive into something we would both enjoy when he stopped and handed me my purse.

"Text your friend."

My brain could not keep up. "What?"

"Your friend. The one keeping an eye on you. Text her. I'm going to need a lot more than twenty minutes once I get a taste of you."

Oh dear. I grabbed my phone and typed out a quick message, asking, "What room are we in?"

Griff growled out a number, his lips too busy kissing up my thighs to enunciate clearly. I still understood, though.

I lied—I went to his room. I'm fine but going to be busy being naked. Room 346 if you never hear from me again.

With that, I tossed my phone to the floor, pushed my purse over as well, and reached for Griff. He was already absorbed in teasing me, growling against my pussy and kneading my thighs.

"Griff."

His hands froze, the pressure remaining but with no movement. "Do you need me to stop?"

"What? No." I ran my hands through his hair, desperate and needy and wanting to ask him to do something but not really sure what to say. I finally whined out a "Need you."

Griff chuckled and dropped a quick, soft kiss right above my clit, making me jump and shake.

"I'll take care of you, my queen. I'm just enjoying the view. You do realize you have a pretty pussy, don't you?"

"You do realize I *am* a pretty pussy, right?" I tried to tug my knees together, to pretend to push him away. "Bad puns aside, I'm going to need you to quit stalling."

"What would you rather I do?"

I glanced down the length of my body, meeting his eyes. The moment was so intense, so dirty. Me still half dressed in a sundress that had fallen all the way to my waist. Knees up, legs spread, with Griff in between them. Holding them open with the darkest, most intense expression on his handsome face.

Absolutely filthy.

And so arousing.

Without conscious thought, almost as if my hands had developed sentience, I fisted his hair and tugged. Pulling him closer.

"Please," I whispered, my entire body trembling with the intensity of my need. "Please just…do something."

His growl rumbled through the room, vibrating against me like some sort of adult toy. I squeaked and jumped, my hips barely leaving the bed, though, because of Griff's hold on me.

"My queen should never have to beg. I apologize for that—I'll make it up to you."

And with that, he dove forward. His lips and tongue attacked my pussy with a power and speed that I was not prepared for. And the growl? The vibration? Yeah…that was a thing. A thing that was going to make me come in an almost embarrassingly little amount of time if he kept it up.

"Griff. Oh, by the fates." I turned my head and upper body as much as I could to the side, wanting to curl up and squeeze my legs around the pleasure building within me. Wanting to slow it down so I could revel in it a little longer.

My handsome mate only growled louder, yanking me back into the position he chose. Tugging me even lower on the bed. He went back to working me over and making me want to scream, but he kept adjusting every few seconds. Kept growling and huffing and moving me, as if this were the wrong position for what he wanted to do. As if he couldn't get enough.

Finally, he proved me right.

"That's it," he said, his voice dark and deep. Slightly scary, to be honest. Without asking, he grabbed me and rose to his feet. Moving up to kneel on the bed as he carried me with him. The man had amazing reflexes because he spun with me, catching me in midair and twisting himself to fall onto the mattress with me…

Well…

With me straddling his head.

"Griff, what are you—"

He smacked my ass and grabbed my thighs, that growl deepening and his fingers digging deep. "Sit."

I couldn't move, couldn't follow such simple directions. My entire body was locked down in some sort of strange demure setting where the very idea of me doing *that* caused an overload. I couldn't even speak.

Thankfully, I didn't need to because Griff seemed to understand my hesitancy. Understand it and know exactly how to knock down that wall.

"Brittani. Sit on my face so I can eat that pussy like it deserves to be eaten." Another spank, this time a little harder. Making me jump forward. "Now."

I may have been a house cat and therefore exceptionally independent, but I knew when to follow orders. I did exactly as Griff said, lowering my body over his face until he made contact. And by contact, I mean he yanked my thighs harder, pulled my pussy to his mouth, and absolutely attacked it. I couldn't even think about controlling my body. A hand landed on the headboard in an effort to hold on to something. My legs spread wider, my weight dipping. I was literally *sitting* on his face, writhing my hips in circles as I chased the pleasure I knew was coming. And Griff, bless him, kept that growl a constant. Kept licking and sucking my clit. He was a human—or, really, not-quite human—vibrator set on level eight, and there was no escaping him. No getting away from the pressure and the tease and the friction. There was no—

"Oh my… Griff!" I reached down and grabbed his head with both hands, curling my body over as the moment of full anticipation stole my senses. As every thought and instinct circled down to that one moment, that one sensation, that one sight. Griff opened his eyes and looked up at me, those pupils dilated wide. The ring of gold around them practically glowing. I was lost in that vision as the pleasure wave finally broke, and I came with a squeal that had to be heard by the neighboring rooms.

Griff didn't stop, though. He kept going all the way through my orgasm, growling the entire time as he laved at me with even more vigor. Teasing me and dragging me through all twelve levels of pleasure in a way I hadn't known was possible. I finally had to rise up onto my knees to escape him.

"Too much," I whispered, still running my fingers through his hair. "You are too much."

Griff growled and grabbed me again, rolling us until we were diagonal across the bed with him on top of me. I could only laugh.

"You do realize I'd move of my own accord if you just asked me, right?"

"What fun is that?" He laid a soft kiss on my lips, giving me a taste of myself before moving down my neck with kisses and licks and small bites. His hips rolled forward, placing his cock at my entrance before stopping. "Is this okay?"

The man and his need for permission... It was so hot.

"Yes," I whispered, tugging his head back down so I could kiss him deeper, use my hands and my body to direct him. I wrapped my legs around his hips and lifted, pulling the head of him inside me just enough to make him sigh and groan. He followed my lead, moving slowly forward. Nudging his way into me at a speed even turtle shifters would have appreciated. I liked it, but I needed more. Still.

"Faster, Griff," I mumbled against his lips, squeezing my eyes shut as he slid in deeper. As he began to truly fill me. "Faster. I don't have all day."

He chuckled, rising up on one arm but again moving his hips to push forward. "Are we in a time crunch I'm not aware of?"

I shrugged and smiled up at him. "I wasn't expecting you to charm me into bed on our first date. I have to work tonight."

"When?"

I glanced at the clock on the bedside table. "In three hours."

He dropped down to kiss me one more time, that growl still rumbling. "I can do a lot in three hours."

And he did. Without a break or a warning, without his customary ass-slap I'd actually enjoyed while sitting on his face. Instead, he thrust right into me, sliding deep on a single push. I gasped and grabbed for him, needing more of a physical connection. Wanting to feel his weight and warmth all around me. Being in Griff's arms was like basking in a ray of sunshine, and I needed more of it. Would always want more.

Thankfully, the man obliged.

"I've got you," he said, dropping to his elbows and slowing his thrusts to more of slow rolls. Using his entire body to bring sensation to mine. And he did—I felt it *all*. The weight, the muscles grinding against me, the hair on his chest and down to his cock bristling in between us. He increased contact until there wasn't a part of me that felt neglected, until I was surrounded by Griff. Overwhelmed with his scent and feel and sounds.

Until I couldn't help but respond with a purr of my own.

"Aw fuck," he groaned, his entire body jerking. "Brittani. That sound."

I laughed and purred louder, reaching up to dig my fingers into his neck. To pull him closer so I could purr right into his ear.

I also made sure to whisper, "How's this for being a pretty pussy?"

He lost control, fucking me harder and deeper than before. Growling in a tone that nearly matched mine. The two of us were lost to each other, our animal souls joining just as our physical ones did. Both of us rocking and thrusting and fucking until there was nothing left. Nothing outside of that moment. Nothing outside of that bed.

I came with a mewl and a gasp that set Griff off even more, making him move in a rougher, harder sort of way. Rhythm off, hips snapping almost violently against mine, he groaned and growled his way until his body locked down and he came inside me. Thrusting deep and roaring toward the ceiling. He was a sight to be enjoyed when he came. More animal than man, and I couldn't help but respond to that.

"We have time," I said once Griff had dropped down to lie on my body, both of us breathing hard.

"Time for what?"

"For more." It was my turn to roll *him* over, shoving and pushing until he complied with my demands. Until I had him on his back while I straddled his hips.

He gave me a silly sort of grin. "I'm going to need a little more time than that, my queen."

I shrugged and grabbed the hem of my dress, yanking it over my head before tossing it to the floor. "I don't, but we still have a couple hours. I'll wait for you to catch up."

6

GRIFF

There was nothing as satisfying as that after-sex glow. Well, unless you counted the after-sex exhaustion that came from having a young mate with a libido that put yours to shame. My shy librarian was a needy little thing, and it would take all my time and attention to keep her satisfied.

The fates, they were good to me.

Well, only partially.

"Why are you getting up?" I rolled in Brittani's direction, wanting so badly to grab her and tug her back into bed with me. To curl up for a long nap with my mate in my arms.

My queen had other plans. "I have to clean up for work. Remember?"

Ugh, of course I did. My inner lion grumbled low in my head, making his unhappiness at the situation apparent. Still, my girl had responsibilities. I would honor that.

I rolled off the bed and headed for the dresser in the room. "Do you need to stop at home first? I imagine you wouldn't normally wear such a pretty dress to work."

She didn't answer me. I finally looked over my shoulder, assuming she'd slipped into the bathroom without my realizing it. Nope. That woman stood right where she'd been, dress in hands, eyes wide and staring…

Well, she wasn't looking at my eyes.

"Are you staring at my ass, love?"

Brittani darted a look up to meet my gaze before quite literally shaking her head once. "Sorry. I was distracted by…"

"My ass. You can admit it. You were distracted by my ass."

She rolled her eyes and slipped her dress over her head, covering that luscious body of hers. "Fine. I was distracted by your ass. Happy now?"

"We are both putting on clothes so we can separate for a few hours. Happy is not what I would call the emotions swirling inside me. But I do like knowing my ass can cause you to lose your train of thought. I might have to find a way to use that to my advantage."

She snorted a laugh. "You already have all the advantages."

I was in motion before she could escape me, landing delicately in front of her and grabbing her hips to tug her to me. "What are you implying, my mate?"

She bit her lip, staring up at me. "You're the predator in this relationship. You have more power than I do."

"Oh, my queen. No." I tugged her into a hug, rocking her softly. "I may be the predator, but you hold all the power in this relationship. I am here to follow, not lead, my beautiful kitty cat."

She didn't look convinced, so I dropped a kiss to those pouty lips and smacked that delicious ass. "You'll see. I'll show you."

And with that, we separated to finish getting ready to walk outside the door of our little love room. I walked her all the way to her car, uncertainty roiling within me. She was leaving. In her own car. Which meant she might not come back tonight. This could be the last time I saw her for a number of hours. That just wouldn't do.

"Why don't I take you?" I finally said, knowing there was no way I could be without her now. "That way, I can bring you back here after work for dinner."

"You don't need to—"

"Yes." I caught her surprised gaze, shrugging in an almost apologetic way. "I have to. Please."

"But my car—"

"I'll handle it while you're at work."

"That's not—"

"Please. Let me take care of it. Of you."

She stood stock-still for a long moment before finally nodding. "Okay."

I took that okay as a win. I also tugged her with me, plopped a kiss on her lips, and opened the passenger door to my car for her.

"Your chariot awaits."

Brittani rolled those hazel-green eyes. "You are ridiculous."

Ridiculously in love with my mate? Getting there.

Once I had her sweet ass in my car, I raced around to the driver side and settled in. I even snagged her hand and held it over the center console, needing to stay connected to her in every way possible. But the longer I drove, the more my good mood faded.

"Griff?" Brittani caught my eye as I glanced her way, looking concerned. "What's wrong?"

My inner lion took over for the briefest of moments, the beast's concerns rolling over into a growl that rumbled from my chest.

"Sorry." I raised her hand to my mouth to kiss the back of it. "I'm just nervous about you going to work."

"I go to work almost every day. I will be fine."

"I could—"

"Stop." She tugged her hand away, moving to sit sideways in the seat. "What you could do is trust that I'll be okay. I'm letting you drop me off because it made sense, but once I'm at work, you need to leave."

The growl rumbled louder and deeper, my hands gripping the steering wheel tightly. "I understand."

"And sitting in the parking lot in your car isn't an option."

I swung into a spot in front of the library, nearly ready to jump out of my skin. My teeth grinding as I said, "I want you safe."

"I will be safe. Safe inside the library."

"You have no security in there."

"I have no threats against me."

This woman was going to drive me insane. "Brittani—"

"Griff." She stared at me, face nearly expressionless. Eyes unwavering. She was standing up to my predator stare like it was nothing. The woman had a backbone that couldn't be broken, it seemed. I was both surprised, proud of her, and irritated as fuck at the same time.

But I was not giving this up yet. "Please, my queen. Let me watch over you. It's not because I don't feel you can take care of yourself. It's because I want to be able to take care of you and show my worth as your mate."

The glare softened, and she reached across the console to grip my hand again. "Fine. But you can't stand around inside or on the porch."

"Fine. I'd like to exchange phone numbers if you don't mind, then. In case you need me."

"Oh. Of course." She fumbled with her bag, appearing nervous all of a sudden. Eventually, she retrieved her phone and swiped to wake it up, handing it to me without a single bit of reserve. "Just type yours in."

I unlocked my phone and did the same, handing it to her so she could type in her info. Once finished, we exchanged phones again. I still wasn't ready to let her go, though.

"If you need anything at all, you text or call me. Okay?"

"I'll be fine."

"Even just a coffee from the diner or a treat from the bakery. Anything at all—call me."

She nodded, looking through the front window for a moment. Her voice quieter as she asked, "Where will you be?"

It was the tone that got to me. The vulnerability and slight anxiety in it. She needed me. She was worrying that I would leave her. That was never going to happen, but the woman needed more than my words. Without looking away from her, I woke up my phone and swiped to her contact info. Once there, I clicked the link to turn on location sharing. She watched me with a furrowed brow, glancing down at her own phone when she received the message that I'd like to share my location with her.

"That way, you always know where I am."

She caught my eye once more, a sense of insecurity still floating around her. "I'm not really comfortable sharing mine—"

I stopped her with a kiss—a deep one. One that I hoped showed her how much I felt for her. How much she meant to me already. Yes, we had only just met, but the fates had brought us together for a reason. I trusted them. And my Brittani was proving to be exactly what I needed and wanted in a partner. I could take my time waiting for her to feel the same.

"Just because we're going different speeds doesn't mean we won't eventually reach the same destination." I kissed her again, softer this time. Slower and sweeter. I also slipped a hand up her skirt to tug at the waistband of her panties before breaking the kiss. "Go to work. I'll be out here."

She nodded, coming to rest with her forehead against mine. "Not on the porch."

"Not on the porch."

One last kiss, and then she was gone. It irritated me not to open her door, not to walk her to the library's porch, but I knew she wanted to keep her work life separate from me right now. My walking her to the door would invite questions from coworkers—she wasn't ready for that.

Once she was safely inside the building, I grabbed my laptop from the back and powered it up. What was a man supposed to do when his new mate had to work and he had a lot of time on his hands? Research. I started with searching for Brittani's name. I wasn't looking for anything private—just stuff she posted publicly. The first hit was a review for a smoothie place down the road. Apparently, Brittani really liked their pineapple and turmeric smoothie after a workout to help cut down on muscle soreness.

I'd given her a workout that morning.

At least, I hoped I had.

Fuck, my poor mate was going to be sore.

I had my phone in my hand and the texting app open in seconds, my thumbs typing out a quick message.

What time is your lunch?

Her reply came quickly. *I only work five hours today, so I won't be having one.*

You'll starve. When is your break?

I tapped on the dash as I waited for her response, nearly jumping when my phone buzzed.

I have stuff at my desk. It's no problem for me to skip a meal.

Oh, hell no. *You will never be a problem unless you get sick from malnourishment. What can I bring you for lunch?*

This time, her answer took forever. Like ten minutes forever. I was about ready to step outside the car and begin pacing when she finally responded.

Griff, you're being bossy.

I'm concerned for your well-being.

Bossy.

Lunch. Snack. Anything.

There is nothing I need except to get to work.

Fuck. That was an obvious blowoff. I was bothering her, but I couldn't help it. I just wanted to prove to her that I would take care of her. That I would be a mate of worth. That she could rely on me. Obviously, the woman had been relying on herself for a long time. It was going to take some negotiations for her to be willing to make space for me.

For today, I was going to have to be a little pushy.

Gacy told his wife that the smell from all the bodies buried under their house was because of mice, and she believed him. When is your break?

GRIFF... Wait. Is that true?

I laughed out loud at that one. *Yes, and WHEN?*

She finally texted me the time, following it up with a *Now leave me alone unless you have more serial killer tidbits to share* message.

I replied with a heart and a *Tidbit: the land Gacy's house had been on could be seen from the hotel OJ stayed in when he was running from possible prosecution for the murder of Nicole and Ron. I'll see you then. Before* tucking my phone away and grabbing my laptop once more. I had a solid two hours before I could bring my woman a treat. Those were two hours I could get a little work done before I needed to make my next move.

Operation *Make Her Swoon* commencing.

7

BRITTANI

I would forever have a fondness for the Night Stalker case. Not fondness because of the horrible things Richard Ramirez did, but more for the way he was caught. The tiny bits of evidence that built up until he was exposed. I especially loved the way the community had come together to chase him down and hold him in place until the police showed up. That was the stuff of legends.

I slipped a couple knitting books onto a shelf, one of my favorite podcasts about the Night Stalker case playing in my ears. I was totally absorbed in my work and the words being spoken, totally distracted from anything around me, when someone suddenly appeared right where I had been standing. I jumped back, blocked by the returns cart I'd been pushing, yelping and tugging out my earbuds at the same time.

"What the—" I froze, trying to get my heart to stop racing. "Griff? What are you doing here?"

He reached out with a plastic cup filled with bright-yellow slushy stuff, handing it to me. "Sorry about that. I thought you might like your pineapple turmeric smoothie."

I glanced at the drink, remembering how I'd been obsessed with them last year. It was definitely a favorite, but...

"How did you know?"

He shrugged, leaning against the bookcase. Keeping his distance, it seemed. "You left a review calling it your favorite for post workouts. I thought perhaps you might need it after our morning."

I felt my jaw drop, staring at him for a couple long, silent moments before spitting out, "You've been web-stalking me?"

His brow furrowed. "No. Of course not. I simply looked up publicly available info on you so I could bring you a treat. I was hoping it would be a positive surprise."

I took a deep breath, reaching inside myself to find reason. To be honest, I should have known something like this would happen. The man was a detective—he spent his days researching people and looking at details most of us would miss. Of course he searched for me online. Heck, I may have done a little internet sleuthing myself when I got to work.

How could I be mad when he hadn't done anything worse than I had?

Plus, he'd brought me a treat.

I sighed and approached him, rising onto the balls of my feet as soon as I was close enough to reach him. "I love this. Thank you for being so proactive."

His smile grew, turning almost silly. "You're very welcome. I know you have to work, so I'll leave you alone. I assume it's still okay that I pick you up?"

"Of course."

"And you're still joining me for dinner, yes?"

"Definitely."

With a growl that made my panties wet, he grabbed me and spun us, pushing my back against the bookshelf and crowding me. Tucking his face into my neck to bite the length of it.

"Griff, I—"

"And after dinner, may I take you back to my room and worship your body again?"

I mean… I couldn't just give in all the time, right? "We'll see."

He dropped a kiss on my lips then backed away. Grinning. "That's better than an outright refusal, I guess."

"Go on, Griff," I said, grinning and still leaning against the bookshelf. "I have work to do."

"Yes, ma'am." He turned and strode away, his confidence something that made my knees weak. His ass doing a good job as well. Without thought, I reached into my pocket and grabbed my phone, typing out a quick message once he'd disappeared down the stairs to the main level.

I hate to see you leave, but I love watching you walk away.

His laugh echoed through the building, making me grin. My phone vibrated at a new message. No words, just two emojis.

A peach and a winky face.

Night made.

8

BRITTANI

Four days. For the four days since the morning of breakfast—and more than breakfast—with Griff, I'd spent every moment possible with him. That meant four solid days of no alone time, no recharging, no...secret lifestyle stuff. Single girl stuff. I woke up with Griff, got ready with Griff, he drove me to work, he brought me lunches and snacks, he picked me up from work, drove me back to his hotel, and then made me scream his name all night. Life with him was amazing.

But I was over all the togetherness.

"Hey, Griff?" I leaned against the bathroom doorframe, watching him put product in his hair to try to tame it. It never worked—that mane of his had a mind of its own for sure.

"Yes, my queen?"

That nickname in his voice still gave me shivers. I slipped in beside him, needing to touch and feel. To be grounded by him because this conversation had the potential to turn not-so-positive.

"You know I'm an introvert, right?"

He chuckled. "Of that, there is no question."

"Well, introverts—we need time to recharge our batteries." I took a step back as he set the brush down and turned my way, his brow furrowed. No stopping now. "I do love spending all this time together, but I'm feeling really drained."

Griff reached out and tugged me closer, holding me against him in a soft, gentle hug. "What can I do to help?"

"Nothing. Well, not nothing." I pulled back, needing to see his face for this. "I'd like to go back to my place tonight. Alone."

Yeah. The reaction that exploded over his face was not positive. Griff wasn't mad, though. He seemed more hurt, but he covered it well.

"Okay." He nodded, obviously processing my request. "I can drive you to work, yes?"

"Yes."

"And dinner. May I still bring you dinner?"

"You don't have—"

"I didn't ask that. *May* I still bring you dinner?"

"Normally, yes, but it's a short shift, so I won't be taking a dinner break."

He sighed, his head dropping. "Right. So, no dinner. And after work, you want to go to your house."

"Yes."

He leaned against the counter, crossing his arms over his bare chest. "How are you getting there?"

"Walking."

He looked up at the ceiling, taking a deep breath. "Will you at least call me? So I know you're safe?"

I couldn't help it—I wrapped my arms around my very overprotective mate and snuggled into his side. "Of course I will. And I'll likely call or text all night. I'll be missing you."

"But you need time alone."

"Yes." Because the stuff I was going to do tonight was not anything I would ever want to do with him around. At least not yet. He'd only known me for four days.

Judgment ran rampant in the big-cat world, and I wasn't ready to be the victim of his.

Griff drove me to work as usual, chattering away and holding my hand as if the day were no different from the last few. I knew better, though. This evening was going to be hard on him. He didn't take well to me being out of his sight, his fears of me being hurt without him there to save me running deep. It would be a little hard on me, too. I really needed this time by myself to catch my breath, but I was still going to have to deal with sleeping alone. With waking up without him curled over me and keeping me warm.

But I needed a break and a night of doing the stuff I didn't usually talk about with other people.

"I'll be around town if you need anything, okay?" Griff asked once he had pulled up outside the library. His voice was tighter than usual, his jaw clenching and unclenching in a way I hadn't seen before.

Today would be hard on him. "I may ask for a snack later. Or a coffee. You won't mind?"

"I won't mind." He stared down at our joined hands, silent for a long stretch before he said, "I'll miss you, beautiful."

I leaped across the console, hugging him to me. "I'll miss you too. I know this seems silly—"

"No. Not silly." He pulled back, smoothing my hair behind my ears as he looked into my eyes. "Your needs—whatever they are—should never be considered silly. Me missing you is selfish and probably makes you feel guilty, which is not my intention. I'll just be worried about you." He inched closer, kissing me softly. Deepening it as he slid a hand around to grab my ass. "And I'll miss you riding my cock, too."

I laughed and smacked his chest, relieved that the mood had shifted. "We'll get back to that tomorrow."

"Promise?"

"Absolutely." I gave him one more kiss before opening the passenger door and stepping outside. "See you later?"

"You bet your sweet ass, you will. I'll at least stop by to say goodnight."

"Perfect."

And with that, I hurried inside, both excited for tonight and a little hesitant. True, I likely could have invited Griff over to spend time with me in my space, but I really did need the break. I had been around people—mostly him—for days. I needed a little solitude.

And a little of the good stuff my inner kitty was a bit addicted to.

The second I was in my office with the door closed, I had my phone in my hand and was tapping to the right contact.

"Rise Dispensary, where all your dreams can come true if you know what to take. This is Margaret."

"Hey, it's Brittani." I sat back in my chair, looking up toward the ceiling. "I need to get a little something for tonight."

"Girl, you know I got you. But first, are we going to talk about that big cat you've been dodging me because of?"

"Not now—I'm at work. But maybe tonight since I'm going to be flying solo for the evening."

"Excellent. I need all the details on Mr. Fated Mate. Now, hang on and let me check my stock." There was a muffled sort of silence over the phone, then Margaret was back. "Okay, so I am out of Hortie Tortie, but there's Siamese Surprise, Tabby Titan, By the Shorthairs, Rowdy Russian Blue, and a new strain called Persian Perfume. What do you want?"

"Give me three ounces of the Tabby Titan, but throw in one ounce of the Persian Perfume."

"Of course. Whatever you need. And hey, let me know how you like the new one. I haven't had the chance to get my nip on with it yet."

Nip. As in catnip. As in a recreational drug that was totally legal but frowned upon by some more restrictive breeds. Domestic cat shifters loved it, though. Big cats...

Yeah, Griff might not be a fan. I'd tell him eventually, but I needed this break from reality. Catnip after a long week was like having a glass of wine for me. It loosened me up, gave me a little buzz, and helped me get an amazing night's sleep. I couldn't wait.

"Oh, Britt—we're closing early tonight. Any way you can sneak over here before seven to pick up your purchase?"

Shoot. That wasn't ideal at all. I had to work until eight and didn't have my car with me. There were two options—I could walk home, grab my car, and drive to the dispensary when I should have been working, not ideal in the least—or, option two, I send the man I was trying to hide my love of the nip from.

Decisions, decisions.

"I'll send someone to pick it up. You've got my card on file, right?"

"Totally. I'll put the purchase through and set your bag aside for your pickup person. I assume I'll be meeting the fated mate today?"

My stomach clenched at the idea, but I couldn't lie to her. "Probably. Be nice and don't ask him a million questions. We're still getting to know each other."

With that, I ended the call and continued to stare up at the ceiling. I'd known I would need to tell Griff about the catnip at some point. It wasn't a bad thing, after all—wasn't addictive or dangerous. It was simply a way to take the edge off, like alcohol but without the dependency that could develop. Domestic cats were given catnip by their owners, and cat shifters enjoyed partaking as well. Big cats...they were too wild and strong for such things. Or most, at least. I had a feeling Griff wouldn't have experience with it, but hopefully he wouldn't judge me for it.

Might as well tell him.

I sent the man a quick text, biting my lip the entire time.

I placed an order at the dispensary in town, but they're closing early. Is there any way you can pick up my stuff for me?

His response was immediate, as I'd expected it to be. *Of course. Anything I should know before heading that way?*

The man—he was a good one. *The place is called Rise, and they're closing at seven. Tell the front desk you're picking up an order for me. If her name is Margaret, she's my safety buddy. Be nice to her. That's it.*

He sent me a thumbs-up emoji in response, and I went about my evening. Working, ordering, researching options, basically making sure the library had the resources it needed to keep the patrons happy. The work took up all my focus, made the time fly by in ways not much else did. Thankfully, Griff sent me a text about thirty minutes before closing to let me know he was on his way and asking if I wanted anything. I shot him a quick *no thank you* then rose to my feet and stretched, groaning as my tight muscles refused to give. Hunching over my desk was not doing anything to help my back. The catnip was needed.

I hurried out of my office, humming to myself, and grabbed a cart of returned books to process so everyone could leave at once. This technically wasn't part of my job, but I hated walking out knowing others had to stay late to do all the things I could have been helping with. I was upstairs in the reference section—a quiet, dark corner of the library—when Griff appeared at the end of the row. My smile was unstoppable.

"I missed you," I said, rushing to him and curling into his hug. "You smell good."

He chuckled and kissed the top of my head. "I like being greeted this way. And I missed you too."

We hugged right there in the stacks for a long moment before I pulled away, still grinning. "I just need to put away the rest of these books, then I can go. Since you're here so late, you can take me home. Sound good?"

"Sounds perfect, but take your time. I wanted to talk to you anyway."

That sounded…ominous. "Oh?"

Griff followed behind me, taking control of the cart. "It's not anything bad, my queen. I was more curious than anything."

"About what?"

"About the catnip." He stopped to help me reach a high shelf, making sure the numbers on the label on the spine fit in the order of the rest of the books on the shelf. "Is that why you wanted time alone, so you didn't do that in front of me?"

My face and neck heated, and I kept my eyes on the books in my hands. "Sort of. I mean, to me, that's single girl behavior, like eating dinner out of a pan while standing at the counter, or giving myself a pedicure on the coffee table. Stuff that I only do alone because I don't want to be judged for it."

"You think I would judge you?"

"Well, I mean… Big cats—"

"I've drunk whiskey and wine around you, which we both know are more mind-altering and addictive than your catnip. Did you judge me for that?"

"Of course not."

"Well, I won't judge you for partaking in your preferred relaxation enabler either."

"Relaxation enabler?"

He frowned. "Everything else felt harsh."

"Relaxation enabler, it is." I put away a few more books, silent. Letting my mind spin for a bit before speaking again. "You're not disappointed?"

"Never. Your friend Margaret made sure I was fully aware of how safe and normal catnip is in the lives of domestics, not that I needed the lesson."

"She's the best."

"She seems very invested in your happiness. In fact, she convinced me that I should try it myself. Someday, I hope you trust me enough to do that with me around and maybe let me experience it."

"You'd try catnip?"

"Maybe. But I'd really like to see how it affects you." He crowded me against a library ladder, growling low as he said, "Margaret told me it can lower inhibitions."

My friend was also my pimp, apparently. "I wasn't aware my inhibitions needed to be lowered any further than they already are."

He grabbed me by the ass and lifted, moving to fit between my spread legs as I rested on a step of the ladder. His growl rumbled through the shadows, making the moment seem even more dangerous. More intense.

"Griff."

Those hands. He was a man who knew exactly where to touch and how. He grabbed my thighs from underneath and spread them wider, pulling them up as well. Tilting my body forward.

"I think I could get you off like this."

He could. He really could. "What are you doing?"

"Tell me more about your catnip. How does it make you feel?"

My brow tightened, my brain sort of skipping a beat. I was about to open my mouth to say…well, something that likely made no sense… when Griff grabbed me and lifted me again. This time, I landed on a higher step, my hips even with his face. My thighs almost resting on his shoulders.

"Someone could see—"

"Do you want me to stop or speed up?" He looked up at me, an evil sort of glimmer in his eyes. "Your choice."

As if there *were* any sort of choice in the matter. "Hurry."

He dove in with a rumble, slipping my panties to the side and letting my skirt fall over his head. Hidden, sort of. It wasn't as if someone walking by wouldn't know what he was doing. They just wouldn't be able to see any parts of me. The parts Griff had latched on to and was fucking with his tongue.

Fates have mercy, but I was going to come and very, very soon.

"Griff," I whispered, running my fingers through his hair to hold him in place. "How do you do this to me every time?"

He kept up the torment, lashing at my clit before sucking on it, slipping two fingers inside me to add delicious pressure. I was a rocking, writhing mess sitting on a library ladder in the middle of the research section, but I didn't care. All I could focus on was Griff and how he was making me feel. How much more I wanted from him. How this beautiful man was so addicted to me that he couldn't wait to leave the library to get me off.

The fates were so very good to me.

"Griff. Now." I came with a squeak, one fist to my mouth to keep from yelling as my body locked down and bowed over top of him. Griff teased me through it, softening his touch and sliding his fingers out of me as my body unclenched. Lapping at my clit until I finally pushed him away.

"Better?" he asked as he wiped off his mouth with the back of his hand then licked his fingers. Filthy, this man. Animalistic. But so very sexy.

"I can't believe you did that here." I leaned over to plant a kiss to his forehead, still breathing hard. "Next time, it's your turn."

"Any time you feel like getting on your knees for me, I will oblige." He chuckled half under his breath. "Come, my sweet queen. Allow me to drive you home so I know you're safe."

But that didn't feel right. Not him driving me home, but him dropping me off. I was shaky with need and in a weird headspace where Griff was my only desire. And though I knew catnipping in front of him would likely cause me a little anxiety, I still wanted him there.

"Come home with me," I whispered.

Griff lifted me off the ladder and set me on my feet, watching me the entire time. The man so concerned with my comfort level, checking in as always. "Are you sure? You had wanted alone time this afternoon."

"I don't want to be alone anymore. I want to be with you."

He clutched me to him, holding me in his warm embrace. Snuggling me. "Whatever you need, but if you change your mind, I'll leave. No matter what time it is—say the word, and I'll let you have your alone time to recharge."

I rose onto the balls of my feet to place a kiss to his chin. "You are such a good man."

"I'm also apparently a drug mule." He smacked my ass nice and hard, getting me to jump. "Come, queen. Your catnip awaits."

9

GRIFF

I liked Brittani's place. Mostly because it smelled like her—walking inside was like taking a bath in her scent—but also because it was such a reflection of her as a person. Books and trinkets, dried flowers, paintings with vibrant colors, and creepy accents of skulls and spiders showcased on her overcrowded bookshelves. Stacks and stacks of books were all over the place, even being used as side tables. The little house where my mate lived couldn't have been anyone else's.

My absolute favorite part, though, was her bookshelves. The woman had shelves upon shelves lined with books in every color and size imaginable and dotted with little collector pieces and art objects. In my effort to stay out of her way as she changed out of her work clothes, I investigated one shelf in the far corner of the living room. It appeared to be eight feet of shelf space devoted to thrillers, mysteries, and nonfiction true crime titles. She even had some books centered around cases I had worked on over the years. I would definitely be sharing more tidbits from big cases as well as the ones I'd had a hand in. She might get a kick out of learning details from the cases I knew about.

I was about to reach for one thick and beat-up paperback which obviously had to be a favorite when my queen walked out of her bedroom. She had her hair up in a messy bun on top of her head and a

63

robe covering her body. A fuzzy, ankle-length robe. She looked delicious.

"Don't judge me," she said, giving me a stern look.

I held my hands up, grinning. "I would never. You look like someone I want to snuggle, though."

"Don't I always?"

She wasn't wrong. "Yes. But especially now. Are you naked under there?"

"Yes, but not for you." She smiled my way, tightening the tie on her fuzzy robe. "I'll likely shift at some point."

Now, *that* got my attention. As did the fact that her body was barely hidden away from me. "Pity that. Should I prepare to shift as well? You haven't seen my lion yet."

Her face went a little pale, and her eyes grew wide. "I'm...not ready for that."

Fear. There was a definite fear in her voice. Prey worrying about being near predator. I couldn't say I was thrilled with such a reaction, but I also couldn't blame her. "Understood. I will stay human until you're ready to see the ridiculousness that is this mane in that form."

She nodded, taking a deep breath. "It's not personal, you know. I just—"

"There's no explanation necessary, my queen. We're building trust here, and I will have patience for that." I gave her what I hoped was a roguish smirk. "Though I truly can't wait to see your tail."

She rolled her eyes, her smile bright enough to cover the sass, and settled onto a fluffy rug in front of the fireplace. Stretching, shuffling, and reaching, she collected a large bunch of pillows to bring down with her. Nearly surrounding herself in soft, fluffy things. Then she grabbed the bag I'd picked up for her.

I settled into a chair at the edge of her pillow pile, ready to observe. "So, what is this?"

"It's catnip."

"And what does it do for you?"

"It relaxes me, lets me zone out for a bit and forget about the stress of life. Have you never taken it?"

I shook my head, fascinated by the comfort with which she handled the drug. I knew about catnip, of course—all cats did—but no one from my pride had ever spoken about actually taking it. That was left to the smaller cats, the lower predators. Not that I saw Brittani as lower—house cat or lioness, the woman was astounding. This catnip was just a part of her life that I wanted to understand.

Brittani—ever the persistent one—held up a small bag of green plant matter that reminded me of herbs. "Do you want to try it?"

"I'm afraid it wouldn't work on me the same way it does you."

She shrugged, the robe falling off her shoulder. "No way to know unless you try."

She was right. She was also not paying a bit of attention to the way her robe had slipped down her shoulder and exposed so much delicious skin. I couldn't have resisted her if my life depended on it, so I didn't. I moved to join her on the rug, pushing a few pillows aside along the way. "You go first."

My mate rolled her eyes again but opened the bag. "So, catnip contains a chemical called nepetalactone. This triggers either a sense of calm if ingested or can be stimulating if sniffed."

"And how do you usually enjoy it?"

"I ingest it. A lady I used to work with made tea from it, but I buy the good stuff that's not too dry or herby. See?" She held up the little bag and pulled out a small, pill-sized piece of green. "This will practically dissolve under my tongue."

"And then you'll be extra relaxed."

"Yup. And I'll likely shift. My inner cat prefers to be in control when catnip is involved."

"Good. I seriously can't wait to see that tail."

She glanced up at me, an excited sort of gleam in her eyes. "You sure you're okay with this?"

"Of course. I may grab a glass of wine to enjoy the show with."

"Feel free." She placed the pill under her tongue, grabbing a pillow and holding it to her chest. I rose to my feet and moved into the kitchen, finding a bottle of red, a wineglass, and an opener with ease. I was probably gone two minutes, tops, but when I returned—glass of wine in hand—Brittani had definitely sunk into…something.

"Baby?" I slipped into the chair, setting my wineglass on the table beside me. "Are you okay?"

My mate was sprawled across the pile of pillows, her eyes locked on the ceiling. Not moving. Not responding. I was both fascinated and worried. Her breaths were coming evenly, though, so I sat back, grabbed my glass, and kept an eye on her. She'd said this was safe. Her friend Margaret at the dispensary had said it was safe. All the research I'd done while waiting to drop off her catnip had said this was safe.

I was not yet convinced, though.

Even with all my attention, I nearly missed the moment she shifted from human to cat form. One second, a woman with pale skin and a gray robe was lying on the floor and the next…

"Oh, you're a pretty one." I jerked as the cat—a Ragdoll, if the amount of fur and the coloring of her points were any indication—stretched and rolled across the floor. She hit my feet without moving to hers, purring loud enough for me to hear her. "Gorgeous, my love. Absolutely gorgeous."

Brittani in cat form immediately jumped into my lap, putting her paws on my shoulders to bump and rub her head into my chin. She was a fuzzy, snuggly thing with a purr that brought me so much joy. Even her cat form liked me. Good.

I ran a hand over her back, following her spine all the way down her body. Relishing in the amount of trust my woman was showing me. Brittani settled into my lap, stretching to allow me to pet her more. Releasing a quiet mewl as I scratched at the base of her tail.

"I was right—the tail is amazing. So glad you showed it to me, beautiful."

She purred extra loud, sort of flopping onto me and simply allowing me to pet her. It was very cute, actually. And also very dangerous for her to be so relaxed and snuggly—I could see why she didn't take her catnip in front of people. I settled in to keep her safe, to rub her fuzzy body and help her relax, and to simply watch with some amount of humor as her eyes went unfocused and she just sort of…lay there.

"A little high, are we?" I chuckled, unable not to as her head lolled and she stuck out her tongue. "You're such a pretty kitty, my love. The dark points are a nice touch for your coloring. I wonder what our babies will look like?"

She raised her head a small amount, mewling softly as if in response. I took it as a question in my own mind. One that could only be answered with brutal honesty.

"Yes, I see us having babies, so long as you do, of course. You're it for me, my love. I'll move my home base to Kinship Cove if that pleases you, and we'll start a life together. I'll still have to travel for work as cases come up, but we can deal with that as we need to. My downtime will be with you—feeding you, watching you catnip, telling you whatever true crime stories you want to hear. All of it. You'll be my queen forever, fair Brittani."

Suddenly, the cat on my lap shifted, and I ended up with a very human—very naked—Brittani straddling me. Her lips crashed into mine, our tongues tangling as her full weight settled.

"Want you," she murmured in between kisses, rocking her entire body into mine. Riding my cock through the material of the sweat pants I wore. "That was so... Yes. All of it. Want you and all of it."

"You've got me," I growled, gripping her ass and helping her chase her own pleasure. Her eyes locked on mine, and I could tell she wasn't quite sober yet. I didn't want to push her boundaries, so I bit my lip and curled my toes, doing my very best to control my reaction to a naked mate writhing in my lap. Brittani didn't seem to notice, thank the fates. She was wholly consumed by her own pleasure. Rocking and jerking and crying out as she used me to satisfy her needs. It was a beautiful sight, one I would certainly put away to replay later when I didn't have access to my mate. Though jerking off in the shower could never replicate what was happening right in front of me.

With almost no help from me, Brittani came with a cry that sent tingles up my spine. I had to lock my body down hard, had to do my very best not to join her. It felt wrong to take pleasure from her when she wasn't quite herself. Maybe another time after we'd had a conversation about it and I understood how the catnip played into those moments, but not yet. Not when I wasn't sure.

But by the fates, was it hard not to expose myself and plunge into the wet heat I could feel through the fabric between us.

Finally, Brittani sagged against my chest, breathing hard and clutching my shoulders. "Griff?"

Words were hard as I was still locking my muscles in place, but I did my best. "Yeah?"

"Can you stay the night?" She had her forehead against my chest, her face hidden, but her voice told me all I needed to know. My queen was needy and off-balance. It was time for me to be her king and support her however she needed me to.

"Of course, my love. Whatever you need."

She sat up, flipping her hair over her shoulder and making my cock ache all the more for her. "What I need is a shower."

Request understood, I picked her up and carried her across the room, grinning as she laughed and pretended to be shocked by my actions. She wasn't—I had carried her around the hotel room before— but I played along because she seemed really happy. Fulfilled, even.

I, on the other hand, was ready to throw her little ass against the wall and pound her pussy from here to Sunday, but I still didn't feel right about it. Still wondered how the catnip was affecting her control centers. We needed to have some serious conversations about the nip and consent at some point because I was going to need to slip away to jack off while she showered. No way could I keep my distance with a wet, naked Brittani on display.

But when we made it to her shower, when I had the water streaming down at the right temperature for my mate, she didn't allow me to leave. In fact, she pushed my sweats down my legs and dragged me into the shower with her.

The woman was testing me for sure.

I closed my eyes and stood as still as I could, thinking through crime scenes and case notes to stay distracted. Kept my hands clenched in fists and my lips pursed shut. Ten minutes of pure hell. This would just be ten minutes of pure—

I felt Brittani drop to her knees, and I broke, making the mistake of looking down the length of my body.

"Brittani." My voice sounded choked and growly even to my own ears, but there was no holding the need back. She knelt before me, her face even with my hard cock. Lips mere millimeters away. I needed to move, to run away, to do something, but I was transfixed by the view of my sexy mate right there. On her knees for me like something from one of my fantasies.

I couldn't help but run a finger down the side of her face as I basically cut off my own balls. "You're so fucking perfect, but I would rather wait until you're clearheaded again."

My girl smiled up at me, eyes clear and bright. Completely focused. "I appreciate your restraint, but I know what I'm doing."

She took my cock in hand, making me groan. Making my knees weak as she rubbed her nose against the tip in the cruelest tease known to man or beast. Trying to kill me, obviously.

"Brittani, I'm not sure—"

"I'm fully aware of what's happening and enthusiastically consenting. Okay?"

Oh, thank fuck. I nodded and wrapped a hand around the back of her head, supporting her as she took me into her mouth. The heat, the pressure, the wet suction. It was all so good. Too good. I'd been worked up for too long, on the brink of wanting to come for minutes already. This sex act would be embarrassingly short-lived.

As if I'd spoken those words out loud, my mate took me all the way into her mouth and hummed. Motherfucking *hummed* around my cock. I was lost. Forget man points and slowing down and holding back—I came just seconds after she started, my entire body exploding into a mass of tingles and tremors that left my knees weak.

"Ah, fuck," I said, my voice more hiss-like than usual. Brittani released me from her mouth but gave me one more kiss to the tip as she giggled. "It's not funny, love."

"Oh, it is. It truly is. Were you on edge, my mate?"

Fucking hell, I loved it when she called me her mate. I picked her up and wrapped her legs around my waist, turning off the water.

Carrying her out of the tub and grabbing a towel to dry us as best I could.

"Yes, I was on edge. You see, this catnipped-out pussy decided to take a ride on my cock earlier. I'm pretty sure the sweat pants I was wearing will never be the same."

She laughed and clung to me, sinking into my hold with a level of trust that warmed me from the inside. I carried her into her bedroom and laid her out on the bed, staring down into the hazel eyes I adored. Running my hand over her forehead as I leaned in for a quick kiss.

"I'm going to grab you some water just in case you need it through the night. Then I'll be back for some serious snuggling."

She tugged the quilted bed covering up to her shoulders and curled herself into a ball, still smiling up at me. "Sounds perfect."

I had a feeling she'd be asleep long before I was ready for her to be, but that was okay. I simply took my time locking up her house and putting the living room back to rights. I did get her a bottle of water for the bedside table, which I carried with me as I turned off the lights. I also grabbed the baggie of her catnip from the floor.

And I looked at it.

Like, *really* looked at it.

She had seemed so happy and relaxed under the influence. More so than when I drank a glass of wine. I'd always assumed the two were very similar, but I had been wrong. And being wrong unleashed my curiosity.

I opened the bag and brought it to my nose, sniffing once. The scent was surprising—light and delicate with an earthy sort of undertone. I sniffed again, deeper this time. Bringing the bag even closer.

I sniffed until the entire room spun, the water bottle dropping from my hands.

And then there was nothing.

BRITTANI

I woke up to the bed shaking and a deep, dangerous growl rumbling through the room. There was no warning, no way to prepare as I went from deep, deep sleep to wide awake in an instant.

Wide awake with a huge lion sitting on the end of the bed and growling at me.

"Griff?" I slowly moved to sit up, beginning to tremble a bit as that growl deepened. His eyes—always so deep and dark—were laser-focused on me. A predator sighting its prey.

Oh, by the fates. This was bad. Very, very bad. Worst-nightmare-level *bad*.

I scooted away from him, trying to remember if there was anything within arm's reach that I could use as a weapon. I was on the wrong side of the bed to grab my pepper spray, which meant my only way out of this was to run and hope whatever had made my mate go lion would dissipate before he took a bite out of me.

Lion Griff allowed me to scooch away, but then, right as I was sitting up with my back to the headboard, he reached forward with a giant paw—claws totally outstretched and stealing my breath. He laid that paw on my legs, possibly holding me in place. Perhaps getting ready to eat me from the feet up. Maybe just wanting to touch. I wasn't sure, but I was about ready to jump out of my skin.

I practically did when his rumbly growl turned into one of those lion roars and he moved as if to take another step toward me.

Instead of jumping out of my skin, though, I jumped out of my bed and as far away from him as I could. I was running the second my feet hit the floor, racing for the living room. I could hear him behind me, giant paws landing and sliding on the wood floors. I had to imagine it was the sliding that gave me enough time to make it behind the couch because I was not all that fast in my human form. My inner cat definitely wanted to come forward, to take control so she could use her speed and jumping skills to get away, but I was too concerned lion Griff would truly see her as prey. I couldn't risk him forgetting who I was to him.

Which meant going one-on-one with a lion as a human.

I turned to face him, couch between us. Heart racing and breaths coming way too fast. "Griff. Stop it. You're scaring me."

The lion stood stock-still for more than ten seconds before he finally sat down on the rug. The rug absolutely covered in catnip. Had he… Oh dear. I'd often heard that catnip affected some shifters in a negative way —making them hyper and a bit more aggressive. Perhaps Griff was one of those shifters. Though why he'd even gotten into the catnip, I had no idea. If I lived past this night, we were going to have to have a long conversation about it.

If being the operative word.

As if on cue, Griff huffed like an angry library patron and groaned, almost like he was trying to talk. He also moved to stand once more, something I wasn't ready for.

"Stop." I threw my hand up and took a step back, nearly crushing myself against the wall in my effort to keep space between us. "Griff, baby. You're scaring me, okay? Do you understand? Can you shift back, please?"

But Griff didn't respond. In fact, he didn't do anything that I would have expected. What he did do was pin me with a very unfocused stare, lie down in the catnip, and start rolling around while licking it off the floor. Likely falling deeper and deeper into whatever altered state the nip was influencing.

My hunter had just become…well, not a hunter.

"You're going to hate yourself in the morning." I sighed, still worried about how he might react. Wondering if I should call the officer to help me keep him controlled or…

Griff rose to his feet, completely wobbly. He walked with slow and lumbering steps around the couch, his head down but his eyes wholly unfocused. Hunting me and yet unable to really fall into that mode. If I weren't so scared, I would have laughed. Drunk Griff was adorable.

"What are you doing, my mate?"

He grumbled a throaty sort of growl, but as he moved closer, I realized he wasn't growling at all—he was purring. And he wasn't hunting me. He froze at the end of the couch, his butt up in the air, his tail whipping around. He looked like a kitten about to pretend to pounce.

My mate was playing with me.

"I am not to be hunted," I said, trying hard not to laugh at how drunk he appeared. "You scare me when you look at me like prey."

Lion Griff stepped right up beside me, his head coming to my shoulder even in animal form. The beast was massive, with a mane that stood out in beautiful, reddish-blond waves. Everything about him spoke of power and strength, of being a deadly weapon. Except for the fact that he couldn't see straight and had a goofy sort of grin on his cat lips.

This was craziness.

"I think it's time for you to sleep this off," I said, carefully raising my hand to pat him on the head. I reached up—slowly, oh so slowly—to massage his ears. Knowing there were acupressure points that brought relaxation at the very tips. Hoping that worked on him as it did on me. Griff purred louder, pushing his head into my touch. Asking for more in the most feline way ever.

"You are so nip drunk." I shook my head, chuckling under my breath.

Griff didn't seem to mind. In fact, he moved as if to walk around me then started head-butting me between the shoulders. Forcing me forward. I followed his directions, stopping when he wrapped his body around mine once more and…wait.

"Are you licking me?"

He was. There was a lion licking my hand. Said lion then fell to the floor, landing with a bit of a crash and rolling on the catnip-covered rug.

"No, sir. We're done with the nip. Come on." I took two steps away, moving toward the bedroom. Thankfully, Griff growled and rose to his feet, following me. Plodding along unsteadily behind me. I still wasn't as comfortable as I would have liked to be, but he no longer seemed like a threat. He seemed really drunk and in need of a place to sleep it off.

I could handle that.

"Up," I said once we reached the bedroom, pointing at the mattress. "Get up there."

Griff snorted his disapproval but leaped. Messily. So messily, in fact, that I had to push his butt to keep him from falling backward off the bed.

"You are definitely going to hate yourself in the morning," I said as he finally settled onto the mattress. I walked around the bed and slipped in on the opposite side, watching him carefully. His lids had drooped a fair bit, looking hooded and super sleepy. He was almost out. Not quite, though, because as I tried to fit myself into the empty space on my side of the bed, he reached out and grabbed me with a paw. I never felt his claws, just the huge pads of his foot against my skin and then pressure. Lots of pressure.

He tugged me across the mattress until I was right up against him, then laid his head on my shoulder.

My mate was a snuggler even in his lion form.

As he released a purr-like sigh, I kissed his nose and settled in against all that fur.

"Seriously, tomorrow will be rough. But I'll make you breakfast and take care of you."

He grumbled a sound that probably meant something to his human brain then began to snore.

I was sleeping with a lion.

And I wasn't the least bit afraid anymore.

EPILOGUE

BRITTANI

Two months. It took Griff two months to convince me we needed to move to a bigger place. One that was ours instead of mine. One he would be paying for. That fact still rankled as I'd always paid my own way, but he certainly seemed happy about me letting him spend his money.

"Let me get that," my big, strong mate said as he grabbed the box I'd been carrying right out of my arms.

I huffed for what must have been the hundredth time that day. "I *can* carry stuff, you know."

Griff kept on grinning and carrying the box that I'd been bringing into our new home. "I am fully aware of that, my queen. But I really like helping you."

No, what he really liked was walking away from me and turning just when I had gotten distracted by his ass to catch me looking. It was a fun game, especially for him. This time, he was all the way to the porch, literally climbing the steps, which just made those sweat pants he wore pull so very tight across his impressive derriere, when he stopped and turned. The smile he shot me, the wicked gleam in his eyes, nearly made my toes curl. I simply shrugged and took one last look before rushing to grab another box and carry it inside.

Barely inside.

"I've got that," Griff said, taking the box from my hands.

"I swear on the fates—"

"The movers are finished with your books. Why don't you head into the library and start unpacking them?" He leaned in close, dropping a soft kiss to my cheek even as a low growl rumbled through his chest. "I know how excited you are to have your own library."

I would have pointed out that he was even more excited to have our own library *ladder* to play with, but I kept my mouth shut and let him finish unloading the truck outside. He was right after all—I had been awfully excited to have an actual library space with bookshelves from floor to ceiling and lots of windows letting in natural light. The space right off the foyer would be a good one to work in during the day but deliciously dark and moody at night. I couldn't wait to set up a couple leather chairs in front of the fireplace and load the shelves with books. To lay a fur rug down on the floor and snuggle with my mate in front of a bright, warm fire. Possibly with a little catnip mixed in.

My lion loved the nip as much as I did.

As I ruminated on how to arrange my books and where to begin, a set of arms wrapped around me, the scent of the man grabbing me one that brought nothing but pleasure to my body.

"Happy?" Griff asked as he pulled me close and rocked me softly from side to side.

"Amazingly so."

"Good." He herded me forward, moving me until I was face-to-face with our own personal library ladder. Until I had to grip the side rails for support as he practically lifted me off my feet with the pressure of his body leaning into mine. "Remember that night?"

I pushed back on him, rocking my ass against where he was so hard for me. "How could I forget?"

"While the whole catnip and accepting my lion were good, eating you out against the ladder in the stacks was even better."

He wasn't wrong. My panties still grew damp whenever I even walked past that darn ladder. "It was amazing."

"And now we have our own ladder." With a growl, he picked me up and spun me, placing me on a step high enough up so his face was even with my hips. Spreading my knees and pushing up my skirt so he could be even closer. So he had a view and access, letting his fingers begin their trek up my thighs. "The movers are leaving for the day, so I think it's time to christen this room."

I chuckled, running my hands through his hair. Definitely not refusing. "Is this why you had to have this particular house?"

"Why *we* had to have this place. It's both of ours."

"Bought with your money."

"Your opinion and happiness mattered a hell of a lot more than my money."

I rolled my eyes. "Fine. It's our place. But you bought it, and I'm beginning to think it was this ladder that sold you on it."

He didn't respond, simply stared up at me with a gleam in his eyes as his hands began to tease me through the fabric of my panties. I didn't need his words, though. He'd been absolutely set on having a library space in whatever house we ended up in, and seeing the ladder in this one had sealed the deal before we'd even toured the rest of the rooms. I didn't need him to admit anything, really, but I certainly liked teasing him about it.

"Griff." I gripped the side rail harder as his eyes darted to mine, already ready to jump out of my skin. "Now that you've got me on this beautiful ladder, what are you going to do with me?"

He roared and ripped my panties from my body, leaning forward to nuzzle into my pussy. "I'm going to be honest. Your smile when you walked into this room was enough for me to buy the house. The ladder and all the ways I could bring you pleasure on it were just an added bonus." He lapped at me, that evil tongue making me tremble and moan before he backed away again, teasing me with a finger instead as he asked, "Can you blame me for loving having this kind of access to my pretty pussy?"

Naughty lion. Though, two could play at that game. I grabbed on to the rungs above my head, leaning back and spreading myself even wider for him. Moaning as I rested one knee over his shoulder to hold him to me. "You have access to your pretty pussy anywhere, but this is a really great house for us."

"It is. The ladder is nice and sturdy for all the deviant sexual acts I've made up in my mind to try with you." He dove in again, making me squeak as he sucked on my clit before popping back off, filling me with two fingers as he rubbed his thumb over my clit and brought me to the edge of orgasm right there in our library.

"Griff, please. You're going to make me come."

"That's sort of the point, my queen. And once I'm done, I'm going to lay you on the floor and fuck you until you cry for mercy." He growled low and long, really pushing hard on my clit with his thumb and making my entire body tremble. "Once I'm done with you, we'll go lie on that soft fur rug in front of the fireplace, get naked, and catnip together."

The man was perfect for me. Positively *purr-fect*, if I was being honest. And punny.

Later that night as we relaxed on the rug with a fire burning in the grate, I was reminded of just how perfect he was. He lay there in lion form, a constant purr sounding from him, while I rested on his arm in my cat form. Both of us covered in the other's scent after an hour of head-butting and scenting each other. Basking in the heat and the connection. Griff eventually shifted, murmuring my name until I followed suit. Until we were both naked and tangled together in front of the fire. Until he maneuvered me underneath him and slid inside. Until we were once again connected.

Just two mates with a deep love for the library.

Bliss.

UNDER THE COVE

KINSHIP COVE: BOOKS & BAES

Kinship Cove welcomes shifters of all sorts, including ones who live beneath the waves. Welcome to the Kinship Cove library—home of real-life fairy tales—where the head of IT is about to meet his match on the shore...but show his true self off it.

Being a bobcat shifter means plenty of people thinking calling me Bob is funny, though that's far from the worst thing a girl living alone in a small town deals with. I'd seen the true crime shows. I knew the dangers of serial killers and sociopaths. But Kinship Cove really was a safe place to be yourself, no matter the shifter type.

At least, I thought so until I met the man of my dreams and the one the fates picked to be my perfect match. He's tall, lean, quiet, and absolutely not telling me the truth about himself.

. . .

What's a girl to do when the man she's falling for turns out not to be a wolf in human clothing but something much rarer and more dangerous. And how is a cat shifter of any type supposed to accept a life partially lived under the sea?

They claim life is better down where it's wetter…and I'm about to find out if that's true.

MARGARET

How's your day going, Bob?"

I swear on all that is holy, I will bite that woman.

"My name's not Bob, but you know that."

The woman in question—the clerk who worked at the front desk of the library—gave me a wink with her wide blue eyes, those thick, red lips turning up in a haughty sort of smile. "We do know that, don't we?"

With that, she went back to smiling and laughing at a customer as I fumed. Damned Siamese cat shifters with their pretty eyes and all their talking—I should have shifted and shown her what I thought about her little giggle and all that flowing, black hair. I should have let my beast come out to play with the little house cat who continually called me by the wrong darn name.

Just because I was a bobcat shifter did not mean you could call me Bob. Ever. That joke wasn't even original—I'd dealt with it since I'd been a little girl in knee-high socks. The least she could do was *attempt* to be unique. Of course, then I might truly attack her right there in the library, and that would get me thrown in jail with all the other criminals. Orange was definitely not my color.

I took a few deep breaths and kept moving, pushing down the urge to bite the Kinship Cove's Snow White look-alike. In a shifter town, a strong-willed predator could get away with a lot. Biting was a no-no, though. As was humping anyone else's leg without their permission, which was a law passed after a particularly squirrelly Chihuahua shifter moved to town. Which had nothing to do with why I was at the library or the Siamese shifter who continually called me Bob.

"Focus, Margaret."

I smiled at the patron who had obviously heard me talking to myself, passing by quickly as the embarrassment flashed under my skin. I mean, everyone talked to themselves, right? Of course they did. They had to. Maybe not out loud but...

"Focus."

I finally reached the door I had been heading for, frowning at the fact that it was closed. That fact was beyond odd. Brittani—my best friend and the intended target of my trek through all the books—never shut her office door. She loved being in the old library as much as I did, loved looking out across the shelves lined with adventures and instructions. Loved watching patrons discover a new favorite or dive back into a classic. The only reason I could think of that her door would be closed was—

"Oh, for crying out loud, you two." I knocked, making sure the sound was loud enough to be heard over whatever shenanigans my friend and her new mate were likely up to, and waited. And waited some more. Just as I raised my hand to knock a second time, the door swung open.

"Finally," I said, pushing right past Griff, Brittani's lion-shifter mate, and beelining for one of the chairs near her desk. "It's almost the end of your shift. You two couldn't wait until you got home?"

Brittani—all ninety pounds of her pixie-looking self—shook her head, her long, pin-straight hair practically dancing with the motion. "We weren't doing that."

"Sure you weren't."

Griff strode across the room and settled into the chair beside me, leaving the office door open this time, I noticed. *We weren't doing that,* my bobbed tail.

"She's having computer issues," Griff said. "I shut the door because of the colorful language she was using to rage against the machine."

"Did you try turning it off and rebooting it?"

If a look could kill, the one Brittani shot me would have definitely been deadly. "Of course I did."

My mother may have told me I was too forward a time or two growing up, but even I knew when not to push someone a single step further. Brittani was toes over the ledge—it was time to distract her.

"Oh, well, that's the extent of my computer knowledge. But hey, I brought you two something." I reached into my purse and pulled out a little brown bag decorated with the logo of the dispensary where I worked. "Happy Friday. This new strain just came in, and I totally thought of you both. It's supposed to be more calming than normal catnip but also slightly aphrodisiac."

Griff leaned forward and reached for the bag. "Sounds intriguing."

Brittani gave me a tired smile. "Thanks, Margaret. I'm going to need that after the day I've had."

"You're welcome. Just let me know how you like it. I'm not about to try anything billed as aphrodisiac, considering I've been single for—" I looked at my wrist as if I had a watch there "—six hundred and fifty-seven days."

Brittani chuckled, staring at her mate with more love in her eyes than I'd ever experienced. "Your time will come."

As if. "Sure it will. Now, what are we going to do about that computer so your day can start improving?"

Brittani sighed, scrunching her adorable little nose as she turned back toward her screen. "I already called Matthew."

"Who's Matthew?"

Griff growled low under his breath, a sound that made the hairs on my neck stand on end. No predator liked a bigger, badder predator showing such aggression. It didn't sit well with us. Brittani, a house cat shifter who obviously had no sense of self-preservation, just rolled her eyes.

"Oh hush, you," she said as I watched them with wide eyes. Brave little kitty. "Matthew is the children's librarian as well as our IT guy."

I settled deeper into my chair, stiffening when Griff turned his head away. Big cats always made me nervous, though that wouldn't stop me from poking him a little bit. "And your man is jealous of the IT guy."

Griff scrunched his nose and turned away. "I am not jealous."

Totally believable. Not.

"Sure thing, big guy." I nodded, nearly purring to myself when Griff growled again. "So, what's this guy look like? Is he a walking, breathing stereotype of glasses and a pocket protector?"

Brittani rolled her eyes hard. "This isn't some '90s high school drama movie. He's..." She glanced at her mate, suddenly looking uncomfortable. "He's definitely not a nerd."

That look on her face and the rumble coming from her mate definitely meant something.

"Well, what is he?"

It was Griff who answered this time. "A wolf shifter."

Brittani nodded. "A big one."

It was my turn to roll my eyes, totally ignoring Griff's almost constant growling at this point. "Ugh, like a gym head? All big muscles and sweat pants? No thanks. I get so many of those guys in at the dispensary."

Brittani shook her head, looking like a woman trying to bite back a smile. "No, not like that. He's got that lean muscle mass thing going on. Like a swimmer, you know?" She waved me off. "Never mind. Wait until you see him, then you'll understand. He looks so darn *strong*."

Griff flat-out roared that time, his lion side blasting through as Brittani and I both started laughing. There was just something so ridiculous about a lion shifter being threatened in any way by a wolf shifter, no matter how big and bad that wolf might have been. I may have been biased, seeing as I, like Griff, was a predatory shifter of the feline variety, but come on. Lion versus wolf? No contest.

As we laughed and Griff pouted, a man walked through the door into the office. Something about him—maybe his energy or his scent— had me spinning in his direction. His very presence stealing all of my attention.

"What's so funny in here?" the new guy asked.

I was about to say…well, something likely a little clever or sarcastic…but I glanced up and met the eyes of the person I assumed to be Matthew. In that moment, all words failed me. The entire world stopped spinning for a long, protracted second as I looked into the deepest, darkest eyes I had ever seen. I definitely understood what Brittani had been saying—the man was tall but not skinny, muscled but not thick. He was handsome, too, with floppy dark hair streaked with gray and a face that allowed me to forget he was wearing a collared shirt and khaki pants. My inner bobcat sat right up and mewled like the hussy I knew her to be, ready to climb that man like a tree. Not because he was hot—which he was—or because we'd been out of the dating game for too long—which we had. No, she wanted him because the pull of the fates told her he was ours. We'd just found our fated mate.

Brittani had said our time would come. It had…right in her office with her and Griff watching.

"You okay, Margaret?" Griff asked, sounding concerned. I tried to look his way; I really did. But my bobcat would not let me turn my head from the sight of our mate. Thankfully, he seemed just as obsessed with us, staring at me with an intense expression that had to match our own. Which was good—this would have been hella awkward had it been one-sided.

"Margaret?" Brittani said, her voice quiet but firm. Something in her tone must have worked its way through the haze for Matthew because he gave a quick headshake then looked Brittani's way.

"Sorry. I think your friend and I need a few minutes alone."

I still couldn't stop staring at Matthew, but I could hear the frown that had to be on Brittani's face as she asked, "Are you sure about that?"

I nodded, knowing the question was directed at me. I choked out a few words to ease her mind. "Yup. Just a minute or two."

With that, I rose to my feet and grabbed Matthew's hand, pulling him out the door. Laughing sarcastically as I heard him call back, "Try powering down your computer then turning it back on."

"She's not going to like that," I said.

Matthew did not seem perturbed. "She'll have to have patience with me right now."

Right. Because Brittani's computer still needed fixing, but we had better things to do than worry about chips and processors. We had just found each other. Fated mate intros awaited.

2

MARGARET

Me dragging Matthew across his own workplace didn't last for long. It only took me pausing one time to get my bearings before my big, strong mate took control, directing me to a small study room at the back of the library. He shut the door behind us, not turning on the lights, both of us breathing a little harder than normal in the close, dark quarters.

And then he growled.

I backed away on instinct, my bobcat ready to hiss if necessary. Sort of hoping I wouldn't need to. Sort of hoping this was some sort of foreplay instead of a warning of an attack. You never could tell in the shifter world.

"Hi," I finally said, the single word totally inadequate but my mind not working fast enough to come up with anything else.

Matthew didn't respond right away, choosing instead to herd me across the room to the corner farthest from the door. A low rumble accompanied him the entire way, and those intense eyes never left mine for a second. Never gave me a break from a stare I could practically feel on my skin. Did the man even blink?

When he had me pressed against the wall, lording over me with all that muscle and attitude, he placed a hand beside my shoulder and leaned in even closer. Making me feel small and weak. Making me feel like I needed him to protect me, which was not at all true.

I swallowed hard and tried again, eking out a tiny, "Hi, Matthew."

"Hi, Margaret."

I blinked, my heart racing as all the years of watching true crime came crowding into my brain. Suddenly unnerved by that short greeting. "You know my name?"

"I do."

"How?"

"You've been in here before." He leaned closer, sniffing my neck. Scenting me. "Your scent lingering in this place has been driving me mad for months."

I shivered from head to toe, unable to resist the instinct to run my hands up and over his shoulders. Needing to bring the two of us together physically. We both jolted when my hands landed on him, reacting to the spark between us. To the pull for more. His skin was so cold under my fingertips, so smooth but slightly chilled. As if he'd been sitting under a vent blowing cold air or something. I shivered again.

"You've noticed me before?" I asked, running my hands over his cool flesh. Wanting so much to use my body to warm his. Needing it for some reason my instincts could not explain.

Matthew slipped a hand down to my hip, squeezing me. Tugging me against him. "My inner beast did for sure. I've been waiting for you to come back."

I let my head fall back as his lips touched my skin for the first time, practically purring as I gave myself to him. As I consented with action instead of words. "Your wolf must be highly attuned to me, then."

Matthew paused and pulled back, staring down at me with an expression I couldn't read but that sent up a red flag in my mind.

"Wolf. Right," he finally said, tucking his head into my neck once more. Sniffing again. "You're a feline, though. A predator."

His touch sent my brain spinning, all instincts except ones revolving around things like mating disappearing into the swirl. I chuckled at the image of a tornado taking all my troubles away, the sound transitioning to a moan as he grabbed me by the waist and pushed me back, tugging the two of us together as he pressed me into the wall. His entire body resting against mine. My mate was definitely a strong one. Physically demanding as well. Why I liked that so much, I had no idea, but I did. Too much.

Words, Margaret. Focus on the words.

"I'm a bobcat," I said just before I gave in to the desires pumping through me and taking a little bite of his neck. Not a hard bite, just a little nip. Letting him feel my canines against his skin. Sneaking in a taste of my mate.

Matthew groaned and mimicked my actions, running his hands over my ass in a possessive sort of motion as he bit down on my neck. A move that broke through my restraint and brought out a long, loud purr from me. One that quickly transitioned to a distinctive yowl. A sound he definitely seemed to like.

"Bobcat, huh?" he asked, running his tongue up the length of my neck before whispering against my ear, "I can't wait to see your tufts."

I laughed. I couldn't help it. Matthew chuckled as well, both of us clinging to the other as if we'd been together for years. Hands and body parts interconnected in ways that would have been deemed inappropriate in human society, considering we'd only met a handful of minutes before. That was okay—humans didn't need to understand our connection, but we did. Both of us knew this was it—we'd found our mate. There was no use denying or avoiding it.

That didn't mean I couldn't play *a little* hard to get. "You're getting ahead of yourself, talking about my tufts. I don't just show them off to every Tom, Dick, and wolf shifter in town."

With a deep and slightly scary growl that rolled out of him in a way I'd never heard before, he grabbed me by my ass and lifted, forcing me up into his arms. I gasped but went with him, wrapping my legs around his waist. Nearly squealing when he turned us, took two steps, and laid me back on the desk as he followed me down. Suddenly, my mate had me underneath him, staring at me with so much want and warmth, it made me forget any sort of social norm or rule. Made me forget where we were and why. All I could see, all I could think about, was the beautiful man practically lying on top of me.

And what we could have been doing in such a position.

"Tell me no, and I'll stop," he murmured before leaning in to run a line of kisses across my collarbone. My entire body warmed and relaxed, knowing we were on the same page with what was coming for us, but stopping wasn't on my agenda. Not in that moment with so much magic and connection floating around us. Shifters waited lifetimes to find their fated mates, and I was not wasting a single day more worried about what he or others would think.

"What if I said yes instead?"

3

MATTHEW

By Poseidon's belt, the woman was going to make me come right here at my job. What if she said *yes*? I hadn't even given the option enough thought to have an answer. Sure, I'd fantasized—especially since the first moment I'd walked into that very building and had scented her. I'd known then, simply from the lightest of remnants of her scent lingering on the air, that my mate was in Kinship Cove. It was why I'd settled down, planted roots, worked the library job. I'd been waiting for her. And thankfully, I'd finally found her. Or really, she had found me. Either way, we were together, and there was an opportunity to fuck her on a study room table. Talk about going from zero to a hundred in a matter of seconds.

I'd never expected to have the opportunity to have sex in my place of work, but now that I did, I didn't have enough blood rushing to my brain to determine if it was the best idea ever or the worst. Her hands grabbing me by the hips and pulling me deeper into the cradle of her thighs didn't help my thought processes in the least.

"Margaret," I said, letting my version of a growl loose with the word. Letting her feel a little rumble through my body.

She bit her lip—the tease—and whispered back, "Matthew."

I loved my name on her lips, but that voice, that tone, was pure sex.

The sound wrapped itself around me and fed the flame of lust already burning me up from the inside out. This woman seemed made from dangerous waters, pure and simple, and I was ready to dive in headfirst.

"You can call me Matt."

"I don't want to."

That saucy answer only made me smile. "Okay. You make the rules."

"I like that plan. Don't even think of calling me Peggy."

"Understood."

By that point, my hands—totally of their own volition and completely out of my control—had begun to explore. Following every curve and dip I could reach to learn about my Margaret. Her hands weren't still either, her touch leaving a trail of tingles in its wake as she teased me with fingertips on my waist, my hips, sneaking around to my ass. I dipped down and breathed her in, unable not to, needing so much more of her already. Wanting to explore every naked inch. That thought brought with it images of my new mate in nothing at all, which fueled the desires running through me. It also knocked a little sense into me. My human side came to the realization that doing anything at the library likely wasn't a good idea. Even my inner beast reluctantly agreed —he wanted his mate alone. On his terms. Where he could have her all to himself. It was time to put on the brakes.

But still, I brushed my lips over hers. Unable not to. Not kissing, just...whispering a touch there. So close.

Alone.

But first, manners. I may have been a beast, but I wasn't an animal all the time. "Can I take you to dinner?"

Margaret blinked up at me, obviously a little off-balance from the subject change. "When?"

"Tonight."

"Where?"

It was my turn to pull back, to feel uncertain. "Wherever you want, I guess."

She stared me down, both of us backing away. Her rising to a sitting position but keeping her hands on my hips. Holding me in place between her knees but forcing space between us. I felt completely at her mercy and wasn't sure whether that was a good thing or not.

Finally, she cocked her head. "Do you like true crime?"

It took me a solid three seconds to make those words make sense. Or try to, at least. I failed at it. "What?"

"There's a new documentary series that just came out today, and I was really looking forward to getting some takeout, curling up on the couch, and watching it."

Disappointment stung, the knowledge that she'd rather sit at home and watch TV than spend time with her mate filling me with a sense of dread over what our relationship would be like.

"Ah, well…okay. So, maybe another night—"

"Want to come to my place and cuddle up with me on the couch?"

I let out a breath, practically sagging under the relief of her invitation. I could not have cared less what we did so long as I got to spend time with my new mate. This was an easy request to fulfill.

"Yes. Absolutely."

Margaret grinned at me, her light eyes on mine and her face so filled with joy that I couldn't resist her. I leaned in and kissed those plump, pink lips, groaning as I got my first taste of my mate. She pulled me closer, both of us deepening the kiss, a sound like a mewl escaping her as I clutched her to me. The animal in me wanted more, pushing me to strip her right there and slake my need even if we couldn't be all alone, but I resisted. There was so much to build, still. So much to learn about each other. A fated mate was not something to take on recklessly. This woman had been deemed perfect for me, and I'd been waiting for her for a long damn time—I would forever treat her as the gift she was.

When we finally broke apart, both of us breathing hard again, she held me close enough to keep our foreheads together.

"That was nice," she said, chuckling under her breath. "We should do that again."

"Whenever you want me to kiss you, just let me know. I'm all yours."

Margaret darted a look up at me, so much emotion in her eyes. Questions, too. I understood her hesitancy—I had to imagine we'd both done the dating thing in the past. This wasn't dating, though. This was more. I would need to get to know her, but we were it for each other. I was 1000% in on a future with her. I could only hope she felt the same.

"You need to get back to work," Margaret said with a sigh. "Brittani was about ready to toss that laptop out the window when I showed up."

I sighed, knowing she was right but still not happy about it. "Okay. Let's exchange numbers so you can text me your address."

We pulled out our phones, unlocking then exchanging them to make the input a little easier. She added a heart to her name, something that made me grin in what felt like a sappy way when I saw it.

"What time?" I asked, gripping her thighs one last time before helping her to her feet.

She led the way out of the room and back into the library proper, heading for my boss's office. "Six sound good?"

Four hours. Not nearly enough time to make it to the coast and get in some swimming. My inner beast would be mad, but I couldn't pass up the opportunity. We would just have to find a way to deal with the wait. "Perfect. I'll bring wine."

"And I'll order food."

"Sounds like a date."

She looked over her shoulder, shooting me a grin. "It does, doesn't it?"

We walked through the library, neither of us rushing. Margaret tugged me to a stop just before we reached Brittani's office.

"I want to give you this before we walk back in there and have to be subtle." She rose up onto the balls of her feet to place a soft, warm kiss against my cheek. "I'm excited to have met you, and I can't wait for tonight, my big, bad wolf."

My stomach dropped. I had so much to tell her, so much to admit. Things I hid from the world. Things no one in this town knew about me. But this was my mate, my one and only. My partner for life. She needed to know.

Not quite yet, though. It simply wasn't safe...for either of us.

"I will see you and your tufts tonight. Now, let's fix a laptop."

4

MARGARET

The rest of the day went quickly, from Matthew finally fixing Brittani's computer—it did not, in fact, need to be turned off and rebooted but instead required some sort of download of a program—to my mate walking me out of the library like a gentleman. My time in the library was practically perfect. Practically because another ten minutes in a study room alone with Matthew would have been ideal. That said, by the time I left the hall of books and headed into town, I was in a wonderful mood.

"Margaret! It's good to see you." The old woman who ran the diner in town hurried over, giving me her motherly smile. "Eating in or taking home?"

"Taking home. I have a date coming over tonight."

"A date, huh? Sounds intriguing."

I couldn't hold back my grin. I didn't really date, and this was so much more. "It's…I mean…he's my mate."

"Ah, the fates finally blessed you." She reached up and kissed both my cheeks, her fox energy high and bright. "Sit down at the counter, and I'll make you a coffee. What sort of dinner do you want?"

"Actually, I have a little bit more running around to do. I wanted to head over to the bakery for some sweets—"

"Misty's there today. She will get you set up right."

"But I wanted to place an order for tonight's dinner before I ran over there."

"Of course. What sort of shifter am I dealing with here?"

"He's a wolf. A big one, from what I understand."

"Ah, a classic." She gave me a wink and pushed me toward the door. "We do a surf and turf—crab-stuffed salmon for you and a classic T-bone for him. I'll make it on the rare side—all my wolves love their steak a little bloody. What time are you picking it up?"

I glanced at my phone, calculating how long it would take to finish my errands before heading home. "Maybe an hour?"

"Good. Go…tell my daughter to come say hello to her mother once in a while. Your food will be ready when you get back."

And with that, she pushed me out the door and onto the sidewalk. The Kinship Cove Diner made wonderful food, but the owner wasn't for the faint of heart. Still, it had been a favorite since I'd moved here, and I put up with the craziness because their food was amazing.

I quickly crossed the street and made my way to my second favorite establishment in the Cove—the Cake-Ily Ever After bakery. Home of the most amazing macarons, pastries, and cupcakes. And the sassiest fox shifter around.

"Hey, Misty," I said as I walked in the door. The woman in question —daughter of the lady who ran the diner—popped her head up from behind a display cooler.

"Margaret! Haven't seen you in a while. How's it going?"

Good. Great. Amazing. Splendid. All the things that I wanted to babble to her, but I kept myself under control.

"Great. I wanted to stop in to pick up some sort of treat for tonight."

Her eyebrow went up—just one—and she began to creep down the counter toward me. My bobcat reacted to that look with a wary sort of attention, making me take a step back.

"Misty?"

"What's so special about tonight?"

"Oh, not that much," I said, retreating even farther. The fox was on the hunt, and her prey was information. "I'm just having company."

"Of the male variety? Are we talking a date?"

The room suddenly felt much hotter, my clothes practically sticking to me. "I mean, yeah. A man is coming over."

She nodded. "Booty call or something serious?"

I swear, foxes have no filters. "Something else. I…met my mate."

The grin that exploded on her face mirrored the joy in my heart at being able to say those words. Fated matings were celebrated in a shifter town, always had been. Misty made sure to let everyone know when there was a new pairing in the cove, which meant the whole town would know by their morning coffee about Matthew and me.

A sudden sense of dread plummeted into my stomach—I hadn't told Brittani yet. She was my best friend, my ride or die. The woman I texted whenever I was out so it wouldn't take days for police to be notified if I went missing. She was my person, and I had just…skipped over telling her about Matthew. In my defense, Matthew *had* dragged me into her office then did this sort of bending lean over her desk, totally killing the brain cells that kind of discussion would have required. I would forever blame him. Still, Brittani and I needed to have a conversation…stat.

"Okay, so your mate is coming over tonight," Misty said, totally pulling me from my thoughts. "What breed is he, and do you happen to know what he likes?"

"He's a wolf, and no. Not at all. We just met."

"Do I know him?"

"Maybe. It's Matthew, from the library."

Misty did that whole head-back, eyebrows-up thing people did when they totally knew who or what you were talking about. "He's a black coffee, cream horn kind of guy."

The best part about being friendly with someone as nosy as Misty was the intel she always provided. "Can I get three cream horns, then? And a cupcake for me."

"Of course. We've got strawberry margarita and an aviation—which is floral with sort of bittersweet cherry notes. We also have what should be a Malibu and pineapple one, but Ginger decided to try that peach whiskey everyone is drinking on social media." She held up a perfect cupcake crowned in a peach-colored frosting with chunks of candied pineapple decorating one side and a big red cherry right on top. "I don't know what this thing is called, but it's amazing."

"Sold. I'll take one of those." I gave the case one last look, making sure I wasn't missing anything. I didn't get to the bakery as much as I would like because the dispensary had been crazy busy ever since catnip had been legalized for recreational use by the township council. Long hours meant stuff like afternoon strolls across town were simply impossible. Except for today. "Oh, and can I get one of those eclairs as well? A girl needs her chocolate."

"You're not lying. I was telling Clark last night that chocolate kept women sane." She glanced up at me, a wide smile on her face. "He claimed nothing kept us sane and we should all just embrace our feminine crazy."

"Sounds logical."

"My mate is a logical wolf." She put everything in a bag, grabbed a cup from the espresso station in the back, spent a solid minute making…something…then headed my way. "Your treats and a cappuccino, all on the house."

I took the bag and cup from her, already shaking my head. "I can't take all of this. Let me pay—"

"Absolutely not. A new mating should be celebrated. Consider these your welcome gift to the mated women club. Long shall we live without trying to kill the men who drive us insane."

I laughed, unable not to. Misty always had been a fun fox to be around. "Well, thank you. I will continue to make sure to send the customers from the dispensary this way to buy the quality munchies."

"You're a good woman, Margaret. Now go—get caffeinated and on a sugar high to be ready for tonight. Are you going out or…?"

"He's coming over to my house. In fact, I'm picking up dinner from the diner so I don't have to cook. Oh, and your mother said you need to stop in and say hello more often."

Her smile fell, and she threw her arms wide. "I was just there for lunch! I swear, that woman is going to drive me to drink."

"But you do drink."

"More. She's going to drive me to drink more."

Seemed likely, to be honest. I knew I'd be drinking more if I had to deal with that family.

With one last thank-you and a wave, I left Misty to her pastries and irritation with her mom and headed out into town. I needed to stop at the dispensary one last time to make sure the night staff had everything they needed, then I could head home with my food, my treats, and my excitement.

I was having dinner with my fated mate.

But first, I needed to make a call. My phone felt heavy in my hand as I pulled it from my pocket, and the screen made my fingers burn. Or perhaps it was the guilt.

"Hey, girl," I said as soon as Brittani answered her phone, my tone so fake even I heard it. "How's that laptop working out for you?"

Her voice came through completely flat and monotone as she asked, "Something you forgot to tell me?"

Six words, and the guilt might as well have set me on fire. She knew. She knew and was mad at me about not telling her. Friend fail.

"Yeah. So…Matthew is sort of my mate."

"I'm aware, no thanks to you."

I sighed. "I'm sorry. It was so crazy—one second, I was talking with you and picking on Griff, and the next, *Bam*. Mated. My entire brain exploded into pieces, and I forgot how to put it back together until just now."

"Good thing he's not a serial killer, then. You'd be dead by now."

"Likely."

She sighed, but her voice sounded much more upbeat as she asked, "Are you excited about this?"

"Extremely."

"Good. He's a great man—I like him a lot." There was a noise in the background, something that sounded suspiciously like a growl, and then I heard her hissing a hush. "Sorry. Griff doesn't like it when I compliment other men. He gets growly."

"I'd say that was manipulative behavior and you should be careful, but I'm pretty sure he's not a danger to you."

Brittani laughed. "No, not at all. Speaking of which, what are you two doing tonight?"

"He's coming to my place."

"What time?"

"Six."

"Okay. And you'll be having dinner?"

I looked both ways before crossing the street, frowning. "Yeah. Dinner then we're watching the new docuseries on Son of Sam."

"Ooh, Griff and I are doing the same. Okay, well, text me when you can so I know you're okay."

"He's my mate…"

"Doesn't matter."

She was right—it didn't. We always had been protective of the other.

"Fine. I'll text."

There was again muffled noise from her end, almost like she was covering the mic of her phone and having another conversation.

"Britt?"

"Sorry. Griff and I were just placing bets."

"On what?"

"What time you'll get naked."

I felt the need to be shocked, but I wasn't—Matthew was my mate, and he was coming to my house. Sex was definitely on the table.

"What are you two guessing?"

"Griff says by eight if dinner is served about 6:30. I figure you'll definitely get through at least one episode of the doc series, which puts you closer to nine in my head."

I nodded, spotting the sign for the dispensary at the end of the block and striding that way. Dinner, treats, docuseries…time calculation wasn't usually my thing, but I had a solid idea of what I wanted to happen.

"I'm leaning more in support of Griff's guess."

"Damn. Well, try not to be a total hussy and jump him when he walks in the door. Think of your friend who really wants to win this bet."

"What are the stakes?"

"Winner gets to pick where we go for our next weekend away. Griff will take me to some fancy hotel or resort where he can spoil me."

"And you?"

"My favorite murder podcast is having a live show in Chicago the weekend of the American Library Association convention."

"So, your weekend filled with murder and books rests on my shoulders?"

"Not just your shoulders, but yeah."

I nodded as I reached for the door to the dispensary, ready to get to work so I could finish what I needed to before it was Matthew time.

"I'll do my best to make it to nine for you."

"That's my girl. Have fun tonight."

"I plan on it." I swiped to end the call, smiling at my staff. "Okay, folks. You've got me for about twenty minutes before I have to leave. Your boss has a date."

Food and treats in hand, I stumbled my way down the path to my front door. I had spent too much time at the dispensary and felt a little more rushed than I would like. Matthew would likely be there any minute if he was prompt, which I had a feeling he was. He didn't seem the type to dawdle or be disrespectful.

I had just set the food in the oven to warm when I heard a knock on my door. I sent a quick text to Brittani—*he's here, the countdown has begun*—then I blew a rogue lock of hair out of my face, took one last look around to make sure there was no secret-single-girl paraphernalia lying around, and crossed the room, grinning when I opened the door.

"Hey there," I said, eyeing my man up and down. "You look nice."

Matthew smiled back at me, his grin disarming. His dark eyes locked on my face. "So do you, though that's not surprising."

I allowed him inside, taking the flowers he offered me. Beautiful blues and purples sat in the cellophane, the green of their leaves a backdrop that seemed to cradle them. They were stunning.

"These look like they're made from the colors of water," I said, taking a moment to sniff them. "They're beautiful. Thank you."

"You're welcome." He grabbed my hand before I could walk away, tugging me closer and dropping a soft, sweet kiss on my lips. "Thank you for having me over."

It took me a second to catch my breath, the butterflies fluttering about in my belly stealing all my air. Even my bobcat had swooned at that one, but she was an easy touch.

"Thank you for being willing to come over and watch true crime with me." I turned for the kitchen, taking a pit stop at the linen closet to grab the only vase I owned so I could put my flowers in some water. "Now come on. I've got dinner from the diner in the oven and some awesome treats for after."

"I like treats."

I stutter-stepped, nearly stumbling over my own feet. His voice had gone breathy, a depth added to it that I'd never heard before but that I liked. A lot. The implication stood out loud and clear—he would like to have *me* as his treat. I wasn't against that.

With a laugh and a deep inhale to clear my muddied thoughts, I began cleaning up the flowers to display as Matthew invaded my little house. The place wasn't anything special—two bedrooms, two bathrooms, little kitchen, nice sitting area with a fireplace on one side— but it had a view of the cove that couldn't be beat. As with most folks when they came over, it only took Matthew about three seconds to leave me behind and head to the patio doors leading out onto the deck that overlooked the water.

"This is quite the view."

I poured a glass of wine for each of us then joined him, looking out over the cove. "It's why I bought the house."

"Do you like to swim in the cove?"

"Not in the least. I'm very much rooted in my bobcat ways with that one. But I've always been fond of water if I'm just looking at it." I turned as Matthew took a sip of his wine, enjoying the view of his lips on the glass. The man was tall, more so than I'd expected or recognized at the library. Tall enough that I had to look up at him, which meant he had to be about a foot over my head. Tall and lean and absolutely enticing. "You look like a swimmer. Are you a water baby?"

He brought his glass down, eyes still locked on the cove. "Very much so. It's my absolute favorite place to be."

"I wouldn't have expected that answer from a wolf."

He darted a look at me, his face going stoic and unreadable. I had a moment of fear, of knowing something was up that he wasn't sharing with me, but then he smiled again and the fear faded. Didn't disappear, but went quiet.

I was so on edge from the whole mating thing. I really needed to relax.

"Wolves like water," Matthew said, his smile widening. "They're not as finicky about such things as cats."

I cocked my head, shooting him a fake glare. "Are you trying to start a dogs-and-cats war?"

He grabbed me around the hips and pulled me closer, pressing our bodies together. "Why would I do that?"

His tone seemed honest and sincere, but his smile gave him away. I huffed and pretended to be annoyed, which just led to more tugging and leaning closer and perhaps even a kiss or two. Maybe. Not that I liked to kiss and tell.

Okay, fine. They were deep, sensual kisses that had my toes curling and my breath catching. The man knew how to kiss for sure. He was also seriously handsy. If I hadn't known better, I would have said he had more than just two arms with how he held me. Not that I was complaining.

"I feel the need to untangle myself from you. I don't want to burn the dinner," I said with a laugh when we finally broke for air. Matthew chuckled as well, one hand still firmly planted on my ass.

"Fine. But just for the record, I like being tangled with you."

I rose onto the balls of my feet and leaned in, dropping one last kiss to his chin. "I like being tangled with you, too. But let's eat—I'm starving."

We strolled into the house, both of us laughing and chatting away as we prepared for our meal. I brought the plates and silverware out onto the deck, while Matthew carried the food for me. He also made sure to bring the wine as any smart man would do. Within minutes, we were sitting down to the surf and turf dinner the old lady at the diner had put together for us.

"Shall we share?" he asked, indicating the two serving plates—one with salmon and one with steak.

"Sure, though you can have all the steak if you don't like seafood," I said while tossing the salad with the dressing Momma had provided.

"I love seafood, actually. This is the perfect dinner for me."

I grinned, a sense of relief pouring over me. "I'm glad to hear that. I was a bit worried, but Momma at the diner said this would make a solid wolf-bobcat meal. I think she intended the surf for the cat and the turf for the wolf, but this works out even better. That steak smells delicious."

He nodded, looking slightly uneasy for a moment. Though everything seemed okay once he took another sip of his wine. "Everything looks amazing. Do you go to the diner often?"

"I do. They have a special now and again of the best macadamia-crusted halibut I've ever had. It's to die for."

He nodded while spreading butter on a roll. "I've had that. It's really good, but this crab-stuffed salmon is my favorite of theirs."

A wolf who loved salmon—he had to be one of those Alaskan interior ones, though I never could remember the different breeds. "That's good to hear. I'm glad she recommended it."

We spent a good amount of time on the deck, looking out over the water and eating our dinner. The conversation flowed naturally, the subjects inquisitive but light—favorite books, funny childhood memories, ridiculous injuries that came along with being a shifter, as well as the most awkward places we ended up naked after a shifting incident. All normal, get-to-know-you stuff in our world. As the meal ended and we moved inside to clean up, the subject switched to my absolute favorite.

"How did you get into true crime?" Matthew asked. The man had his back to me as he washed the dishes, refusing to allow me anywhere near the counter to help. I wasn't even supposed to dry.

Seriously, if there was a moment to make me fall in love, that was it. I hated doing the dishes.

"I grew up in a human town, and the man two doors down killed his wife when I was a little girl. My parents were obsessed with the case, so I heard a lot about it."

Matthew glanced over his shoulder. "Did the guy go to jail?"

I took a sip of my wine, releasing an irritated huff. "For like five years. Then he was back on the block, tormenting neighbors and killing people's pets."

"What?"

"Yeah, he was a real piece of work. Eventually he moved, but as a teenager, I spent a lot of time looking for more records of his exploits and sort of cyberstalking him. I found others like him. Everyday men—well, usually men—who suddenly snapped and murdered someone. At least that's how they're portrayed to be, but the truth is, they usually showed signs of cruelty and control early on, particularly in their romantic relationships. The guy on my block had been violent for decades, but no one ever held him accountable for it. At least not until he killed someone, and even then, the sentence seemed like a slap on the wrist."

Matthew finished washing, turning and resting a hip against the counter as he began to dry the plates, an inquisitive expression on his handsome face. "Like when doctors say the kids who hurt animals have more of a chance to grow up to harm humans."

"Exactly. And once I delved into that sort of thing, I moved on to the more sociopathic offenders. The Ted Bundys of the world—seemingly totally normal and even well liked, yet doing horrible things."

"The ones that are harder to pick out from the crowd."

"Yup. I love going down the rabbit hole of investigating their lives and looking for any signs of how bad things would wind up being. It's my favorite hobby. Totally useless, but seriously enjoyable."

He finished the drying and even put everything back where it belonged before hanging up the towel on the handle of the oven. He then moved to stand right in front of me but across the counter, arms braced, eyes locked on mine with a serious expression on his face. One that enraptured me completely, making it impossible to look away.

"What?" I finally whispered, almost trembling under the weight of that stare.

"I can't decide if your interest in murderers is adorable or terrifying."

I shrugged, giving my bottom lip a little bite before saying, "Why can't it be both?"

Matthew used that long, tall body to lean across the counter and give me another sweet kiss. "Maybe it can. Come on, show me your murder shows."

"Let me just put the desserts on a plate. Can you grab the wine?"

"Your wish is my command."

We were on the couch and snuggled up within a minute, neither of us shy about our desire to be close. I grabbed the remote and turned on the television, clicking through to the streaming service with the new docuseries I had been so excited to watch. Truth be told, if Matthew had requested we do something else—especially something with a little less clothing and a lot more physicality—I would have jumped at the chance. But spending time with someone who at least pretended to be interested in your interests was nice, too.

Plus, it was only quarter-past eight. I had to hold out until nine for Brittani to win the bet.

But even just a few minutes into the first episode of the deep dive into Son of Sam, I felt myself growing more and more distracted. The story was good, the evidence fascinating, and the narrators the perfect blend of gritty former cops and emotional family members of the victims, but Matthew had his arm around my shoulders and his thumb brushing over my collarbone. That was impossible to ignore.

I finally grabbed his hand, pulled it close to kiss the back of it, then pushed it down my arm. Conveniently, that damn traitorous thumb ended up resting on the side of my breast. This time, when it started its torturous back-and-forth, it was against the swell, just above the cup of my bra.

"You are the devil," I said, snuggling deeper into his side.

"Why's that?"

"Because your thumb rubbing over my skin does evil things to me."

He chuckled, never stopping the motion of said thumb. "I can go sit in the chair if you'd like."

"That's not happening. I like snuggling with you."

He kissed the top of my head, squeezing me close. "I like snuggling with you too."

But snuggling became getting handsy, and getting handsy became far more distracting than just a thumb. Eventually, we ended up with Matthew lying on his back and me on top of him. He had both hands running up and down from my shoulders to my thighs, practically dry humping each other simply from the pressure of his hands. Not that I was complaining—I moaned and groaned with every pass, wanting more. Needing it.

Finally, I cracked.

I snatched up the remote, turned off the television, and grabbed Matthew by the neck to pull his face closer to mine. "Forget the show."

He kissed me immediately, wrapping his arms around me and holding me close before breaking away from the kiss to whisper, "Was I too distracting?"

"Yes, but in a good way." I spread my legs over his hips and rocked my body against his, unable to resist the attraction for another minute. Needing to touch and feel even more.

"Are you sure you want to do this?" he asked between kisses, even as he reached up under my shirt to unfasten my bra with surprisingly agile fingers. I might have been a little impressed.

Focus, Margaret.

"I'm sure. Are you sure?"

"Yeah, but I want to make sure you're good. This *is* a first date."

He wasn't wrong, but he also wasn't telling the full story. "True, but we're fated mates. The universe designed us to do this together."

He grabbed me and rolled me under him, nuzzling into my neck before biting his way up to my chin. I dropped my head back. Mewling like a cat in heat—which I sort of was—and clawing at his shoulders.

"I love the way you think," he whispered before arching up to pull away. He slid his hand under my shirt and tugged, watching me the entire time. "Can I take this off?"

I glanced at the clock, disappointment a heavy weight on my chest. "No."

His face fell at my whiny response, and he moved as if to roll off me. "Sorry. I didn't mean to push."

I laughed and grabbed at him, wrapping my legs around his hips and refusing to let him separate us. "That's not a permanent no—but I can't be naked until nine."

He followed my head nod, looking toward the clock on the wall near the doors to the deck with a most confused expression. "Is this like a Cinderella turning into a pumpkin at midnight thing?"

"No, it's a Griff and Brittani bet how soon we'd end up naked, and I want Brittani to win."

He chuckled and dropped his weight back onto me, kissing me with soft lips again, one, two, three times before pausing. "Ah, well, she is my boss. I should make sure she wins the bet."

"Exactly. Plus, it's not that far away. We can resist the draw of nakedness for a few minutes."

He huffed and bit my neck again, making me shiver. "I've been wanting to get you naked since I saw you in Brittani's office."

I moaned, tightening my legs around his hips to better cradle him. Rubbing myself against where he was so hard and hot for me. This night had been planned as a get-to-know-you, and we were definitely about to get to know each other. Physically. Sexually. Nakedly.

The man drove me to make up my own words—deal with it.

Matthew grunted as my hips rotated against his, rocking into me to increase the sensations. "So, when is this magic time that means Brittani won, and what should we do until it's time to get naked?"

"Nine. We have to stay clothed until nine." I dropped my head back as Matthew slid a hand up under my shirt again, this time yanking down a bra cup to massage my breast. Even tweaking my nipple and making me jump.

"You didn't answer me," he said, a deep growl in his voice as he sat back onto his heels and pulled me closer, spreading my knees wider around him and trailing the evil thumb to my clothed pussy. "What should we do until nine?"

I glanced at the clock—fifteen minutes left. Plenty of time to have a little fun.

I reached for the waistband of his pants and slipped a finger underneath, quickly finding the head of his cock to rub against. To tease. I dropped my other hand over his, directing his touch to my clit. Giving him license to touch me the same way I was touching him. It took him less than a second to take over, his touch turning aggressive in a way that had me groaning and arching into him. Had me slipping my hand deeper so I could wrap my fingers around him.

With a wink, I squeezed him tight, rubbing my thumb over the tip on the upstroke. "You've got fifteen minutes—I think you should get creative."

The smile that appeared on Matthew's face was one that both scared me a little and had me ready for whatever he had in mind.

"You may regret saying that."

5

MARGARET

Matthew wasted no time slipping his hand under my skirt and up my thighs. I followed his lead, wrapping my fingers as best I could around his cock while angling my arm to stay out of the way. It was both the best and worst feeling ever, sort of like a tease that you knew wasn't going to go anywhere.

"Matthew," I moaned as he shifted his weight, dislodging my fingers from him. He moved again, pulling his hand from where I so wanted it to grab my arm and tug. "But I want to play."

"Your turn first. That's the rule in my house and should definitely be in yours."

I grinned up at my handsome mate, running my fingers along his cheek. "A rule, huh? About who gets to come first?"

He leaned down to kiss me just as he once again slipped those long, careful fingers into my panties. His smile when he pulled away melted my heart. "Rule, yes. You will always come first with me. In everything, but especially this."

I threw my head back as he slipped one finger inside me, his wicked thumb finding purchase on my clit. Everything in the world narrowed down to that moment—to him and me on that couch all warm and snug together. To his hand doing wonderfully awful things to me as I tried

113

harder and harder to spread my legs for him. I never even attempted to slow him down. I gave myself to him without thought, without pause. Without a moment of overthinking. This was my fated mate, my one and only. Why would I hold back?

"Fuck, Margaret," Matthew murmured, pressing himself against my thigh. I wanted so badly to figure out a way to grab him, too. To give him the sort of pleasure he was giving me. I wanted us naked and writhing on a bed together. Wanted to see him come because of my body. I wanted...

And waiting was the stupidest thing I had ever done.

"Stop," I said. Matthew froze immediately, staring down at me with eyes that held more concern than I had intended. "Not in a bad way, but we're taking this to my bedroom."

"Oh, okay." He pulled away from me and rose to his feet, helping me to mine as he said, "That was awfully sudden."

I grabbed my phone and shot Brittani a quick text. *Still not naked. Tell Griff he's going down.*

"Texting my boss?"

"Yeah, and setting an alarm for nine. She and Griff are going to get a talking-to next time I see them, too. Lying here unable to touch you was driving me crazy. No bet is worth keeping these clothes between us, but we still have to make sure she wins." With that, I yanked my top over my head and dropped my skirt, leaving me in a *thankfully* matching bra and panty set. One I knew made my boobs look amazing. One that my mate obviously liked if the growl he released was any indication.

"Marga—"

"Come get me, pup." I grinned then hurried off, rushing toward my bedroom. Matthew followed, his footsteps quickly taking over mine. He caught me at the door to the room, spinning me around and pressing me into the doorjamb. Practically attacking my neck with his lips, his tongue, and his teeth.

"Did you just call me a pup?"

I groaned, my entire body attuned to his. Needy and wanting and so very wet. "Fuck, Matthew."

"Oh, we'll definitely be fucking Matthew. But first, we're going to be eating Margaret." With that, he picked me up to toss me over his shoulder, ignoring my laugh and even smacking one big hand on my ass. He carried me straight to my bed then threw me down, chasing me up the mattress. His legs spread over mine. And then he waited, watching me. Not moving.

I was far too impatient for that. "What are you doing?"

With a wink, he nudged his knees between my legs and spread them wide, dropping down to place kisses along my stomach and hip bones, moving lower with every second.

"Matthew?"

"Brittani wins at nine so long as we're not naked, right?"

My brain sputtered, having no idea how we'd ended up back here. "Yeah."

"Naked means both of us with not a stitch of clothing on." He tugged on my panties, slipping them down my legs. Moving so he could pull them right off me.

He made it so hard to actually think. "I mean, in the literal sense. Though I have a feeling the naked thing mostly applies to me."

"Then we do this." He rose to his full height and stripped, baring himself completely to me in that moment. I drank him up as if I'd been walking through a desert for days, thirsty as all hell for those long muscles and tight abs. His cock jutted from his hips, looking just as long and thick as he did. As I watched, he dropped a hand and wrapped it around himself, tugging once, twice. My mouth watered at the sight. By the fates, but I wanted to taste him.

"Matthew," I whined, moving as if to sit up. He dove and pushed me back down, sliding lower along my body until he was once again lying between my spread thighs.

"Hush, my mate. I'll take care of you. Just keep that bra on for now."

Brain…not working. "Huh?"

"If you keep the bra on until nine, Brittani wins the bet." He jumped up my body, stopping at my chest to ravish the satin-covered flesh with his tongue. Even tweaking a nipple through the fabric and chuckling as I jumped and moaned. "Don't worry, I'll be back to spoil these. I want to make you come on my tongue. First, anyway."

With that, he disappeared back between my legs, spreading me wide and baring my pussy to him. I felt no shyness, no sense of awkwardness at being so exposed. Instead, my entire body tingled in anticipation, time slowing as he moved in. Every brush of his hair on my skin lifted me higher; every breath blowing across my heated flesh brought my pinnacle closer. I was going to come embarrassingly fast, and I didn't even care.

"Matthew," I moaned as he finally made contact, as his fingers spread me and he took one long, wet lick from opening to clit. He didn't go slow after that, oh no. He powered through, sucking and licking my clit at a frenzied pace. Pushing my hips down with one arm as I rose up, as if I couldn't decide whether to ride his face or pull away. He stole that option from me in the best way, giving me everything I needed and making sure I took it all. I was a writhing, sweating, screaming mess in seconds. Completely focused on the pleasure the man was drawing out of me. Climbing toward my breaking point faster than ever before.

It was just as my alarm rang, just as we hit that nine-o'clock deadline, that I broke and came. My fingers wove into Matthew's hair of their own volition, tugging him into me. Refusing to let go as my entire body seized. He kept licking, kept pushing me. Kept teasing me through my orgasm until I finally pushed him off me. It took him less than a second to reach up and unfasten my bra, the fabric flying across the room in the next moment. Matthew attached himself to my nipple and fitted his hips between my spread legs, his cock right there. Ready to enter. Both of us driving toward that mate bond moment.

"Get up here," I finally said, pulling on his shoulders. Matthew released my nipple with a pop and rose over me, slipping his cock inside me. Just the tip to start. Staring down at me with a constant, wavering growl rumbling through his chest.

"Grab your phone," he said, holding still. That tip making me crazed with need.

"Why?"

"Text Brittani that she won."

I laughed, the motion making him slip a little deeper inside me. I also reached for my phone, tapping out a message that said *You won, now leave us alone so we can get naked* before tossing the device across the room. Matthew's smile turned soft but heated, his stare back to that intense look that made me feel as if he were looking inside my soul.

"Are you sure?" he whispered just as he began to move his hips in tiny increments back and forth.

I nearly rolled my eyes, ready for a lot more than just the tip. "I just came on your face. Yeah, I'm pretty sure."

He smiled down at me, looking ridiculously young and so very handsome in that moment. "You're so much fun."

"You, too." I reached around and smacked his ass. "Now, get to work."

The man didn't need to be told twice. He plunged into me, the thickness of him stealing all my breath as he split me open. He gave me no reprieve, no time to adjust. Going all the way deep before pulling out to thrust in again. Over and over, fucking me hard and fast, following me as my entire body shifted up the length of the bed from the force. Head back, legs spread, arms reaching for any part of him, I gasped and cried out and lost myself to the emotions and sensations taking me over. At one point, Matthew pulled my legs up over his shoulders, bending me in half before plunging into me once more with a growl that would have terrified me if I'd been in my right mind. Thankfully, I was not—I was in my *going to come any second* mind, where little things like the noises my partner made didn't even matter. All I could think about was how tight my pussy felt wrapped around him, how he kept a constant pressure on my clit with the swirl of his hips. All I could focus on was the pain-pleasure he brought me as he twisted my body to suit his needs and dropped dirty words from his lips.

"So fucking wet. I just want to bury myself inside you." He plunged deep and held still, pushing up into me in a way that should have hurt but instead made stars explode behind my eyes and had my mouth falling open on a silent scream. "That's it. Fuck, I'm going to fill this pussy up. I've felt you come on my tongue, now I want it on my cock."

There was something so ridiculously hot about the children's librarian saying the word cock. I couldn't get over it.

"Again," I gasped, grabbing hold of his hips to pull him deeper. "Say it again."

As if he knew exactly what he was doing to me, he leaned in close. Rocking those hips to push up into me again as he whispered, "My cock is so deep in you. Your little pussy is just swallowing me up, though. Were you made for my cock, my pretty kitty?"

I keened and jerked, letting the words bathe me in a sense of want, so close to finishing already. So needy for him to just make me come. My mate didn't disappoint. With a chuckle, he went back to his pounding pace, reaching between us for a second to spread my lips apart so he could rub himself over my clit on each thrust. By the third one, I died. Not literally, but in the Shakespearean context. I came with a scream that would have scared the neighbors if I'd had any, my entire body shaking underneath him. My pussy clenching all around him as he jerked and lost his rhythm.

"Fuck, Margaret. Fuck...so tight. So good." He practically roared, thrusting all the way in then pushing deeper again, holding still as he came inside me. As he released all the tension and buildup of the past half an hour.

When he was done, when he had finally finished and released my legs to slide down his ribs and hips, he sighed and fell on top of me.

"I need a nap after that."

I laughed, cuddling him. Basking in the heat and the weight of him as I ran my fingers through his hair. "Out of practice?"

He glanced up at me, his expression serious. "I've been waiting for you, love. I knew my mate was close. I could feel your energy when I moved here—so yeah, I guess I am out of practice."

I wrapped myself around him even more, joy and relief filling me with a sort of happiness I had never experienced. "I'm so glad we finally found each other."

"Me too."

After a moment, Matthew pushed off the mattress and rose to his feet. "Come on, my sexy mate. Let's clean ourselves up before we fall asleep."

I followed him, snuggling into his side as we walked toward the bathroom naked. Knowing I'd finally found my person, my soul mate, and we would never be alone again.

Never tempt fate. Wasn't that what people said? Don't put things out into the universe that you think will never happen because fate will slap you in the face with them. Something like that. A rule I should have remembered, apparently.

I struggled with the trash, the morning air cool on my skin. The sun shining down in total mockery of me.

"Shut up!" I yelled to the birds who seemed far too chipper for such a dismal day. "Just shut up and let me be miserable."

They didn't stop, so I headed inside. Ready to shower, get dressed, and do my best to forget about what I thought I'd found.

I had been arrogant and put it out into the universe that Matthew and I would never be alone again. I shouldn't have been so hasty. As I walked through my empty house the morning after a night filled with sex and love and so much pleasure, I had begun to grow angry at the fates who had tied me to that man. The man who had obviously woken up before me and left. No word, no goodbye, no note.

I woke up alone in an empty house, having been left behind by my fated mate. And I still had to go to work.

"Joke's on me, huh, fates?" I said as I walked back into my little house, ignoring the couch where Matthew and I had basically dry humped each other and totally not looking out onto the deck where we'd had such a nice dinner. No way. And my bedroom? Completely off-limits. I grabbed clothes from the laundry area and headed into the shower, needing to wash the remnants of his scent off me. Needing to find a way to get through this day without crying.

I'd been stupid enough to believe I'd never be alone again because I'd met my mate.

Too bad Matthew hadn't felt the same.

Where the hell did he go, anyway?

6

MATTHEW

The water had been especially cold that morning, far different from the hours I'd spent under the blankets with Margaret. Her body had been so warm and soft, so perfect against mine. I couldn't get her out of my head. I also couldn't stop feeling like a major asshole for slipping out of her cabin the way I had.

"Should have just told her," I whispered to myself as I grabbed my clothes from the rocks. I tugged them on roughly, growing more and more worried about my mate and how disappointed she would be upon waking. Would she hate me? Would she be angry? I didn't know her well enough to be able to guess, but there would be pain for sure. Pain that I had caused. I felt like a failure of a mate already, and I'd only just met her.

But the swim had been necessary.

"Shut up, beast."

Once redressed, I hurried to my little cabin to grab a quick shower. It had the same basic setup as Margaret's, but my views were of the woods surrounding the cove. Not being too close to the water helped quell the needs of my beast, but not by much. I still had to return to the sea daily or he'd get particularly cranky. Something none of us wanted.

I showered quickly to get the scent of the sea off my skin and the salt out of my hair, then threw on clean clothes and grabbed my keys. It was already breakfast time, and I still needed to find my mate. To apologize. To…

"What are you going to do? *Tell her?*" I shook my head, locking the door behind me before jogging for my car. I would eventually need to tell her for sure. My shifter side had been a secret for so long, though—had been surrounded by this air of a need to protect, to hide, to lie to keep us safe. Telling Margaret was a definite need—she was my fated mate, after all—but it would not be an easy conversation. Neither would the one about why I had left her without a word that morning. But I needed to have it, too, now that I was back in control of myself. Immediately, in fact. Which was why I went tearing out of my driveway and sped along the dirt roads toward hers, ready to pour my heart out to her and beg for forgiveness.

I pulled up to her cabin, noticing immediately that her car was no longer in the driveway. It was too early for her to be up and about, and yet that car had been there when I'd arrived the night before. I was sure of it. Which meant she wasn't home. Still, I climbed out of my car and walked up onto the porch and toward her front door. I could hear the waves from the cove in the distance, feel the pull to go back to the sea, but it was nothing in comparison to the sudden fear that I might not ever see my mate again. Impossible, really—she had a job in Kinship Cove. Friends. A life. She wouldn't just…walk away.

Would she?

"Margaret!" I pounded on the door, peeking inside. There was no sign of her. No sign of us either. She had obviously picked up her place and gotten rid of any evidence I had been there, including the flowers that had been sitting in a vase on her counter before. Even the blanket on the couch that we'd mussed while playing around had been neatly folded and draped across the back. She'd erased me already. Fuck.

"Okay, okay. If she's not at home, she has to be in town." I hurried to my car and dove inside, peeling out of her driveway and heading down the hillside toward Main Street. There weren't really a lot of places she could be that early in the morning—the diner, the bakery, her store.

Maybe the library if Brittani was there before we opened. I just had to do a sweep, to look for her car. Then I would find her.

Thankfully, I didn't have to drive all over town looking. I found her car in the public lot across the street from the dispensary on my first pass around the block. Thankful and yet terrified at the same time, I quickly parked beside her and raced across the street, banging on the front door of the shop until I saw her peek out from the back room.

She did not look happy to see me.

"Okay, Matt. Play it cool," I mumbled under my breath as she walked toward the door. I pasted a small smile on my face and tried my hardest to look the opposite of a threat, even cocking my head slightly when she opened the door by about two inches. She wasn't welcoming me back—noted. "Hey, Margaret."

"Can I help you?"

Cold. Angry. But mostly hurt. All my fault. And I deserved every ounce of that sharpness in her voice. I had definitely earned her distrust.

"I know you're mad about my leaving the way I did—"

"Oh no, honey. You put far too much weight into how your actions can affect my life. I'm not mad—I'm disappointed. You're not important enough to deserve my anger."

I paused, letting her words land the way I assumed she wanted them to. Taking the hits from them. This was going to be even harder than I had thought.

"Noted. But do you think I could come in and talk to you? I'd really like to apologize."

"You can apologize from out there."

"Please." I leaned closer, refusing to let her look away from me. "Just for a few minutes."

She sighed but stepped back, letting me grab the door handle to open it so I could step inside. I'd never been in the dispensary, but it was not at all what I had thought it would be. I had imagined patchouli incense burning and cases of paraphernalia out, sort of a hippie vibe to the place. What I got was a high-tech medical office with a few rows of neatly placed boxes along shelves behind the sleek counter where I had to assume the business was handled.

"This is nice," I said, looking around at all the soft gray and black. "I wasn't expecting it to seem so high-end."

"You assumed a dispensary would look like dirty hippies ran it?"

The anger in her voice told me to tread carefully.

"Not specifically. I just expected more of a homey vibe. This is super medical and high-tech."

"It should be. Catnip has a long, proven history of medicinal properties, from pain management and reducing inflammation, to helping to ease the symptoms of anxiety and depression. When a customer walks in here, they are escorted to a private room where one of my trained staff members can speak to them about their needs for the nip and help them pick the perfect product to ease whatever symptoms they are experiencing."

"Impressive." And it was, but I wasn't here for a lesson in the business of selling catnip. I took a deep breath and met her eyes, frowning. "I am so sorry I had to leave the way I did this morning."

Immediately, Margaret's lips pursed and her expression went hard. No matter what she claimed, the woman was hurt and angry, and it was my fault. I'd done that to her.

"Why did you leave, then?" she asked, not budging an inch.

"Because I needed to shift."

"You could have shifted at my house."

"No, I couldn't. And I already know that's a shit thing to say without a full explanation, but I've kept a lot of secrets for a long time. Most of my life. It's not going to be an immediate thing for me to just be willing to…open up to someone."

She cocked her head, curiosity dancing across her features. "So, I'm just a random someone?"

Oh, hell no. I closed the distance between us, herding her backward. Growling under my breath as I moved us until I had her pinned to a wall.

"You are not *just* anything. You're my mate, and I want to share my world with you. I want to tell you all my secrets. But I couldn't do that this morning before I left because my inner beast had woken me up. He was screaming at me and took control before I could react. It's always a battle with him, and he won this time."

She sighed, her eyes looking suspiciously glassy. "I didn't expect you to tell me your life story in one night, but you could have at least let me know you needed to go and said goodbye."

"You're right, and if I could go back to that moment, I would have found a way to do that. But I was so far gone when I woke up in your bed. We didn't want to scare you."

"Why would your shifter side scare me?"

And wasn't *that* the question of the day.

"I promise, I'll tell you. But not now. Please. This is so new, and I'm so excited to get to know you and for you to get to know me. I don't want anything messing that up."

She leaned closer, surrendering finally. Wrapping her arms around my neck as she said, "You know what will mess up us getting to know each other? You leaving after a night of what I thought was good sex without even saying goodbye or hey, I have to go or thanks for the ride."

I chuckled and cuddled her closer, relief flooding me at her silly joke.

"You are one-hundred-percent right. Next time, I'll wake you up and say thanks for the ride."

"Good." Her smile fell, her expression shifting to something more serious. Something that screamed I'd truly hurt her. "Don't do that to me again."

"Never." And I meant it. Never again would I make her doubt my feelings for her. I held her tight, rocking her back and forth in an attempt to soothe whatever hurt I'd caused. Thankful to the fates that my beautiful mate wasn't kicking me out of her life on our second day together. I also kept up a string of profanities and threats against my inner beast, making sure he knew he had to learn to control himself, especially when it came to her. I'd given him far too much leeway—we would not be losing our mate because he didn't have enough patience to hold off on his daily swimming long enough for us to have a damned conversation.

My anger at my beast must have been reflected in my body language. Margaret kept shushing and rocking me, rubbing her hands over my body as if to calm me. I soaked in every sound, every touch. Thankful for another chance.

"Hey," she finally said, reaching up to tug on my hair. By the fates, did I love that. "I actually have work to do this morning, but would you like to go with me to the bakery for some coffee and—"

"Yes."

She laughed, the sound a soothing balm to my soul.

"You didn't let me ask my question."

"You said would I like to go with you—the answer is yes. I don't care where we are going so long as I get to be with you."

She shot me a super-phony glare. "You're trying to charm me."

I leaned closer, letting my lips brush against hers as I whispered, "Is it working?"

Her answer was to weave her fingers through my hair and tug me against her, kissing me deeply right there in the lobby of her business. I grabbed her and lifted, placing her ass on the counter and pushing her legs apart so I could fit between them. Needing to touch her, taste her, feel her wrapped all around me. Every breath a gift, every mewl a sign that we would be okay. This was my mate, my one true love, and I would never make such a stupid mistake in regard to her again.

The second I broke apart from her, I placed my forehead against hers and took a deep breath.

"Come to my place tonight."

She chuckled, the sound more sarcastic than I would have hoped for. "Are you going to leave me there this time?"

I grabbed her thighs, holding her in place as I stared down into those amazing green eyes I was quickly falling in love with. Knowing I couldn't lie to her.

"Yes, but only because I have to. And I'll tell you before I go."

She tried to yank away from me, but I held her in place.

"Matthew—"

"Please," I said, totally cutting off whatever she had been planning to say. "Come to my place tonight. Let me spoil you the way you spoiled me last night. And then, when I've got you fed and maybe a little drunk, I'll explain everything."

She stared up at me, eyes hard. Not trusting. "You swear?"

"I do. I promise—you will know everything tonight."

Her shoulders finally sagged, and she let out a big sigh, almost collapsing into me. "I swear, Matthew. If you run out on me again—"

"Never. Not without you knowing exactly why I have to and when I will be back. Okay? I swear to you."

"Fine." She pushed me back, hopping down from the counter then straightening her clothes. "Well then, let's go get some coffee and pastries. Otherwise, I'm going to take you in the back and do naughty things to you."

"I mean, if that's an option…"

She shot me another one of those sarcastic glares over her shoulder as she headed for the door, making me follow behind her like a little puppy.

Funny thought, considering I had told her I was a wolf shifter even though the truth was practically the opposite of that.

But that would be handled later. For the moment, it was time to live a lie while indulging in coffee and sweets. Just a few more hours of deception.

MARGARET

I t's in the woods. Like, really in the woods." I gripped the steering wheel tight enough to make my knuckles white as I followed the dark, curvy, dirt road. "Brit, this is like some sort of murder hideaway."

"I doubt it." My best friend laughed, likely at something in the background, but was back to being serious when she spoke again. "It's Matthew—I've known him for years. He's a great guy and totally not a serial killer."

"That's what they said about Ted Bundy."

"And Richard Ramirez. Dahmer, too."

"You're not making me feel any better."

Her laugh made the phone crackle. "I know, but come on. It's *Matthew*—sweet, kind Matthew. He's a children's librarian, for fate's sake. You'll be fine."

"Sweet and kind, my ass. That's what they all say, and then, *Bam*—I'm dead, and you're crying to some news reporter about how much I lit up a room."

My best friend's voice was completely deadpan as she said, "You don't light up a room."

"Exactly. My anxiety is more about turning you into a liar on national television than my own safety. I'm the bestest friend ever."

Brittani huffed a laugh then sighed, the static preceding her words. "Send me a pin when you get there just in case. Griff and I will be on the way if either of us feels something is off."

That promise took a little of the edge off. "Okay, yeah. I know nothing will happen, but…I'm nervous."

"I can tell, but don't be. No one is making a skin dress out of my best friend."

"I would hope not." I pulled into what had to be Matthew's driveway, his car parked up close to the little house and the golden glow of lights coming from inside.

"Hey, Margaret?"

I put the car in park as I said, "Yeah?"

"He's your mate. Relax and enjoy getting to know him."

I grabbed the phone, still feeling tense and unsure. Likely more because Matthew had snuck out after our night together than him possibly sitting inside with an extension cord and some sheet plastic taped in place, ready to do all sorts of untoward things to me.

Ah, the joy of watching so many serial killer documentaries and then finding yourself in a situation that caused anxiety.

"Hey, Brittani," I said, switching the phone off speaker mode and bringing it to my ear as I fought to find my calm. "You are the best. I'll drop a pin now."

"Have fun. Griff promises to avenge you should anything happen."

"He's a good man…without a cabin deep in the woods to kill you at. You should keep him." With that, I ended the call, sent her my location, took a deep breath, then opened my door to head inside. Matthew was already on the porch, smiling down at me.

"Hey there, beautiful," he said, hurrying to give me a gentle hug and soft kiss. Nothing too demanding or assuming. I liked that. Needed if after how I'd been abandoned that morning.

"Hey, yourself," I said, fighting back the anger remembering that morning brought up in me. "That's quite the drive."

He shrugged as he led the way inside. "It's a bit far out, but I like my privacy."

I was halfway through the door—sort of sliding past Matthew, who stood back to hold it open for me—when he leaned closer and whispered, "No one can hear you scream all the way out here."

I dropped my phone and spun, ready to fight. But Matthew was smiling at me, hands up as if in defense. His goofy expression a huge sign that he intended his words as a joke. He wasn't the only one with a sense of humor.

"If they can't hear me scream, they can't hear you either." I shrugged then reached into my bag, pulling out pepper spray and a set of brass knuckles that had what looked like a unicorn horn mounted in the middle. Perfect for stabbing. "And I'm the one who came prepared."

Matthew glanced at my weaponry and laughed, closing the door behind us before bending to grab my phone so he could return it to me. "Noted. You look amazing, by the way. I'm a fan of the skirts on you."

I swooned a little on the inside, finally paying enough attention to him to notice that he was also looking mighty fine. Low-slung jeans, a soft gray tee, and that wavy hair of his deliciously tumbled and tossed as if he'd been swimming all day and had let it air dry. The man was one fine specimen. And mine. He was mine.

"I was just thinking the same thing about you." I slipped in close to him, grabbing hold of one of his belt loops to tug us together so I could rise up to give him a kiss. He moaned softly against me, grabbing my hips with gentle hands and hanging on. Both of us trying to move closer, to eliminate the space between us. His hands felt cold as he tucked his fingertips up under my shirt, making me shiver.

"Sorry," he whispered against my lips. "My hands are always cold."

"It's okay." I dropped one last kiss on his lips then pulled away, dropping my head to his chest so I could breathe him in. But something other than the scent of my Matthew caught my attention. "It smells amazing in here. What have you been up to?"

He chuckled and wrapped an arm around my shoulders, leading me toward his kitchen. "I made paella."

"You can cook?"

"Of course. You can't?"

I hopped onto a counter stool as he moved to the other side to attend to the huge pan on his stove. "I fed you surf and turf from the diner. No, I don't really cook."

"Not a bobcat trait?"

"Not a Selvaggia family trait. My parents didn't cook when I was a kit. They lived a little more…wild."

He glanced over his shoulder at me, eyebrow raised. "They embraced more of the bobcat side."

Not a question. In the world of shifters, some things didn't need explaining. "Yup. I grew up in the mountains, hunting prey and climbing trees for fun."

"Sounds sort of amazing."

"It was, but I eventually grew up, got bored, and decided I wanted something a little different. So, here I am, living in a shifter town, selling medicinal and recreational catnip at the dispensary, and doing all the fun human things I never knew existed. What about you?"

Matthew hummed and reached for the bottle of wine, pouring the deep red liquid into two glasses. "I had more human experiences as a child than not. We kind of kept to ourselves and avoided strangers."

"Sounds traumatizing."

He shot me a grin over his glass. "It didn't make me a murderer—I promise."

"So you say." I took a sip of the wine, moaning as the warm, luscious liquid danced over my tongue. "Oh, now that's delicious."

Matthew leaned across the counter, placing his hand on the back of my neck to pull me closer. Forceful but not overly so, rough but gentle. He kissed me deeply, his tongue tangling with mine in a way that screamed aggression and had me practically writhing right there at his kitchen counter. But just as suddenly, he was gone, giving me a wicked grin as he licked his bottom lip.

"It really is. You should drink more of it."

Catch your breath, girl. Catch. Your. Breath.

"Trying to get me drunk?"

He laughed, turning off the flame on the stove and grabbing two large, flat bowls to serve the paella in. "Not intentionally, but I'm up for a little drunk Margaret in my life."

"I actually don't drink much, but I do partake in the nip now and again."

Matthew led the way to his table, bowls in hand. "I'm up for that as well. Can you grab the basket of bread on the end of the counter?"

"Of course." I hopped down and did as he'd asked, carrying the bread and my wineglass to the table. Matthew pulled out my chair as I approached, giving me a smile that turned my insides warm and gooey. In a good way—like a lava cake or something.

"What's that look for?" he asked as I took my seat.

I shrugged. "Just thinking about how you make me feel like cake."

He chuckled and took his seat, laying his napkin across his lap as if we were at a restaurant. "I can't say anyone has ever said I made them feel like cake."

"Good, because then I'd have to be jealous. So…paella. Did you pick a seafood dish for the bobcat in me?"

Matthew spooned some of the steaming rice and seafood into my bowl, the smell practically making me drool. "Partially yes. Partially I prefer seafood over most other meats."

"Really? Most of the wolf shifters I know are more red-meat eaters. How'd you get hooked on sea life?"

His face froze for a second, his eyes darting away from mine. "Just what I grew up eating, I guess. Try the bread. I made it myself."

Subject change—activated. I brushed off the unease his answer had given me and focused on the food. The spices, the crusty bread, the perfectly cooked scallops and shrimp…all amazing. All showing a skill set I had no idea how Matthew had obtained.

"So how did an IT professional slash children's librarian learn to cook like this?"

He shook his head, looking almost sheepish. "I spend a lot of time in libraries—there are cookbooks there."

"It's a weird mix, though. Computers, cooking, kids books."

"I didn't intend to be all the things. I was hired by the city to handle IT for the park district, the public works department, and the staff at city hall. They didn't have an office for me and I couldn't get strong enough internet speeds out here to work fully remote, so I would spend a lot of hours working out of a study room at the library. When the city cut costs and decided to outsource my job, Brittani hired me. She didn't have the budget for just an IT person, though, so she asked me to handle the children's section as well."

"It was that easy?"

"Hell no. I spent an entire winter holed up reading everything from board books to middle grade chapter novels to learn the different authors and series and concepts in them. The basics of the job are easy enough—the recommendations and research are a bit more than I had been prepared for. I love it, though. Those little readers get so excited when I can help them find a new book they might like."

I sat a little deeper, my ovaries falling in love with the man across from me. Handsome, kind, smart, an amazing cook, and good with kids? He was quite the catch.

"So, after all that research, what was your favorite?"

"Overall or by age group?"

"Overall."

"Easy. *Don't Push the Button!* by Bill Cotter. It's an excellent book for parents to read with their kids."

"I don't know that one."

"I'll buy you a copy."

I looked up at him over my wineglass as I took a sip, my smile unstoppable. "I'd like that."

We finished our dinners in a similar fashion as the night before—both of us getting to know the other through questions about what we did now and why. We didn't delve too deep into our past selves, but I figured that would come with time. No one needed to dig into childhood trauma on a second date, even if the first one did involve a whole lot of naked time.

But as the evening wore on and we cleared the food, as I sat at the counter while he cleaned up from cooking even though I had offered to help, the unease I had been experiencing since I'd woken up alone began to build once more. Finally, as Matthew tossed the towel he'd been drying the pans with into the laundry room and came back to grab his wineglass, I broke.

"All right," I said with a nod. "Let's hear it."

"Hear what?"

"All of it, starting with why did you leave me all alone this morning? If we're going to be mated, then we shouldn't have secrets. What are you hiding?"

The look of pure panic that flashed across his face told me everything I needed to know.

I was not going to like what came out of his mouth next.

8

MARGARET

I'd never seen a man look so guarded—almost afraid—as I settled onto the couch with my glass of wine and the rest of the bottle. No way was I leaving that behind. I had a feeling we might have to open another one with the way Matthew was fidgeting as he took a seat in the chair opposite me. He looked good, though. Casually sexy, that man. I wanted to purr for him, but the timing was far from opportune.

"Tell me," I said, keeping my voice low but firm.

"Okay," he said, blowing out a breath and finally looking right at me. "I'm not a wolf shifter."

I sniffed on instinct, my bobcat growling soft and low as the scent of canine surrounded us. "You smell like one."

"I know. It's a…life skill." He sat a little deeper, closing his eyes. For the briefest of moments, I would have sworn the color of his skin changed. That he almost began to blend into the background. But then that sight passed, and I was again staring at a normal-looking Matthew…

Who no longer smelled of canine.

"What is that?" I leaned forward, sniffing harder. My bobcat truly awake and alive and ready to take control as my survival instincts burst into life. "You're something dangerous."

"Not to you." Matthew put up both hands and shook his head. "I would never be a danger to you."

I sniffed again, unable to place the scent. "You smell kind of like the sea."

"I know. It's because I'm…" He licked his lips, an air of discomfort blanketing the room in an oppressive sort of heat. I couldn't move, could barely breathe. I sat on the literal edge of my seat, waiting for him to say something. To tell me. To admit—

"I'm a cephalopod shifter."

It took me far too long for those words to filter through my brain and begin to make sense. When they finally did, I still had so many questions.

"What kind?"

"Octopus."

That word stole the rest of the air from my lungs, leaving me silent and staring and in a sort of shock I hadn't experienced before. Even in a town full of shifters, some things you simply didn't see. You heard rumors, of course—knew the urban legends—but that was all they were supposed to be. Octopus shifters were not supposed to live in Kinship Cove. Hell, they weren't supposed to live anywhere around people who weren't their kind.

The only words I could find were not nearly adequate to express my shock.

"You're rare."

"That's one way to describe my kind, yeah. Endangered is another. Threatened. Unsafe, even when surrounded by other shifters…"

The way his voice trailed off could have been an entire novel. He was worried about how I would take this admission. If I could be trusted. If I would keep his secret.

"I would never tell anyone."

He nodded, not looking convinced. "You have to understand, even telling Brittani could be dangerous for me. Collectors would swarm the cove and begin net fishing it if there were even a hint of a possibility that we were here."

"We?"

He glanced up, his eyes sharp. His gaze locking me in place. "I'll tell you my story—I won't tell you theirs. Not yet."

I may not have liked that, but I had to respect it. "Fine. Then tell me yours."

He sighed again, looking almost tired. "I grew up in a clan of cephalopods—mostly squid, but a few octopi like me. We protected one another, kept an eye out for any sort of collectors, and never stayed long in a particular place. Some of the elders taught me to hide my coloring, my scent, everything."

Memories of high school biology classes came whispering into my mind. "Octopi can make themselves blend into their surroundings, even their texture."

"Even our scent."

"So you honed that skill set to stay safe."

"To stay free. If I'm caught, I'll end up in a private aquarium, being forced to shift on command like some carnival sideshow character."

The growl that rumbled up from the deepest parts of my chest was unavoidable. "I won't let that happen."

Matthew shot me a tired smile. "Good, because the idea of keeping my true self from my fated mate is exhausting."

The word mate used so causally made my heart beat a little faster, but we weren't done yet. "Why wolf?"

"It's the easiest scent for me to mimic. Plus, with the sheer number of wolf shifters compared to other animals, it's a pretty easy breed to copy. No one asks a lot of questions when you say you can shift into a wolf."

"That's smart. Whenever I tell people I'm a bobcat shifter, they always want to talk about my tufts." I cocked my head and raised my eyebrows. "Or want to see them."

Matthew grinned, his expression a little sheepish. "I meant what I said—I do want to see your tufts."

"Only if I get to see your tentacles."

"We can make that happen."

My neck grew hot, memories of naughty stories about humans and creatures with tentacles dancing across my brain. *Bad timing, Margaret.*

"So, why did you leave this morning?" I asked, trying hard to cover up the way my entire body seemed to have woken up in the last few minutes. Ignoring the purr coming from my bobcat and making my voice a little rougher than it should have been. Matthew cocked his head, eyeing me. Obviously missing nothing of my reaction but, thankfully, ignoring it. For the moment.

"My octopus is very strong and requires a daily swim. I should have gone before I came to your place, but I was so distracted at having found my mate and I hadn't wanted to push back our dinner. It was really poor planning on my part."

"I would have understood."

He sighed, leaning forward. "I wasn't ready to tell you all about me yet. My human side knew we needed to be cautious, even if my octopus was already madly in love with you."

Well, that was a turn in the conversation. "Your octopus loves me?"

Matthew immediately moved off his chair, creeping across the space between us to kneel before me. He placed his hands on my thighs and rubbed then tugged, spreading them. Sliding in between them so he could be close to me.

"He does," he said, his voice low and rumbly in a way that sounded more like the waves on a rocky shore than any sort of predator growl I'd ever heard. "So much. How could he not when you're his mate?"

I ran my hands through his hair, needing to touch him. "And the human side of my mate? How does he feel?"

Matthew dropped a kiss on my thigh and moaned. "He's madly in love with you as well. Since the very first moment we made eye contact in Brittani's office."

That was it. The moment I broke. I grabbed Matthew by the shoulders and tugged, making my intentions clear. The man was a champion at following instructions because he nearly jumped up onto the couch, twisting me to lie underneath him then settling his weight on me. There were no more words needed, no secrets left to dive deep into. All that was left was a need to rebuild our connection on the physical level.

And maybe play with tentacles, though that would come later.

It didn't take long for Matthew and me to find a rhythm that meshed our bodies together. That put us in tune with the other. He kissed me deeply, hands bracing on the couch as he rocked his lower body into mine. All the weight, the heat, and the pressure combined with his scent —his real one—to intoxicate me more than the wine ever could have. I was drunk on my mate, writhing underneath him and chasing a release as my mind went quiet and unfocused.

Matthew's soft grunts and mine joined together to make a soundtrack to our dirty little dry hump. And when he started whispering, when my name dropped from his lips along with words like *soft* and *sweet* and *fuck*, I was gone. My entire body arched into his, a keening mewl escaping from my lips as I came underneath him. As I clutched at his shoulders and gave myself over to what it was my body wanted. Matthew didn't stop teasing me either. He kept going, his chants changing to include phrases like *give it to me* and *all of it* and *love to watch you come*.

And when I was finished, when I collapsed into the couch with a sigh, tugging Matthew on top of me, there was only one thing I could think of to say.

"That was nice."

Matthew dropped his head to my shoulder and laughed, his body vibrating against mine. "Thanks, I guess."

I chuckled as well, still a little out of it from the orgasm this beautiful man had given me. I reached up and ran my fingers through his hair as we cuddled, keeping my legs and arms wrapped around him. Needing to feel him.

"So, am I spending the night?" I finally asked, almost afraid of the answer. Remnants of the disappointment I'd woken up to lingering.

Matthew's heavy sigh and serious expression as he raised his head to stare down at me did nothing to quell my anxiety.

"Oh," I said, looking over his shoulder when his stare grew too intense. "Got it. I can just—"

Before I could push Matthew off me, he shifted slightly to hold me in place, uttering a quiet, "Wait."

So, I did. I waited as he took another deep breath and caught my eye once more, his expression so very serious. Too serious for having just dry humped me into his couch.

"What is it?" I finally asked when the waiting became too much.

"I'm trying to fight him."

Him. His beast. "He needs to go swimming."

"Yeah," he whispered, the fight he was having suddenly clear. "He wants to go to the sea and bring back treasure for you to prove he's a good mate."

I ran a finger down the side of his face, my brow pulling tight. "Tell him I don't need presents to think he's a good mate."

Matthew leaned in to drop a sweet kiss on my lips. "He's far more animalistic than that, my love. If we were in the sea, he would bring you clams and things to eat while waiting to see if you would mate with him and kill him or just kill him."

I laughed. How could I not? The very image of such a thing was ridiculous, and yet, I understood. I was best friends with a librarian—I knew way too much about the most random subjects. One of those happened to be the mating rituals of octopi. In the wild, we would both soon be dead from that night at my place. Talk about a one-night stand.

"Is it hard for you?" When he raised his eyebrows at me, I rolled my eyes and clarified. "Fighting him, I mean. I know *you're* hard, Matthew."

"Just making sure." He kissed me again, almost as if needing a taste of me for reassurance. "It is very difficult to fight against his instincts. Our relationship has never been one of balance, you know?"

I did know. My inner beast came out to play when she wanted and definitely had her opinions on things, but she never overpowered me. I had a feeling, if I felt threatened, she might. But otherwise, she let me drive and gave me the occasional verbal or physical cue in my mind. Not having the freedom to live my life by my rules would be torturous.

Which meant I needed to give up something myself to ease his suffering.

"Go," I said, keeping my voice soft.

Matthew practically jerked away, his eyes wide. "What?"

"Go. If he needs you to go and you're fighting him, don't. Just go."

"But you—"

"I'll be here when you get back."

"You would be okay with that?"

I shrugged, running my hands over his shoulders to help ease his tension. "Okay might be a stretch, but I understand and don't want you suffering just because I want to hoard all your time. How long will you be gone?"

"I don't know for sure. He'll want to swim for an hour or so. Until he's ready to let me come home."

"And bring me presents."

"Yes. And bring you the presents he's collected."

"I like presents."

He kissed me again before rising from the couch and taking me with him. "I'll make sure they're the best the cove has to offer."

I nodded, suddenly nervous. Not wanting to be left alone but also knowing this was what he needed. What his inner beast had to have. My bobcat snuggled up against a wall in my mind, her fur a comfort to me as I said, "You should go. The sooner you leave, the sooner you come back."

Matthew kissed me once more before pulling me toward the door. As he leaned over to put on his shoes, he said, "Make sure to lock up after I go. I'll have my keys on me."

"Okay."

"And don't answer the door for anyone. I don't know my neighbors, and it's way too late for anyone to be needing a cup of sugar or something."

"Does that really happen? People borrowing sugar?"

He stood back to his full height, tugging me into a hug. "I have no idea, but your serial killer show has me a little more worked up than I'd normally be."

And that, I could understand. "Don't worry about me. I've got Brittani and Griff on speed dial."

"Is there another bet for tonight?"

"No, sadly. But don't worry—I'll be naked the minute you're out the door. Naked and waiting for your return."

Matthew stared for about two seconds, face slack as if my words had just scrambled his brains, and then he grabbed me. Pulling me into his hold and lifting me right off the floor to kiss me. His tongue tangled with mine, that ocean scent wrapping around me. Enthralling me. Making me moan my desire for him. When we finally broke apart, he was practically panting.

"Poseidon's belt, do I love you."

My entire body warmed, my bobcat purring in my mind. "Yeah, yeah. That's what all the mollusks say. Now, go swim, so you can get back to me."

"Naked you," he said as he opened the door, eyebrow up as if in question.

I tugged my shirt off right there, backing away when he growled and seemed ready to pounce. Shaking my head with each step. "Naked me will be waiting for you. Go swim."

With that, he took one last look at my chest then rushed out the door, slamming it behind him. I hurried to the door and locked it, watching through the glass as he jumped into his car and drove away into the night.

Off to swim in the cove as an octopus.

"What is this life?" I asked to no one, not that I expected an answer. Still, I laughed and stripped off the rest of my clothes. I had made that man a promise, and I was going to keep it.

Which meant sitting around, watching true crime shows on his streaming service, and texting with Brittani. Naked.

"Come home soon, my love," I whispered before grabbing a blanket, snuggling into his couch, and reaching for the remote. I had to make the hours pass somehow.

9

MATTHEW

Tucked into a crevice in the lee of a large stone at the bottom of the sea was not at all where I wanted to be. Sadly, that was exactly where my octopus wanted to be. At least for the moment.

"You promised her presents," I whispered, reminding him that we still needed to find something to give to our mate. He lifted our head, eyes focusing on the most minute details of things that littered the floor around us. I was pretty sure he'd spotted what he wanted to grab—a large, shiny obconic shell about thirty feet away from our resting place —when he zeroed in on something else. Without my even realizing what he'd become focused on, we were off, flying across the bottom of the cove on some sort of hunt.

"Get 'em, big guy." I watched through his eyes, still having no idea what it was he was after. At least until he reached a shell and grabbed it with one long, tentacled arm. A clam, it looked like. I tucked myself away as he ate his prey, never having enjoyed the act of injecting venom into the shell and then tearing into the creature within. Besides, I had no need to eat at that moment. I just wanted to crawl out of the sea, shift to my human form, and hurry back to my Margaret.

My animal form grunted at me, catching the "my" in my thoughts in regard to *our* mate.

145

"Sorry, man," I thought back to him. "Habit."

And it was, but also, we hadn't spent any time with her in our animal form yet. Hell, I hadn't even seen her bobcat yet. Our beasts needed to meet, to get to know each other. We needed to take our beautiful Margaret swimming.

That thought caught the attention of my other half, his head popping up and his tentacles bursting out as if to take up space, to make himself look bigger. Meaner. Yeah, he liked the idea of bringing his mate into the sea with him. He would protect her, fight for her, make sure she stayed safe. But first, he needed to bring her a gift.

"Good. Then we can go home."

We took off again, this time sticking to the floor of the cove, moving quickly but not flying through the water. The beast needed to hunt. He managed to find our way back to where we had been resting then looked around. The second he spotted that obconic shell, we were off again. He came to a pause over the shell, stirring up the sandy bottom from the current his own body created. He grabbed the shell with a tentacle and tugged it close, a sense of pure masculine pride racing through our shared mind, before swimming deeper into the cove. Heading for shore. Looked like we were heading home.

We passed a handful of other creatures swimming out to sea. Creatures like us—rare and threatened, ones who would keep our secret solely because they knew we would keep theirs. There were far more shifters in the water around the cove than any of the residents knew about, including an old shark shifter who preferred telling stories of his days in the deep, open waters than hunting down his food, and a woman who lived her life underwater as about twenty different seahorses. The chaos in her mind had to be almost impossible to handle.

And then there was me, my octopus a predator under the water, our ability to match our surroundings and defend ourselves from attack legendary. We swam a lot in these waters—daily, really—and kept an eye out for threats to our underwater world. But tonight, the trip needed to be cut short. We had a woman to go home to.

And ask about going swimming with us.

We made it to the wall of the cove about where we'd entered. There was a long-forgotten ladder leading up from the water that no one seemed to pay attention to. Still, I shifted in the water, making sure to pop up a time or two before reaching the ladder just in case anyone was watching for me. I climbed out—stark naked, mind you—and hurried to where I'd tucked my clothes. I did a quick dry-off with a microfiber towel meant for swimmers, yanked on my clothes, and was racing for my car in just minutes. I wanted to be home more than anything, needed to know our mate was still there. Needed to see her, smell her, touch her.

"Almost there," I said to the anxious octopus filling my thoughts with images of our mate. He definitely seemed just as restless as I was, at least until he pictured the shell he'd grabbed for her. I ran my fingers over it, having secured it in the passenger seat. "It's a beautiful shell."

Yeah, he liked that. He would have liked it even more coming from Margaret.

We arrived home in record time, my need for Margaret growing with every passing second. I raced from the car to the porch then to the door, struggling with the keys in my haste to get inside. But once I did, once I walked in and was again surrounded by the scent of my mate, I calmed.

"My love," I whispered, unable not to.

Margaret stared up at me from a spot on the couch, her naked shoulder visible over the blanket she held up to cover herself. Her smile growing. "Welcome home, my mate."

The growl I released was far louder than I would have liked, but it didn't matter. Margaret was not afraid of me. I shut and locked the door then slipped off my shoes, the shell in my hand. I held it out as I walked toward the couch.

"We found this for you."

She took the shell and grinned, looking at it like it was some sort of precious gem. "It's gorgeous."

My inner beast preened at that, proud that he'd pleased our mate. I wasn't much better. I would always bring her gifts if they put that look on her face.

"*You're* gorgeous." I leaned down to place a kiss on those plump lips, needing a little taste before I had to walk away from her again. "I need to shower."

She hissed, the sound taking me by surprise, then rose onto her knees. Letting the blanket fall to reveal her beautiful body to me.

"No. You came home to me like this."

Resisting her felt near impossible, though I tried. I really did.

"I smell like the sea."

"You smell like my mate. Be with me as such."

That was all it took. I growled again, the sound rolling through me as I reached down and grabbed my gorgeous mate by the thighs. I lifted her in one motion, tugging her legs to wrap around me before striding toward my bedroom. Her naked body against me felt so warm, so hot and soft. I wanted to touch it all, taste it. Be inside it. I needed hours discovering it.

"Need you," I murmured as I fell onto my mattress with her underneath me. "Need every part of you."

"Then take, my love. I'm yours."

I didn't have to be told twice. I dropped to the floor, kneeling before her spread legs, and yanked her closer. My big hands pressed her thighs apart, my eyes zeroing in on my prize. She reached down to run those wicked fingers through my hair, drawing me closer. Wanting it almost as bad as I did. Knowing exactly what was coming.

How could I resist that?

"I've been dying for another taste all day," I said, and then I dove in. My mouth on her pussy had to be my favorite thing ever. The taste of her, the way her body rolled against mine, the needy sounds of pleasure she made. All of it had become my happy place, my sweet heaven. A place I never wanted to leave.

But as she broke against me, as her pussy trembled and pulsed along my tongue, I moved again. Pushing her up the bed and climbing on top of her. Giving her no relief between my mouth and my cock. I slid inside with ease, the heat nearly making me come. The squeeze definitely making me groan.

"Matthew," she whispered, and I nearly lost it again. My name on her lips was a siren call, a magical spell whispered across the waves. But answering wouldn't kill me as the fables told. It would bring me life. For she was my siren, made by the fates just for me, and I would cherish that bond forever.

"Stay with me," I said as I began to move inside her, pulling out in long, slow strokes before plunging back into her heated depths. "Be mine."

Margaret dug her claws into my back, the pain steeling but addictive. The growl in her chest adding fuel to my fire, to my desire.

"Only if you show me your tentacles." And then she bit my neck.

I came with a yell, arching through it, slipping a hand between us to pinch and rub her clit so she came with me. Fuck me, the woman was a sorceress for sure.

"You're evil," I said as I continued to rock inside her, dragging out the pleasure for both of us. "Pure evil."

My siren purred, the song one that enraptured me. Would never let me go.

"Maybe. But you love me anyway."

I did, and I planned to show her how much for the rest of the night. Starting with me rolling us over so she could ride me.

Planning out when and how we could show her our tentacles while finally getting a good look at her tufts.

MARGARET

The next morning, we both called off work and headed to the shore. I knew he wanted to see me as my bobcat self, but I was far more excited to see him as an octopus. That was much rarer than me and my tufts. Still, Matthew seemed so impatient, begging me to shift in the house, in the car, on the walk to where we hoped we could be alone on the beach long enough for me to shift and be able to run on the sand.

"You're like a toddler on Christmas Eve," I said after he again bemoaned the fact that he had yet to see my tufts.

"I can't help it. I have the sexiest mate on the planet. I want to know everything about her." He raised my hand to his mouth, kissing the back of it. "Even the furry bits."

I laughed, unable not to. Feeling so very connected to the man. And so very tired. He'd kept me up almost all night again, fucking me up one side of the bed and down the other. Showering my pussy with so much attention from his mouth and fingers that it continued to buzz hours later. Not that I minded or that I hadn't followed suit, sucking his cock and riding him until near exhaustion. We had been ravenous for each other, both of us losing ourselves to our animal sides more than once. He'd definitely felt my ears go fuzzy, and I had a couple bruises from suckers that had formed along his fingers and latched on to me. It had been a wild night, one that ended the way the first one should have—with us waking up in each other's arms.

But today was less about our human sides getting to know each other and all about formally introducing our animal selves. I couldn't wait.

"Here we go," Matthew said, pulling into a clearing and putting the car in park. "That beach should be empty for most of the day."

I followed Matthew out of the car and down the hill, excitement building with each step. "Who's up first?"

He grabbed my hand and helped me over a large tree that had fallen, clinging to my hips once my feet were firmly back on the sandy soil. Staring down at me with the most heated look I'd ever seen.

"Tufts. Show 'em."

I laughed and reached down to pull my dress over my head. Exposing my naked body to the world in one swift move. Matthew's eyes nearly bugged out of his head.

"Okay," he said with a nod. "I wasn't ready for that."

"You've seen me naked."

"I have, but it's always a gift when I'm allowed to again." He ran a hand down my side and over my hip, leaning closer to bend and give my nipple a kiss. "I'll suck on you later. For now, I need to see some fur."

I laughed and yanked myself away from him, spinning into a shift just to show off. I landed on four feet, yowling loudly. Moving almost immediately into a hunter stance.

Matthew seemed to approve.

"Those tufts are amazing." He reached for my ears, running his fingers up the long hairs that formed the tufts of my ears. He continued petting me, tugging on my facial ruffs gently before moving to run his hand over my neck and down my short back.

I changed my growl to a purr, leaning into his touch. Closing my eyes as he explored my fur. He sat down in the sand beside me, giving me the opportunity to crawl right into his lap. I met him at his level, our eyes locking. My purr constant.

"You're gorgeous," he whispered, still petting me. "And the tufts were absolutely worth the wait."

I shifted right there in his lap, my purr turning into a chuckle. My body wrapping itself around his as I came back to myself.

"You're ridiculous," I said, filled with a joy that nearly brought tears to my eyes. "How did I get so lucky to find you?"

"I'm the lucky one," he replied, tugging me closer. "And I'm about to be the one getting lucky if you don't get that hot-as-sin, naked body off my lap."

I leaned back and wiggled my hips against his, just enough to tease him. "I mean…we have all day."

He grabbed me by the neck, his touch bold and strong. Pulling me closer as he whispered, "If you'd rather this than see my tentacles—"

"No, sir. I will happily take a spin on your disco stick later tonight." I was up and moving away from him in an instant, grabbing my bag and digging for my swimsuit. I slipped on my little bikini then snagged my dress, tucking it into the bag I would leave on the sand. Once ready, I hurried back to him, my grin unstoppable. "For now, I need the octopus."

He smiled and rose to his feet, tugging his T-shirt off in the process. "You only want me for my tentacles."

"I want you for a lot of reasons—your tentacles are only one."

He shook his head, laughing. Dropping his shorts right in front of me. Man, I was one lucky bobcat. My mate was thick but lean, tall, and muscled like an Olympic swimmer. He was also hard as a rock, which didn't seem to bother him much.

"C'mon," he said, reaching a hand my way. "The tide is on its way out. I should be able to find a good pocket of tide pools to play in where you'll be protected from the worst of what's out there."

"You mean like sharks?"

"Yeah, though the local shark shifter is old and not really as aggressive as he used to be."

I pulled him to a stop, my brain needing a second. "There's a shark shifter in the cove?"

He smiled and yanked me along behind him. "Of course there is. Now, come on. I want to swim with you."

Matthew pulled me along the rocky shore, helping me over some larger stones before he finished stripping. Naked and oh-so handsome, he led me to an outcropping that he deemed acceptable. I had to admit, the man knew his coastline. The spot was rocky but filled with pockets of deeper water, consistently about knee- to waist-deep with some spots where I wouldn't have been able to touch the bottom.

"These will be tide pools once the tide is out," he said, directing me to a section where I stood in water only up to my mid-thighs. "They'll be teeming with wildlife, but we've still got an hour or so until that happens. For now, it's plenty deep for us to swim."

I crossed my arms and cocked my head. "Then swim."

He gave me a cocky grin then dropped into one of the deeper sections, disappearing underwater. I stood in the chill morning air, waiting and watching. For what, I had no idea. The man was an octopus —it wasn't like he would breach the surface on a jump or pop his fin above the water. I kept my eyes where he'd dropped and waited. And waited some more. It wasn't until I was about ready to yell his name that I looked down.

And I screamed.

"Fates alive." I jerked away, absolutely shocked to see a creature sitting just under the water at my knees and staring at me. Staring hard. "I… Is that you?"

The creature—looking quite like a large ball—began to unfurl itself, arms slowly gliding under the water. Eight of them. Definitely him.

"I wasn't prepared to see you staring at me like a creeper," I said, dropping down a little to place my hand underwater. "Aren't you cute."

The creature froze then spun, stirring up the water as if mad. That only made me laugh harder.

"Okay, okay. You're a fierce, vicious, terrifying creature of the deep. I bet you're the baddest predator in the cove, aren't you?"

Matthew calmed and slipped closer, one tentacle coming to sit in my outstretched hand. The suckers pulling on my skin in a way that made me giggle. It also changed colors right there, lightening and seeming to almost blend with my skin tone. I stood in the sea, holding hands with an octopus, which was far beyond what I had thought I would ever possibly do in my lifetime, but there we were. Even my bobcat seemed enthralled by the dance of the tentacles below the waves, pushing against my mind to see, though not wanting to take over. She never had been the biggest fan of water.

With a tug from my mate as guidance, I stepped carefully across the outcropping, enjoying the feel of his tentacles rubbing against my legs as I moved toward deeper water. When the water rose to my waist, I looked at Matthew one last time and pursed my lips.

"No funny business, mister. We're here to swim together."

A tentacle slipped up my thigh and over my hip, finally wrapping itself halfway around my waist. He tugged me closer to him then squeezed, lifting me with that one arm while others came to support my back and legs. I went from staring at my mate to staring at the sky in seconds, the change disorienting. The feel of so many suckers against my skin absurd.

"I'm swimming with my octopus mate," I said with a laugh. "This is so surreal."

We swam until the water began to grow too shallow, Matthew always touching me. Never letting me go. When the waist-high water became knee-high, Matthew tugged me out farther into the sea. Again helping me stay afloat as we reached water where I couldn't touch the bottom. Together, we swam around the rocks and toward the shore. At one point, he slipped underneath me and flipped me over, forcing me into a float instead of swimming. He stayed right under me, holding me up, wrapping tentacles around me and tightening them. A full-body hug from my multiarmed mate. I grabbed the tentacle around my waist and ran my hand over it, the slickness of his skin a bit of a surprise. The coldness even more so.

But the feelings shifted, the creature below me slipping away and being replaced by a human man with only two arms and two legs. Still holding me in the water, of course. Still hugging me. Just in his human form. When he stopped us so we could stand in the water—my feet finally reaching the bottom again—I spun and wrapped my body around his.

"That was amazing."

"Not too weird for you?"

"Oh, it was weird, but not in a bad way. Your octopus is magnificent."

Matthew laughed, hugging me tight as if he'd been afraid I might not have a positive reaction to what I'd just experienced.

"You're going to give my beast a bigger ego than he already has."

I pulled away, smiling up at him. "Is he a badass?"

"The baddest." He leaned down to press his lips to mine, deepening the kiss and tugging me into his arms. I wrapped my legs around his hips and held on as he began to move us toward the shore. Loving the warmth and the touch, the feel of his muscles bulging and stretching under my touch. The confidence of my mate.

I finally had to break away before I started writhing against him right there. "I really wish water wasn't so bad for sex."

Matthew raised an eyebrow, his smile turning knowing. "Is my mate feeling needy?"

I chose not to answer with words but to let my bobcat make a sad, mewling sort of noise. The sound of her desire. Of her need. Matthew responded as if he knew that sound, reaching underneath my ass to tease me. To spread my thighs a little and rub his knuckle against me.

"I'd fuck you right here if I weren't afraid of someone watching us."

"Not an exhibitionist?" I asked, leaning in to bite his lip.

He growled against my mouth, moving faster toward the shore. "Not particularly, no. I want to keep you all to myself."

I reached down and grabbed his ass, squeezing hard. "Same."

He planted another kiss on my lips, this time sealing us together and pressing his hand on the back of my neck to hold me in place, before falling forward. I kissed my mate in his world—under the sea—with both of us tangling our bodies together. I could have sworn I felt a tentacle wrap around my legs, would have thought there were a few suckers massaging my thigh. But then we were both above the water again, and Matthew—fully human—was carrying me to the beach.

"Come, my little kitty cat," he said when he set me down in the ankle-deep water at the shore. "Let's get you home where I can have my way with you."

I gripped his arm and pulled him to a stop, turning us to look out over the water. Snuggling close while the waves lapped at our feet.

"This is our future, isn't it?"

He kissed the top of my head, holding me tight. "Yeah, it is. You, me, your bobcat, and my octopus. Are you okay with that?"

I grinned and leaned into him more, looking up to meet his worried eyes.

"You, me, a bobcat, and an octopus living in a cabin along the shore. Sounds like heaven to me."

And it did. A heaven where land and sea met. Where both could come together to explore the worlds they loved. Heaven right there in Kinship Cove.

EPILOGUE

MARGARET

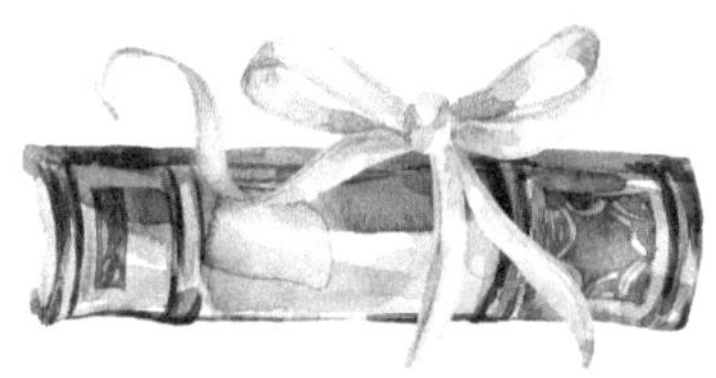

Midsummer in Kinship Cove happened to be one of my favorite times. From the festivals to the boats on the water to all the people walking the streets and enjoying a meal or a drink on the patios of the restaurants. Kinship Cove truly came alive in the summer.

"What's on the menu tonight?" Matthew asked, bringing the back of my hand to his mouth to kiss it in that habitual, almost unconscious way he tended to do.

"I was thinking we could grab a bunch of appetizers from that small plate place. Maybe a glass of wine or two."

"Or four," he said with a laugh.

I shrugged. "No point in wasting a bottle once it's been uncorked."

He laughed again, directing us to the restaurant in question. We were seated quickly at a table on the back patio, looking out over the cove. The perfect place for the two of us.

"Land and sea," I said, reaching for his hand. He turned my way, his eyes still a little wistful from looking out over the water.

"You and me."

I sat back as the waiter poured our drinks, giving him time to move on before asking, "Do you need to swim tonight?"

Matthew turned his head toward the water again, frowning. "Definitely. And soon."

"Then it's a quick dinner." I motioned for the waiter when I spotted him, holding up my menu. "Can we get every plate that has seafood, please?"

"A mermaid dinner. Absolutely. Is that all?"

I glanced at my mate—my very distracted mate—and shook my head. "No thank you. That will be all we need."

Once he left again, I tugged on Matthew's hand, forcing his attention back to me. "Give me thirty minutes, and then you can go."

He shook his head. "I can make it through dinner."

"Baby, you look like that water is screaming your name. Thirty minutes is all I ask for."

The relief on his face was enough for me to know I'd just said exactly what he needed to hear.

"I love you, Margaret."

"I love you too. Now, I'm not sure if you—"

"Hey there, Bob."

I growled under my breath, unable not to. Matthew and I both turned toward the woman in question—his coworker and my nemesis. I'd learned the Siamese shifter's name was Arabella and that Matthew thought she was really nice. I still hated her, mostly for always calling me Bob, but also because Matthew thought she was *nice*. Jealousy wasn't a good look for me, but what could I do? My inner bobcat was a territorial little bitch.

"My name's not Bob, but you know that."

Arabella turned those wide eyes on me, smiling with those bright red lips in the most sarcastic way possible. "We do know that, don't we? It's nice to see you two out on a date. I thought Matthew here just sat at home playing video games when he left work."

Matthew laughed as if what she had said wasn't rude but funny. "I mean, I do like a good video game now and again, but dinner out with my mate is my preferred evening activity."

I purred under my breath, catching both of their attention. "Is it now?"

His grin turned wicked, his eyes sparkling. "Preferred activity for when we leave the house."

Arabella laughed, the tinkling sound grating on my nerves, the bounce of her long, black hair annoying. "You two are adorable. Well, I'm meeting a friend for a few drinks. See you at the library, Matt. Bye, Bob."

With that, she strode off, hips swinging and hair bouncing. So annoying.

"Stop," Matthew said as he leaned across the table. "She's not important to us."

"She bugs me."

"I know, but you shouldn't let her get to you."

"She always calls me Bob."

"It's her sense of humor."

"I don't like it."

"Should I convince her to go swimming with me and drown her?"

By the fates, did I love this man. "No. But thanks for offering."

He shot me a wink then sat back. "Speaking of murder, there's a new docuseries coming out this weekend about—"

"Yes."

He stared for a second. "Yes, what?"

"Yes, I know it's coming out. And yes, I want you to make paella and get a good bottle of wine so we can sit on the couch and watch it together."

He laughed, head thrown back and as loud as he wanted to be. Attracting attention and obviously having no shame in that.

"You know me so well."

I leaned across the table, meeting him in the middle for a quick kiss. "I do, my tentacled love. So yes, let's plan a night in with a serial killer. But first, let's eat a delicious dinner, drink some amazing wine, enjoy these stunning views, then get your naked butt in that water so my tentacled friend can relax."

His eyes softened, his gaze going almost hazy. "I am so lucky to have found you."

"I'm the lucky one."

He smiled again, leaning forward for one more kiss before whispering, "Come swimming with me tonight?"

I nodded, sitting back as the waiter arrived with our food. Unable to wipe the smile off my face. Of course, I would go swimming with my mate. He would take me to the deeper waters, swimming down with me in my snorkel gear and him in his octopus form. He'd never let me out of his sight, never stop touching me. Those tentacles would be hanging on to my arms and legs and waist the entire time we played in the warm water. The feel of those suckers against my skin had become one of my favorite things, the pressure they caused something that couldn't be replicated. Even my bobcat loved to head out into the water with him, paddling her paws and snarling at the fish that swam by. Our swimming dates had truly become a family affair.

And when we were done, when my Matthew was back to his human form and we had returned to the shore, he would take me home and fuck me right there on the deck overlooking the water. The closest to being an exhibitionist he would ever be.

And I would be in my personal version of heaven. Just Matthew, me, and the cove.

Perfect.

SNOW RED

KINSHIP COVE: BOOKS & BAES

Kinship Cove protects their own and is a popular spot for fairy tale heroes, heroines, and even a villain or two. Welcome to the Kinship Cove library where the sassy library clerk is about to have all her secrets exposed during story hour.

Siamese cat shifters are known to be chatty but I don't always live up to that stereotype, mostly because talking means telling secrets. That's not what I should be doing. I may have run away from my own version of the evil queen to hide among the shifters of Kinship Cove, but that doesn't mean I'm safe quiet yet.

Mirror Mirror, on the wall…how can I hide from my past when my fated mate is going to hunt to uncover it all?

1

ARABELLA

There was something about farmers markets that always brought me such joy. The excited children running around, the people sniffing and investigating crops grown by farmers who lived right down the road, and the unending patience of the vendors working the stalls as they were asked for the millionth time how much something with a price sign right in front of it was. I'd been attending farmers markets since I was a wee kitty, both as a shopper and a booth worker, and they never grew old for me.

"Mom, look. She looks just like Snow White."

Neither did comments like that, especially when I'd been sent to the market specifically because I looked a lot like the movie version of Snow White.

I turned and smiled at the young girl who'd pointed me out, dropping down to her level and wagging a finger at her until she approached.

"Do you like fairy tales?"

The little girl nodded, her eyes wide. I glanced up at her mother just in case, seeing nothing but happiness on her expression. Not a bit of fear or worry. Excellent. Time for the sales pitch.

"There's a reading club at the library just for people who like fairy tales. Every week, I or one of my princess friends come to talk about where fairy tales come from, read ones you already know and love, and explore others that you may have never heard of. Does that sound fun?"

"Yes. Mommy, I want to go to the fairy-tale club."

I gave the girl a quick hug and handed her a rose. Around the stem, Matthew—the children's librarian—had tied a simple piece of paper with the information for the fairy-tale club he'd created.

"Here's your invitation, young miss. Do come and see me this weekend."

I rose to my feet and reached into my basket, pulling out a postcard Matthew had printed. "And this is for you, your highness."

"Thank you," the woman said, grabbing her daughter's hand. "We'll be there for sure."

Mission accomplished. I nodded before turning, my long red skirt billowing out in what I already knew was quite the show, and moved on through the crowd. One family invited to Matthew's story hour. The children's librarian loved to use me as bait for the little readers, and I loved putting on a show for them. Especially in what my mother had always called my love letter dress.

My stomach clenched a little at the thought of my mother, and my hands began to shake. I never thought about that woman, about that time in my life. I hated to. Yet that little whisper of a memory had found its way inside my head. Ugh.

I gripped my basket tighter, lifted my chin, and banished those thoughts from my mind. That girl—that child who had been forced to put up with her mother's horrible treatment—was long gone. I was Arabella Snow, I worked for the Kinship Cove Library, and today, I needed to pretend to be Snow White to entice children into a summer reading program. I could not fail because of old memories.

"Arabella!"

I spun as I heard my name, my heart jumping for a moment. *This is why we don't think about her.* I took a deep breath and found my smile, keeping it wide and bright. There, across the sea of people, was my friend Sebastian, with his trusty camera in hand.

"Hi, Sebastian," I said once I had walked close enough to be heard over the noise of the crowds. "Working on a story?"

"Just a light piece about the farmers market. Nothing too crazy." Sebastian shrugged, his cheeks already flushing. The man was nothing if not predictable. He always had that camera and would forever blush around me. He was the most bashful person I'd ever met, but I found that endearing.

"Just photos this time or the whole thing?"

Another shrug, more blushing. "The usual."

Which meant more than just pictures. Sebastian was the local newspaper reporter. And their photographer. And their editor. Pretty sure Sebastian was the only person who worked for the paper, but I would have never asked. I wouldn't want to insult the man—he worked really hard to post stories with local interest. He also would have blushed painfully red.

I nodded and looked up, totally ignoring the flush on his cheeks and squinting into the sun for a moment. "Well, it's a wonderful day for the market. This weather has drawn a good crowd."

"Totally. It's just so...repetitive." He sighed and looked around the crowd. "I wish something would happen around here, you know?"

I did know, and deep down, I hoped for the opposite—that nothing ever *did* happen. I wanted a quiet, calm life. No drama, no craziness, no wild histories or town horror stories. I wanted exactly what I had in Kinship Cove, but Sebastian wasn't one to agree with such thoughts.

"Well, perhaps one day you'll get your wish."

"Perhaps." He frowned, looking me up and down. "Hold on."

Within a split second, Sebastian had his camera up and was clicking away. I smiled at first then turned away, uncomfortable with so much attention. It was my turn to be the bashful one.

"I think you have enough pictures of me."

"Not in that dress. You look like a fairy-tale princess." He took a few more shots. "After the big battle scene, though."

"After the what?"

"The battle scene. You know—the fight to win her hand sort of thing." He pointed at the bottom of my skirt. "That fade to black on the very edges makes your skirt look like a fire."

The market spun, my breath catching. Yes, my skirt did look like that. Intentionally, though most people didn't notice the ombre edges as much. I hated that he'd picked up on the meaning.

Before I had to explain or brush him off, a commotion at the other end of the market caught both of our attention. Without words, we drifted closer, Sebastian likely wondering if he'd finally catch a decent story and me simply curious and looking to avoid more conversations about my skirt. Together, we pushed through a small knot of shoppers who'd obviously run into one another and wanted to chat in the middle of the path between booths, then made a turn before seeing the cause of the commotion.

There, at the end of the row, stood a man bigger than any I'd ever seen. Thick and tall with salt-and-pepper hair and taking up all the space he could, he was impossible to ignore. As was the small child at his feet, crying. The market, the dress, the tears—memories of my own childhood flooded me. The fear I had lived in, the tears I'd cried at night when no one could hear me. Child me had needed protection I hadn't received—I would not allow a Kinship Cove youth to be put in the same situation.

"Hey!" I pushed through more people, picking up speed. "Hey, you! Leave that boy alone!"

The second I made it clear of the worst of the crowd, I started running. I knew I had to look a little crazy—black hair flying in the wind, bright-red skirt with darkened edges fanning out behind me. I didn't care, though. I'd make a spectacle of myself if it meant that little boy could stop being so afraid.

The second I reached the two, I jumped in between the man and the little boy, arms out in a protective stance. My basket of flowers flew from my arm, the roses falling to the concrete. Splashes of red dancing at my feet. Something in the man's hand distracted me for just a moment, though. Only long enough to reel in all the wild worries flying through my mind. It was a teddy bear. A small, tattered bear with a missing eye but a clean bow tie around its neck. I glanced down at the boy who seemed intent on the bear...and totally free to walk away. A large arm invaded my sight path, handing the stuffie back to its rightful owner, who immediately stopped crying, gave me a watery grin, then ran off into the crowd.

Oh. Ooooohhhhhh. Well, this was embarrassing.

I slowly turned to look up at the beast of a man, to apologize for rushing in the way I had, but the second my gaze met his, all thoughts disappeared. There, in the depths of chocolate brown staring down at me, I found a connection I'd never expected. A link to another person I knew was possible but had thought I'd missed out on. A tug deep in my gut and a sudden pounding of my heart sent my soul spinning while my brain practically shut down. I could only focus on one thing.

I'd just met my fated mate in the middle of a farmers market dressed like Snow White.

I had not been prepared.

The man, my mate, held my gaze as he bent forward, reaching down between us and retrieving a single blood-red rose. Holding it out to me with a soft smile lifting his lips.

"I believe this is yours."

Oh, that voice. It sent shock waves up my spine.

"You're..."

I couldn't speak, couldn't put my thoughts in order. I took the rose from him simply out of instinct, but my mind had scattered and my inner cat had started yowling in my head. I had no room for things like words and making sense. No synapses firing enough to string together syllables and sounds.

Thankfully, the man seemed to understand my lack of verbal acuity.

"It's okay, princess. I know this is shocking. Let's start at the beginning—I'm Mateo. And you are?" He gave me a gentle smile. Almost as if he were inviting me to speak to him.

Here goes nothing.

"Arabella," I whispered, proud of myself for finding the clarity to give him the right name at least.

"Beautiful. A name fit for royalty." He looked me up and down, inching closer. "Truly beautiful."

As the market moved on around us, the space between us disappeared, the two of us growing closer without any thought or intention on my part. It was as if we were caught in each other's orbits, slowly revolving around each other until we crashed together. Oh, and we definitely crashed together. The moment our bodies met, my mind exploded into an array of colors and smoke. Like fireworks behind my eyes, bright sparks flew across my mind, coloring Mateo in reds and blues, bright greens and hot pinks. He was it—my one and only. My gift from the fates. This was *fate*.

"Arabella," he said, moving even closer. Pushed right up against me. "Can I—"

Sebastian suddenly appeared at my side, jostling me away from Mateo. "That might be the best picture I've ever taken in my life."

The sound of Mateo growling under his breath distracted me from the camera Sebastian was holding out to me, the abrupt noise of the market invading the silence I'd been living in. Our little bubble of fate popped, so it was back to reality, it seemed.

"Yes, it's…" I looked up at Mateo, still unable to think clearly. Unable to find words.

Thankfully, he seemed to understand my dilemma. "Beautiful. It's stunningly beautiful."

"I'm totally putting this on the wire," Sebastian said, staring at his camera. "This may be a chance to put Kinship Cove on the map."

I had a moment of fear, of cold terror, before Mateo placed a hand on my arm. That touch, the warmth from it, banished all negative sensations. And as Sebastian rushed off, I almost wondered what had bothered me in the first place.

"So," Mateo said, leaning in even closer and lowering that sexy voice of his. "May I take you to lunch?"

I nodded, words still hard. Ready to take the next step toward a future I'd never thought possible.

With a fated mate.

"Sure."

2

ARABELLA

M ateo seemed to be the sort of old-school gentleman I hadn't thought existed anymore. He escorted me to the diner, making sure to walk on the street side of the sidewalk. He even opened the door for me, guided me to our table with a hand on my lower back, and pulled out my chair, too. Such small actions that meant so much to me. I truly appreciated him because, even though we were only having lunch at the local diner, he was treating me like a princess.

Perhaps he was a prince.

"So," Mateo said once we were seated. "That's quite the eye-catching dress."

Oh. I'd almost forgotten my costume even as the red fabric danced along my ankles. "I was working the market for the library. This dress catches the kids' attention."

"I'm sure it does. It certainly caught mine."

The smile he shot me made my entire body warm. Before I could respond—not that I had any idea what I might say back to that—the waiter appeared to hand us menus and tell us about the specials. I couldn't focus on him with Mateo there, so I continued to stare at my mate instead. Waiting impatiently for the young man to leave. The second he did and I had Mateo's full attention again, I relaxed into my seat.

"You okay?" Mateo asked.

I nodded, opening the menu as if my heart weren't beating so loud I had to worry about him hearing it from across the table. "I'm good."

"You looked uncomfortable there for a minute."

"The idea of having to share your time with others right now makes me anxious. I'm sure it will pass."

Mateo stared at me for a solid ten seconds, his face closed off. Emotionless. But then his eyes lit up and his lips began to rise in a slow smile that promised so many wonderful things to come.

"I hope it doesn't. What would you like for lunch?"

I frowned at the menu. "I think I'll just have the tuna salad stuffed tomato. They have the best Greek pickles here."

"And to drink?"

"Milk, of course."

"Let me guess—you're a cat shifter of some sort."

"Of some sort."

The waiter returned, making me clam up again. Thankfully, Mateo spoke for both of us, selecting a large salad for himself and glancing my way when he ordered my plate—including extra pickles—and glass of milk. I simply smiled and nodded, happy to have that task handed off to someone else.

Once the waiter disappeared across the room, I relaxed again. "That is so weird."

"It's territorialism," he said, looking smug. "You don't like others being close to me."

"Oh." I stared at my water glass for a moment, pushing down the disappointment trying to claw its way up my throat. "But you don't feel that way with me."

He laughed, loud and long. "Oh, my dear Arabella, no. I absolutely feel that way for you. That waiter is smart. If you noticed, he hasn't spoken to you directly or even looked your way."

I frowned, not understanding. "So?"

"So...he's given me no reason to be territorial with you. Now, if he had dared to even give you a smile…" Mateo leaned over his side of the table, a deep rumble coming from his body. "You would definitely have seen my protective side."

My neck and cheeks warmed, my entire body suddenly in tune with his. "Oh."

"Yes, oh. Relax, princess. I'm just as smitten as you."

With that, I did relax. We chatted and laughed with each other, talking recent events and Kinship Cove stories. Our food came, and we spent a good ten minutes on the merits of what made a good pickle. All solid, surface sort of topics.

It was when the questions turned a bit more personal that things got more awkward.

"Where did you grow up?"

I froze, unable to breathe. I knew what I was supposed to tell him—the same story I'd been telling people since I moved to Kinship Cove. The lie. That I'd been brought up outside of Atlantic City—a vague enough spot most people brushed off as somewhere they may have been but nowhere they actually knew. I didn't want to lie to my mate, though.

"I…uh…Indiana. LaPorte."

Not a lie. I'd actually told someone the truth. By the fates, that seemed like a really bad idea, but my truth was now out there.

"Arabella?"

I set my hands on the table and frowned. "There are some things I'd rather not talk about just yet."

He nodded, looking concerned. "Are you okay?"

I took a deep breath, trying to focus on the now instead of falling into my memories. "I try to be. Not thinking about that place helps."

The look on his face turned raging mad, the fury practically its own pulse in the air. He took a few deep breaths, seemingly ready to fight something that wasn't even there. I thought for sure he would be jumping to his feet and throwing tables in a second, but instead, he visibly calmed. Another few breaths, these much more soothing in nature, and then he coughed.

"Sorry about that. I've got a bit of a temper. I've been working on controlling it."

"Let me guess…wolf shifter."

He huffed a laugh before taking a sip of his water. "Not even close. Bull."

Oh. Oooohhhhh. That explained a lot.

"So, you're not kidding when you say you have a temper." I glanced down at my lap, frowning. "I definitely wore the wrong color today."

"You are stunning in red."

I blushed again, unable not to. "Thank you."

"So, now you know I'm a bull shifter—"

"Do you have horns?"

He eyed me, that dark gaze going positively wicked. "Yes. Big ones."

"I want to see them one day."

"I promise that you will." He shook his head, his expression quizzical. "What about you—cat shifter. Domestic? Tabby?"

I grinned and sat back. "Siamese, to be exact."

"I've heard they're quite talkative."

"I have my moments, but I'm quieter than most. My mother lives up to that assumption, though. She can talk your ear off with the right conversation."

"What would the right conversation be?"

I took a deep breath, fighting to keep my hands from shaking. This was normal, right? Chatting about our pasts as newly fated mates was normal…safe. I hoped.

"Local legends."

He cocked his head, looking inquisitive. "LaPorte… That has to be the Lonely Hearts Murders, right?"

My stomach twisted, the room growing almost unbearably hot. It took me a few more seconds than I would have liked, but I found the strength to whisper, "Yes."

Mateo grunted, his eyes locked on me. I didn't know if he saw something that told him this wasn't the path to stick to or if he simply made a turn in the conversation, but whatever the catalyst, he wrenched topics back to Kinship Cove events. I listened as he chatted away, answering questions when asked, but otherwise almost completely distracted by memories from Indiana. I couldn't even finish my lunch, my thoughts were so bad.

Thankfully, Mateo either didn't notice or ignored my rudeness. We finished eating—him paying for the meal even after I argued I could pay for my own—then he rose and offered me his hand.

"I assume you need to return to the library."

I nodded, shaky but refocusing. Fighting to ignore the old stuff that tended to shut me down. "Yes, actually. I still have a few hours to work."

"May I walk you there?"

I placed my hand in his, looking up into his deep, dark eyes and smiling. "I would really like that."

Mateo escorted me outside, both of us saying goodbye to the older lady who ran the establishment and who told us to come back for their meatloaf special. Once on the sidewalk, he placed my hand in the crook of his arm, once again making sure to walk on the street side of the sidewalk. Such a gentleman.

The fresh air did me good, blowing off the stink of the depths my mind had tried to drag me down to. I wasn't in LaPorte anymore—I was in Kinship Cove, home of shifters of all sorts. None of whom I was related to. A safe place for me.

And I had my new mate beside me.

"I like this," I said, letting myself drift a little closer to him. "Walking with you."

"I'm glad."

"I feel safe with you."

"I'm even more glad. You should feel safe with me—I would never let anything happen to you."

That promise did a lot to reassure me. Of course, he could always change his mind once he learned my truth. Once he found out all my secrets. But for the moment, he seemed to genuinely care for me even though we'd just met. So far, I'd have said the mating was going swimmingly.

Of course, that was until we actually reached the library and I realized I had to let go of him. I might have sighed my displeasure at the thought. I definitely pouted.

"Well…this is me."

Mateo grunted, seemingly as upset as I was. "May I see you again?"

My answer exploded out of me, bright and vibrant and with no hesitation. "Yes."

"When?"

"Tonight?"

"Yes. I like that. What time should I pick you up?"

I bit my lip, knowing I should direct him to my cottage but unhappy at the thought of even one extra minute keeping us apart. "I get off work at five."

"I can be here at five to walk you home or right to a restaurant. Whatever you like."

I took a deep breath, psyching myself up to be far more outgoing than usual. Once I felt brave enough, I rose onto the balls of my feet and dropped a soft little kiss on his cheek. "You are the sweetest man."

Mateo snuck an arm around my waist, pulling me up and into him. Tugging me close. His lips were a whisper away from mine, his breath warm on my face as he murmured, "May I kiss you, sweet Arabella?"

My whispered "Yes" was all it took for him to plant a kiss on me that had my toes curling and the blackness behind my eyes exploding into lights and colors again. The man kissed like a beast—strong and demanding—but also not overly aggressive. I had a feeling kissing him when we were alone would have me melting on the spot, and I was definitely looking forward to that.

For the moment, I had to be happy with a quick, deep kiss and feeling the rumble of his growl reverberating through my body from his.

He took a deep breath when we broke apart, still holding me close as he whispered, "I'll see you at five."

"Right here," I replied, hating the thought of letting go of him. Wanting to feel his arms around me every moment of every day. I had never in my life felt so safe. So protected.

But I actually did have to work, so I pulled out of his hold, staring up at him.

He gave me a soft smile. "I promise, I will be right here when you're done with work."

I nodded, slowly turning and heading for the stairs. I stopped when I reached the top one, meeting his eyes for one last time. "Don't be late."

"Never."

I had a feeling he truly meant that.

3

MATEO

I'd never been so happy and yet so filled with rage in my entire life. Happy because I'd finally—*finally*—met my mate. Living alone for so long had left me feeling as if the fates had skipped me over, but no. They'd been waiting to drop the most beautiful, sweet, amazing Siamese cat shifter in my lap. Arabella could stop the world with a smile, and she was to be mine. There were not enough words to proclaim my joy.

But the rage...that came right along with the mating. Mostly because I was a fucking idiot.

I jumped into my car once I knew Arabella had made it safely inside the library and pulled out my phone. I needed to score a reservation at the nicest spot in town, which, from my research, seemed to be the restaurant at the hotel right on the water. Not the place I was staying but I'd looked up every detail about this town before I'd arrived, and that search had shown me picturesque views and food that looked pretty enough to smell through a monitor. Seemed like a solid choice.

Once I secured a reservation for Arabella and me to have an intimate meal together, I took a deep breath. Stared at my phone for a solid two minutes. Then I pressed and scrolled until I reached the contact I really didn't want to speak to. My client.

The phone rang and rang, finally clicking over to voice mail. I ended the call, not wanting to leave this in a message. I might have been able to pull off an actual conversation, but not a message. I had no way to judge the old biddy's reaction to what I was saying. Instead, I again tapped on the screen and pulled up my email. Sending a written missive was in no way my preferred method of communication, but it would have to do.

"Don't be an idiot," I said to myself, and then I started to type.

I've chased your information across the United States but had no success in locating your target. Unfortunately, something personal has come up for me, and I can no longer continue this investigation. I will be refunding your deposit as this failure to continue is entirely my fault. Thank you for your business.

"Yeah, that's solid. Not suspicious at all." I sighed and sat back, sending the email and hoping the client would accept my resignation without a fuss. I had a wickedly rough feeling in my gut, though. One that told me my hopes would not come true.

I had known when that creepy old shifter woman had hired me that I should have turned her down, but I'd been stubborn and had thought the job would be easy. Arabella had just made sure that wasn't the case, though.

Thinking of my mate reminded me that I had a lot to do to prepare for our date. First up, flowers. As much as it pained me to leave Arabella alone at the library, I wanted to spoil my pretty kitty. Thoughts of my mate bombarded me, memories of that first sight of her—long black hair blowing out behind her, the look of absolute fierceness on her face as she moved to protect the child at my feet, and that skirt. Long, red, and entirely too enticing to a bull shifter like me. My inner beast pawed and grunted in my head, making enough commotion for me to shut down my memories.

"Knock it off," I said as I made the turn onto Main Street and started heading toward the only florist in town. "You're going to give me a headache."

My bull snorted his displeasure but quieted. Which was a good thing because I needed to focus on the task at hand. I needed to pick out beautiful flowers so I could court my lady.

Did the kids say court anymore?

"Has anyone in the past century said court, you idiot?"

My brain needed an update.

I pulled into a spot outside the Enchanted Rose floral shop and took another deep breath. I had to calm down. If I busted into such a small, quiet place with my personality on ten as it was then, I'd probably scare the hell of whoever worked there. That wouldn't do. I just needed to relax a little. To focus on what I needed to accomplish.

"Calm down, you jackhole." A few more deep breaths, a little meditation-style relaxation, and I was ready to go. I hoped.

A little bell rang over the door when I entered, tinkling softly in the fragrant space. I took a deep breath before heading for the counter, ready to deal with the woman who likely owned the place.

It wasn't a woman who came out from the back, though.

"What's up, man?" the tall blond shifter said, smiling broadly. "How can I help you?"

I blinked and froze for just a second before coughing. "Yeah, um…I need some flowers."

The man's smile grew wider. "Then you're in the right spot. What's the occasion?"

"A date…with my new mate."

That gleamingly white smile grew wider. "Ah, a new fated mating in the Cove. Excellent! I can absolutely put together a bouquet to set the stage for a night of courting. What do you know about her?"

My smile came unbidden, his energy and good-naturedness pulling it from me. Plus, he'd used the term courting. I wasn't the only one.

"She likes red."

"Good start. Is she local? If she's been in here, I might know the flowers she likes to buy."

"She is local. Arabella—works at the library."

He let out a laugh. "Arabella Snow? Ah, great catch, my friend. She's an amazing woman. She comes in here every two weeks to buy herself a few daisies, but she loves my roses. How about half a dozen roses with some daises intermingled for that touch of whimsy?"

I didn't know whose whimsy he'd be touching, but I wasn't about to argue with the man. "You're the professional."

"Damn straight." His expression grew serious, and he leaned across the counter as if about to tell me a secret. "Do you really want to knock her socks off?"

I nodded. What man wouldn't? Of *course* I wanted to do everything I could to make the best impression possible.

The florist obviously understood that. "Here's what you're going to do. While I pull this together, you head over to the Cake-Ily Ever After bakery. It's a block down the road. Ask for Ginger. She knows Arabella best and will put you on to her favorite treat."

Damn, the man was good. "Great plan. Want me to pay now or…"

He scoffed and waved a hand in my direction. "When you come back. I'll even give you the new fated mating rate."

"You have one?"

"I do now. Go. Buy your woman something sweet. Come back to me for the flowers."

"Thanks. I really appreciate it." I rushed out the door, on a mission to find the bakery. If flower dude said I should buy my woman a treat, then I would buy my woman a treat. But when I walked into the bakery, it wasn't a woman named Ginger at the counter. It was a man. And if my nose wasn't playing tricks on me, he was a dragon shifter.

Fuck me.

"Can I help you?" he asked, his tone flat and somewhat aggressive already.

"I'm looking for Ginger."

The dragon's eyes went red, and his nostrils flared. My bull perked up, recognizing the signs of an impending fight when he saw them.

"What do you need Ginger for?"

I looked over the cases filled with treats then brought my eyes back to his. "I need her assistance in picking out a treat."

"You don't know what you want?"

"No."

"Then why are you in a bakery?"

"The florist dude sent me."

"Seems sketchy."

"Yeah, well, so does a dragon shifter hanging out in a bakery, but I'm not such an asshole to call that out."

The man looked ready to climb over the counter at me, but thankfully, the door to the kitchen opened and a redhead came rushing through.

"I need your help with the mixer, Kingston. The damn thing—" She stopped dead in her tracks when she saw me, slowly moving her head as if looking between the dragon and me. The eye roll she finally performed was the stuff of legend. "Who are you pissing off now?"

The dragon huffed. "I'm not pissing off anyone."

"Yeah, he is," I said, giving the man no grace. "You don't happen to be Ginger, do you?"

The woman shot the dragon a scowl then turned a wide smile on me. "Sure am. How can I help you?"

"The guy at the flower shop sent me to you. Said you might know my new mate's favorite treat."

"Who's your mate?"

"Arabella, from the library."

Ginger grinned and jumped up and down, clapping her hands. "Oh! I love Arabella. She's a feisty one. Okay, her favorite thing to buy is our dulce de leche cupcakes. I don't have any out here, but you're in so much luck. I was about to frost some in the back as tomorrow's special flavor. Give me two minutes, and I'll have a couple ready for you."

"Thank you. I'd appreciate it."

"No problem." She elbowed the dragon at her side. "Come on, Kingston love. You need to fix this mixer so he can spoil his mate."

The dragon huffed, following behind Ginger, though never taking his eyes off me until the door closed between us.

"Nice place. Real welcoming…other than the guard dragon," I said to myself, taking a breath. I pulled out my phone, expecting an email response from my client or a call or…something. There was nothing. No response to my resignation. Maybe I'd escaped any sort of retaliation for not finishing the job.

Maybe…but doubtful.

I couldn't think about that, though. I had a date to prepare for. Once Ginger returned with my cupcakes—and the dragon stopped glaring at me—I headed back to the florist to pick up Arabella's bouquet. I wasn't a flower sort of guy, but the red blooms mixed with the big white ones did seem really pretty.

By the time I was finished, it was close to five. I drove back across town to the library and parked right in front, leaning against the hood of my car with the flowers in hand to wait for my sweet mate. I checked my phone again while I waited, just in case. Dread built in my gut. No calls, no emails. Radio silence from the woman responsible for putting me on the path to Arabella. That just…seemed off.

At five till, I took a deep breath, knowing my girl would be exiting the building soon. I didn't want her to see me distracted with my phone when she appeared, so I tucked it back into my pocket. I needed to focus solely on her, to make sure she knew she was the only thing that mattered in that moment. I needed to be prepared.

And I thought I was prepared, thought she'd be the one surprised by the sight of me, but I had been so very wrong.

Arabella walked out of the library looking like a princess, with her hair pulled up, dangly earrings drawing my attention to her long neck, and a smile on her face that stole every bit of breath from my body. All thoughts of what had brought me to Kinship Cove—my client, my resignation, and how messy things could get if people knew my intentions—flew right out the window. That girl looked amazing, and she was all mine.

I rushed up the stairs to help her down, reaching out my hand for her to take. Nearly sighing when she did.

"Hi," she said, all sweet and smiling and so damned adorable.

"Hello. You look absolutely stunning."

Her neck grew pink, and her smile bloomed right in front of me. "Thank you."

"Ready for a nice dinner?"

She nodded, then slipped her hand into the crook of my arm, looking up at me as if I was some sort of Prince Charming. I wasn't—I knew that one—but for one night, I felt okay letting her think that. I could play the role. For one night, I could pretend to be the man she deserved.

Tomorrow. I would tell her the truth tomorrow.

4

ARABELLA

I had never been to the hotel on the cove for dinner, and the second I sat down at the table, I knew why. The place was fancy with a capital F. No way could I have afforded it, and since I hadn't really dated since I moved to Kinship Cove, no one was taking me.

Until Mateo.

My big, handsome mate helped push in my chair then moved to his own, dropping into it with a grace his size belied. A waiter handed each of us a long, stiff piece of paper, whispering something about the wine list. Mateo glanced his over before giving me a smile.

"Do you like wine?"

"I've never had it." I glanced over the long list of wines, having no idea where to even begin. "Do *you* like wine?"

"I do, but we don't have to have any if you don't want to."

I shook my head, handing him the menu. "I would like to try it, if you don't mind. Whatever you usually drink."

He nodded at the waiter. "Let's go with a Pinot Grigio. Something crisp."

"Of course, sir. I know just the one." The waiter disappeared, leaving me alone with Mateo. Well, as alone as we could be in such a big space. I glanced around, unable not to. Soaking in the candles, the white tablecloths, the waitstaff in tuxedos or shirtsleeves and bow ties. It was all so…

"Fancy," I said, giving Mateo a shrug when he cocked his head inquisitively. "This place is really fancy."

He looked around as if only just noticing it. "I guess it is."

The waiter returned with a bottle of wine, presenting it to me as if I had any idea what the label meant.

"It's…pretty." I glanced at Mateo, nearly panicked.

He gave me a reassuring smile. "Agreed. It's a pretty label."

The waiter nodded. "It's one of our most popular brands. Allow me to pour you a tasting—"

"That won't be necessary," Mateo said, still smiling my way. "I'm sure we'll love it."

The waiter nodded once then poured two glasses and set the bottle in a small container filled with ice before taking our orders. I hadn't even looked at the menu, but it didn't take me long to find a seafood dish that appealed to me. Mateo ordered a pasta dish that also sounded amazing. When the waiter had left once more, I took a sip of my wine. It was dazzling—sweet but not too sweet and just the tiniest bit sharp on my tongue, sort of like a Granny Smith apple.

"This is delicious," I said to Mateo. "Thank you for picking it."

"I'm glad you enjoy it."

"Do you drink wine a lot?"

"No. I rarely drink, to be honest. Don't eat meat either. I don't really live up to the stereotype of a PI, I guess."

"You're a PI?"

His face froze, eyes locking on mine. A sort of fear in them. The look passed quickly enough.

"I forgot that we haven't gotten that far yet."

I would have shrugged if it wouldn't have been a move that felt completely out of place in the room of fancy. "That's okay. You know I work at the library."

"I do. And now you know I'm a private investigator."

"Are you here on a case?" I frowned, my brain spinning. "Do you even call them cases?"

Mateo laughed, a hearty, rough sound that warmed my heart. "I use the term jobs. So, yes, I was here on a job, but it's over now."

"What are you planning to do with your free time?"

"Spend it with you, of course."

Oh. That line hit me hard. My entire body felt energized, as if such a simple statement had sent electricity shooting up from my toes to the top of my head and every place in between. Every. Single. Place.

I shifted on my chair, not missing how Mateo raised an eyebrow at the action. Ignoring it entirely.

"What sort of job brought you to Kinship Cove, anyway?"

He broke eye contact, looking off to the side as the waiter approached. "Normal missing person stuff. Looks like our food is here."

That felt like a brush-off, but the waitstaff truly were approaching the table so I let it go. Besides, there were likely confidentiality rules about his cases. I had to imagine he couldn't just go talking details right there in public.

Once our food had been placed and the waiter had checked to make sure we were happy, the staff left us alone again. This time, I had questions for him that did not involve work.

"So...you're a vegetarian?"

Mateo glanced up at me, still twirling pasta onto his fork. "Mostly, yes. I sometimes eat fish, but my diet is primarily plant-based."

"So, my eating meat in front of you is no big deal?"

"Not at all. You're a predator—your body was built to eat the flesh of prey. Mine was not."

I sat a little deeper in my seat, getting even more comfortable. "I never thought of it that way—your not being a predator. You're just so... big and bold."

"I fit the predator stereotype."

"Well, yeah."

"Bulls aren't predators in any way, but they are mean. They will fight —" he shot me a wink across the table "—but only for the ones they care about."

My neck and face got warm. "Good to know. How's your pasta?"

He sat up a bit, refocusing on his plate and the pasta twirling around his fork. "It's amazing. Would you like to try a bite?"

"Thank you, but no. My halibut will be far more than I can eat. Would you like some?"

"No thank you, princess. I'm fine with this. Would you like a little more wine?"

And so, the evening went—both of us on our best behavior but truly relaxing into the meal and having a great time. We talked about all the trivial things you did on a first date—favorite colors, animals, life in the Cove, silly stories. Nothing too deep. Nothing that could ruin the buzz of excitement around us. The wine disappeared quickly, both of us raising our glasses to our final sips. The waiter appeared at that moment as if the empty bottle had summoned him.

"Another bottle?"

Mateo glanced my way and smiled when he caught me shaking my head. "No, I think we're good on this. I would love a cappuccino, though. Arabella?"

"Oh yes, please. A cappuccino sounds perfect."

"Excellent." The waiter nodded toward my plate, reaching for it when I sat back. Doing the same to Mateo. "I'll wrap these up for you and have the barista make you two cappuccinos. Would you care to see the dessert cart?"

It was my turn to answer. "Oh. No thank you. I couldn't eat another bite."

"Agreed," said Mateo. "That meal was outstanding."

"Thank you, sir. The staff appreciates the compliments."

With that, the waiter swept across the room, leaving Mateo and me alone once more. I couldn't hold back my grin as I watched him. Something he definitely seemed to notice.

"What's that smile for?"

I shrugged. "I like how kind you are to the waiter. Some people…"

As if he could read my mind when I faltered on my words, Mateo said, "Treat those serving food like lower-class individuals?"

"Yeah."

He shook his head. "I would never. That's hard work, right there. My mom was a waitress for a lot of years—she would put in miles on her feet every day. I respect the profession."

I nodded, agreeing. My own mother had not been so kind, treating anyone who in any way served her like dirt. Landscapers, delivery people, waitstaff, stylists—all of them tormented by her sharp tongue.

"What just happened?" Mateo asked, looking concerned. "You went from a sappy smile to looking as if you'd seen a ghost."

I realigned my face, making sure to paste my smile back on. Kicking all those old memories into the closet in my mind where I tried to hide them. "Nothing. Just thinking how rare it is to find a kind man like you."

The waiter delivered our cappuccinos at that moment, quietly asking if we needed anything else before disappearing back across the room when Mateo said no thank you. My mate's face did not look happy, though.

"Did someone hurt you?" he asked, his voice hard and his words clipped.

I shook my head, not intending to go down this road. "Oh, no. Not like that. I'm fine."

He reached across the table, weaving his fingers with mine. "It's okay if you're not fine, you know. I'm here now—I'll take care of you."

Oh, my heart. It wanted to break so badly. Wanted me to swing that closet door wide open and let all my secrets come spilling out. But this was our first date, and such a nice restaurant wasn't the place to have the discussion that could darken his view of me. No, those secrets needed to stay hidden away for a little while longer.

I squeezed his hand. "I appreciate that. I'm here for you, too. That's what mated couples do, right? They take care of each other."

His dark gaze grew deeper, stronger. As if untold emotions were swelling inside him. I could almost feel the energy shift between us, sense the deepening of our bond.

"Yeah," he said. "I guess they do."

The waiter appeared at that moment, breaking the spell between us. "Can I get you anything else?"

Mateo's soft smile remained, his eyes still locked with mine. "Just the check, please. I believe it's time for me to take my beautiful mate home."

Bill paid, waiter generously tipped, Mateo pulled out my chair for me like the gentleman I was learning he could be and held out his arm. I slipped my hand up and over, hanging on to him tightly. Not wanting an inch between us anymore. The man had completely charmed me, leaving me feeling all soft and gushy inside. But the date was over, which meant it was close to time to be separated again. A thought that did not sit well with me.

"I should call a car," I said, the very thought making my chest hurt.

Mateo looked down at me with the most confused expression on his handsome face. "Whatever for?"

"For a ride home."

"I can take you."

"Oh, no. You don't need to drive me home. You're already at the hotel."

He looked back as if surprised by that fact then frowned down at me. "I'm not staying here."

That took me by surprise. "You're not?"

"No. I'm staying out at the motel on the edge of town."

I knew that motel—had started there myself when I'd first come to town. It wasn't anywhere near as nice as the hotel on the cove. "Then... why did you bring me *here*?"

"This restaurant is supposed to be the best in Kinship Cove. You deserve the best."

My heart fluttered a bit, my body turning to face his as if of its own volition. "I'm a simple girl, Mateo. I would have been happy with dinner at the diner."

Mateo stared down at me, that deep, soulful connection back. The energy between us zapping and zinging along my skin. The man had a look that bypassed all my walls, that made me feel as if he could see straight into my soul. He looked at me like he could truly *see* me, something new and exciting. I'd never felt so paid attention to, especially not with just a look.

"You're perfect for me," he whispered, moving us slightly to the side and into a shadowy spot in the foyer. "I don't want to presume here, so I'm just going to come out and ask—may I kiss you?"

I nodded, my heart exploding and my body ready. But Mateo shook his head all slow and deliberately.

"That's not enough, princess." He pulled me closer, bending his body over mine and bringing his lips so very close to mine. "I want enthusiastic consent. I want to taste your yes."

The tone of those words, the growl behind them, made my knees go weak. Thankfully, Mateo had the strength to hold me up so I could whisper a soft but firm, "Yes."

His lips met mine in a gentle kiss that quickly turned stronger and more heated. Right there in the foyer of the nicest hotel around, Mateo kissed me as if he'd been dying to do so. As if he had needed my kiss more than air. He kissed me until I could barely breathe and could no longer make sense of things like time and space. Until I forgot where we were and simply did what I wanted. My hands wandered, my brain shutting off and allowing my body to do what it felt like. And what it felt like doing was wrapping itself around my mate and letting my hands run over his broad shoulders, his trim waist, and the backside that filled his pants far better than most men's did.

Mateo was no different. He took full advantage of having me so close, pulling me in and letting his hands wander as well. I loved feeling his skin against my thighs, my waist, up my back. Loved knowing that I felt as good to him as he did to me. Loved feeling his hardness pressed between us and knowing that was all my doing. The man was a hunter for sure, seeking out all the parts of me that brought him pleasure. And I truly relished being his prey.

"We have to stop," he said with a gasp when we broke apart. "I don't want anyone to see us like this."

I nodded against his chest, still holding on to him. Practically shaking with need. "Take me home, mate."

He took a deep breath then murmured a soft, "Okay."

But I hadn't finished my demand just yet. So, with all the confidence I could wrangle, I pushed off my mate and began backing away from him, leading him out the front doors by the fingertips. I grinned at him once we were fully outside.

"Take me home...and stay the night with me."

ARABELLA

I'd never been more anxious as I walked into my house. Not because I'd been gone so long or thought someone would be in there, but because my mate was with me. Right behind me. And I'd invited him to stay the night with me.

"Sorry," I said as I dropped my keys for the second time. "I should have left on my porch light."

Mateo didn't respond with words. Instead, he quietly shone the flashlight from his phone on the door handle for me. Because he was a gentleman. And I was the one he proved that to.

"Thanks." I finally opened the door—hands shaking like mad—and ushered him inside. I'd never had a man in my space, so watching him look around felt important. Felt like the little cottage needed his approval in some way. That my wild, natural decorating and comfortable furniture had to meet some sort of rule book I had never read. At least it was clean. "Welcome to my home."

Mateo glanced down at me before devouring my place with his gaze once more, looking oddly surprised but in a good way. "It's beautiful. You have so many plants."

I tried to see the space through his eyes—to take in all the greenery as new instead of just something there. "Yeah, I guess I do. I like nature."

He took a few steps inside, leaning over to look into the birdcage that held my sun conures. "I wouldn't have expected a cat shifter to have birds as pets."

I shrugged. "They chirp and sing during the day, making me feel as if I'm outdoors even when I'm inside. Plus, they keep me company."

"Alone a lot?"

I swallowed hard, the three words making up such a simple question practically a kick to the gut. "Yeah. I am."

"Me too." He moved to a different cage, one with my cockatiel in it. "Who's this guy?"

"His name's Dopey."

"Really?" He pressed a finger to the cage wires. "Hi there, Dopey."

"Cookie," Dopey said before jumping to grasp the cage wires right below Mateo's finger. "Dopey cookie."

Mateo's jaw dropped. "He talks?"

I reached past him to grab a cookie for the bird. "Not like conversations, but he can say a few things if he hears them a lot. He says his name, cookie, love, apple...I think that's it."

I slipped the cookie to the bird so he could have his snack, still watching Mateo. The man had stood up, smiling softly, and started moving deeper into my space. I followed along behind him, both of us stopping right outside of my little kitchen.

"This is very you. Right down to the bright-red apples on the counter." He turned and gave me a smile. "I've only ever seen you in red."

I gave a little curtsy, letting the red pleated skirt I'd changed into at the library bounce a bit. "It's my favorite color."

"I see that."

I would never be able to say what made me do what happened next. One second, I stood just outside of my kitchen space, smiling at my mate. The next, I spun. Twirled, perhaps. I moved in a circle and let my short skirt fan up and out, likely revealing the lacy white panties underneath. Maybe I'd thought I would tease my mate, or that he wouldn't notice the panties. Whatever had fired in my brain and made me do such a thing had sorely underestimated the needs of a bull shifter seeing something he wanted in red.

"Princess, stop." His voice had grown deeper, rougher. A warning in his tone even though his words were benign. I felt that threat down to my bones.

I did as I was told, coming to a full stop right in front of him. Staring up into those deep, brown eyes. And then I smiled.

"My consent is still as enthusiastic as at the restaurant, you know."

He gripped the back of my counter stool, looking as if he were fighting not to crush the wood under his fingers. "Arabella."

My name in that tone had me shivering, had me ready to run out the door or jump into his arms. That sound was a warning, and those were my only two options. I chose the first option, but only sort of.

I took a few steps back. "Mateo, what—"

"Arabella," he said, following me. Tracking me. Practically hunting me. "Whatever you do, don't run."

I had never wanted to run more, but the heat in his eyes and the intensity in his energy kept me locked in place. He herded me until my back hit the wall. Until he had me trapped. And then he kept coming, moving to press his body against mine. To breathe in my scent as I trembled against him.

He was just so big.

"Tell me to stop," he whispered as he brought a hand to my hip and clutched at the fabric of my skirt. The air hitting my upper thighs startled me, and I reached up to place my hands on his chest. To hold on to something solid and firm because my world was definitely going sideways. As was my brain.

"What?"

He took a deep breath, bringing his nose all the way to my neck and rocking his body into mine. Making me shake all over.

"I am going to kiss you so deeply, my mate. Tell me to stop, and I'll back off."

The trembling increased, almost my entire body touching his. I had been hunted by my mate. Caught by him. Surrounded and scented and made prey by a non-predator. And by the fates, did I like it. I just needed to make sure he knew that.

"There's no need to stop."

Before I could even finish my sentence, he fulfilled his promise. Kissing me so deeply that he rocked my very soul. He dropped his hands to my thighs and lifted, pulling me off my feet and into his arms. Pinning me between him and the wall. I wrapped my legs around his hips on instinct as he plundered my mouth. As his tongue tangled with mine in the most aggressive kiss of my life. No, it wasn't a kiss. Wasn't *just* a kiss. Mateo had invaded my body and overtaken my mind with his lips. Never before had I wanted to writhe against someone the way I did with him. Never had I been so ready and willing to strip naked and let another person do whatever they wanted with me. This man was my mate, my fated partner, and he wasn't just kissing me. He was claiming ownership.

And I had no problem with that.

"Mateo," I whispered as he finally released my mouth to attack my neck. To lick and bite up and down the length of it as I groaned against him.

"Tell me to stop, princess," he growled, the sound more vibration than anything.

I still wasn't afraid of him. "Don't stop."

He growled low and deep as he lifted me higher, striding across the room to the kitchen island. With one swipe of his big hand, he cleared the counter, sending my fruit bowl flying. Bright-red apples rolled across the wooden floors, escaping his wrath. But I was trapped. Happily.

"Lie back," he demanded, using one hand to push softly on my belly. To tell me what to do. I did as instructed, lying back on my kitchen counter. Skirt rucked up to my hips and my entire upper body likely flushed and red as the heat rose through me. I lay back and spread my legs around him, even bringing one foot up to rest on the counter. Presenting my body like a gift for the conquering hero.

Mateo grunted and stared down at me, watching his own hands as they pushed my skirt up even higher. As he exposed my panties to his greedy eyes. Without warning, though, one hand slipped right up the middle of my stomach to the buttoned front of my blouse. In a second, the man had ripped my shirt open, leaving me lying there with the tatters hanging from my shoulders and my bright-red bra on full display.

"Mine," he grunted, tugging me down until my hips practically dangled off the edge of the counter. "You are so beautiful and all mine."

I nodded, barely able to squeak out a "Yours" before he had me moaning as he ran those naughty hands up my thighs to tug on my panties.

"I'm going to taste you," he said as he worked his thumb against my clit through the thin fabric. "Right now. I'm going to kiss you here—" he pressed hard on my clit, initiating another squeak from me as my legs shook "—if you let me."

I shook my head, groaning. Unable to think beyond the needfulness building inside me. "You don't have to."

Mateo ran his hands down my thighs, spreading them wider, bringing one hand back to my pussy to push aside the fabric and nudge a thumb inside me. I gasped and jumped, trying to push back against him. Trying to escape. Unsure which was the right option.

"I'm going to ask you again," he said, bringing that naughty thumb to his mouth to suck on it with a groan before slipping it back inside me and pumping it in and out. "May I taste you?"

The reality of his needs hit me like a ton of books. He wanted permission, not submission. He wanted me to give explicit permission to him for all the debauched things he planned to do to me. I had a feeling the man could just take anything from me and I'd likely let him, but that wasn't enough for him. That wasn't what he needed to get off.

I had to be an active contributor to my own defilement.

"Yes," I whispered even as my legs clenched as if to close of their own accord.

Mateo clucked and shook his head slowly, staring down at where his thumb was now deep inside me. "That's not enough, my pretty princess. And you know it."

I did know it. I'd already figured this out. He wanted my enthusiastic participation, not just my consent. He wanted to make me beg for it.

If I weren't already sprawled before him like a holiday feast, I would have dropped to my knees in a heartbeat. Instead, I reached between us, locking my eyes on his as I grabbed his hand and pulled his thumb from inside me. I didn't let him go, though. Instead, I directed his long, thick fingers to where his thumb had been playing. Used his hand as my own personal toy as I directed one of his digits inside me, following it up with one of my own. Both of us working over my pussy together. I arched and writhed at the intrusion, at the pressure, closing my eyes and letting my body do the talking for the moment. Letting him feel what he did to me.

"Fuck, Arabella," he said, his grip on my thigh growing stronger. I would have bruises there in the morning, and I would love every one of them. I would wear them with pride, knowing I received them pleasuring my mate.

"Do you feel how wet I am for you?" I asked, keeping my voice low, practically purring my words.

"You're so fucking wet. So wet."

"I've been this way all day because I couldn't stop thinking of my stubborn mate. And now you're here but still not satisfying me." I pushed his finger deeper then pulled mine from inside me, bringing it to his lips and smiling when he sucked on it. When he groaned at the taste of me. "This is my consent, Mateo. My wet pussy is showing you my enthusiasm."

His groan practically shook the counter, and he dropped to his knees immediately. With a quick tug, he ripped the panties from my body and tossed them to the floor. They landed on one of my apples, the white practically covering the red. Innocence over sin.

There would be nothing innocent about tonight.

Without a word of warning, Mateo grabbed me by the knees and pulled me closer to him, and then he was there. His face between my legs. His overpowering kiss directed at my most delicate flesh. There was no small lick or tease, no cautious beginning. The man devoured me from the start, slipping a second finger inside me as his lips and tongue attacked my clit.

I arched and yowled, reaching down to grab hold of his hair and tug him tight to me, the anticipation breaking over me. The pleasure cresting almost immediately. The heat of his mouth on me, the feeling of his tongue laving my clit, was all it took to throw me right over the edge. I came with a scream that couldn't be held back, my entire body seizing as Mateo continued to assault my tender flesh. As he dove in even deeper, filling me completely and sucking on my clit. I shook beneath him, my hands clutching at his hair as if they had minds of their own, not sure if I wanted to pull him closer to push him away. Thankfully, he didn't make me choose.

"Now," he grunted before yanking me into his arms—my knees over his elbows and my legs spread around him—and striding from the kitchen through the house. "I need to fuck you now."

"Second door," I whispered, still fuzzy from my orgasm. Still fighting the conflict of sinking into the fogginess or pulling myself from it. Luckily, I didn't need to make that decision. Mateo took me straight to my bedroom, tossing me on the bed before stripping off his clothes. He climbed on top of me, pushing my skirt up, settling himself between my thighs. And he did as he promised. He fucked me. Good and hard and repeatedly. Him fully undressed and me like some fallen princess, skirt around my hips and blouse hanging in shreds. He fucked me up the mattress and down, flipped me over and took me from behind. Gave me more orgasms than I could count as he filled the silence with his grunts and heavy breathing and filthy mouth. Telling me all about my wet pussy, how deep his cock was, and how much I was made for him.

At one point, as I rode his cock toward an ending that I was almost afraid to reach, the bed groaned and cracked, the entire head of the mattress falling to the floor. A broken bed didn't stop my mate, though. He simply flipped us over to where I was underneath him then spun us around, thrusting into me again and again.

Stubborn to the very end.

6

MATEO

Waking up in my mate's bed with her in my arms might have been one of the most amazing moments of my life, had I not felt as if I were somehow slipping off the mattress. I opened my eyes, squinting at the sunlit room, to find the entire head of the bed on the floor with the foot still supported.

"Ah, fuck," I groaned, memories of the night before resurfacing. She'd been so hot, so wet. So delicious. I hadn't been able to pay attention to something as trivial as breaking the bed. That was definitely something I'd need to address today, though. Especially since my feet were basically on the floor. And Arabella…

Well, Arabella lay next to me, soft and sweet as ever. I moved a lock of that jet-black hair off her pale face, amazed at how red her lips were even without makeup. Probably slightly bruised. I hadn't been gentle with her the night before—kissed her hard, handled her roughly, and fucked her brutally. She'd definitely seemed to enjoy every second of it, but I should have tried harder to be sweeter. Softer. I wasn't good at that, but I could have attempted it. Could have held back instead of going all in our first night together. I'd been an animal with her—barely giving her a break. What had I been—

Arabella sighed, breaking the downward spiral of my thoughts and bringing one hundred percent of my attention to her. By the fates, she was beautiful. Stunning, really. And mine. My inner bull snorted at that, the bastard proud as fuck that his mate was so lovely. There was so much more to her than her looks, though. She was kind and sweet, funny and engaging. The woman had it all...

And she was stuck with me.

"I promise to do everything I can to be good to you," I whispered, running a finger down the side of her face. She sighed again and rolled toward me, cuddling closer. My heart nearly exploded. She wanted to be near me. Even in her sleep, her instincts kicked in to stay at my side. Our mating would be a strong one for sure. Strong and happy. I'd do everything I could to be certain of that fact. I'd never woken up so happy in my life, and I would protect that. And her.

Which meant I needed to deal with my client.

Before my thoughts could take off in the direction of work, Arabella shifted in her sleep. Raising a leg to tangle with mine. All felt well and good until said leg brushed against my already aching cock. I tried not to move, to stay still and silent, but my hips had a mind of their own. They rocked forward, passing my cock over her knee once more, which made me groan. I did it again. And again. Hating myself with every pass. Growing needier for the real thing with every move. I was an animal to bother such a sleeping angel. A beast. A dishonorable hunter. I was—

"Mateo," my angel whispered in her sleep. Her gorgeous eyes opened and locked on mine, her red lips rising into a smile. "Good morning."

Ah fuck.

I couldn't help myself. Couldn't resist her. I dove in for a kiss, demanding entrance into her mouth and going to war with her tongue. My little mate battled right back, wrapping her arms around me and pulling herself up my body. Up because the bed was still sort of hanging there. It didn't take Arabella long to be distracted by the fact that we were lying at an angle with our heads at the foot of her mattress. She pulled away, looking down the length of our bodies before returning those gorgeous eyes back to meet mine with the most adorable pout on her lips.

"My bed—"

"It's fine."

"But we broke it."

"We did." *Don't be proud of that, you animal.* "I'll fix it. Or if I can't, I'll buy you a new one."

"You don't have to buy me a bed." She started to unwind herself from me, looking absolutely distracted, which wouldn't do.

I rolled with her, keeping her underneath me so I could gain all of her attention again. Practically grinning when her concerned pout turned to a smile. "I broke it. I'll replace it."

That smile turned softer, her fingers coming to dance along the side of my face in the gentlest touch I'd ever experienced.

"*We* broke it. Together."

Fuck me. I couldn't control myself. I dove in for another kiss and manhandled her until I had her exactly where I wanted her. In the perfect spot for me to gain access to that sexy body of hers. Once I had her positioned, I grabbed her leg and pushed it out, spreading her, before slipping a hand between us. Using my fingers to tease her clit. She was already wet for me, already primed and ready, and I groaned when my fingers slid right inside her without a hint of resistance.

"Were you dreaming of me, mate?" I growled, diving in to give her neck a little bite. "You're awfully wet already."

Arabella gasped and arched, seeming to like the attention I gave her pussy. "I woke up wet. And needy. If I hadn't been distracted by the broken bed, I'd already be riding your cock for sure."

Dead. I was dead. My mate had just killed me with a filthy mouth that did *not* fit her sweet persona. I loved it, though. I snatched my hand from her pussy, grabbed her by the hips, and flipped us over. Placing her on my hips as she spread her legs to accommodate me. Lying back with my hands behind my head once she was good and stable.

"Go ahead, mate. My cock is yours to use. Pleasure yourself on me."

And fuck me, but she did. Arabella shot me a wicked smirk then reached right between us, holding me in place as she slid down the length. I died right there—the confidence, the heat, the pulsing grip of her pussy, the smirk on her wicked, red lips. All of it led me to my death. Old Mateo was dead and gone. New Mateo had been reborn to do nothing but take care of the woman riding his cock like a goddamned pro. The woman the fates had deemed perfect for me.

The woman I had come to Kinship Cove to find, though not because of the fates.

"You were made for me," I groaned, trying hard to hold on to any sense of reality before I made a fool of myself and spilled before she'd gotten hers.

Arabella didn't disappoint. She leaned over and gave me a little kiss, biting my bottom lip like a vixen before sitting up once more and letting her pussy swallow my cock whole.

"And you for me, my big, strong mate."

Big and strong. Yes. That was me. And she was small, fragile almost. Something to be protected.

As my mate began to twist her hips in a way that had me groaning and grabbing hold of her, had me arching so I could try to be just a little deeper inside her, my mind went right into protective mode. As much as I wanted to stay in Arabella's bed all day—to fuck her for the next week without letting her out of my sight—I had one last job to do. Once last task. I had to protect her.

Which meant making sure the woman from LaPorte who had sent me to Kinship Cove to look for her was off her tail. Permanently.

ARABELLA

The only problem I could see from spending a solid two days in bed with a mate three times your size was the fact that walking afterward became an issue. A big one. It was almost comical how I had limped into work that morning. Thankfully, none of my coworkers had said a word. Brittani had even brought me a stool so I could sit while checking out patrons, not mentioning at all how I might have hurt myself. I appreciated her as a boss even more in that moment.

Her friends, though…

"Good morning, Bob."

The bobcat shifter shot me a mean glare, looking as if she were ready to shift and fight me. I just smiled. I knew the name bothered her, but the look she sent me when I called her that was well worth the irritation. At least to me. She might have disagreed. Bobcats were just so dramatic, though.

"Hey, Arabella." Matthew approached the desk around halfway through my shift, staying back a good five feet from the other side. At first, I wondered if something was wrong, then I realized that I must have positively reeked of Mateo. A mated male would never challenge another, and Matthew was far too smart to put his scent on me in any way, as that would be seen as a challenge.

The fact that I was now a mated shifter hit me as a surprise once more, and I had to bite back the silly grin wanting to explode across my face.

"Good morning, Matthew. Something I can help you with?"

"Maybe. I was wondering if you'd be willing to dress up and play the Snow White role again this weekend. There's a street fair—"

"Absolutely."

The man smiled, stepping almost to the edge of the counter. "Great. I'd really appreciate it. The families that have been coming in have…"

Matthew kept talking, but at that moment, Mateo walked into the library, and every bit of my attention locked on my mate. He was just so big and overwhelming. He seemed to fill the space of the foyer with ease, seemed really comfortable in his size. Other people looked and moved away, obviously scared of him, but I wasn't. In fact, if Matthew hadn't still been talking to me, I would have hopped over the counter and run into Mateo's arms.

If my thighs allowed. Those hips were thick, like the rest of him. I was going to need to do some serious yoga to increase my flexibility.

Mateo looked right at me, his expression solid and…mean. Angry, even. He flicked a glance to Matthew, who was still chatting away about the fair, and the heat in his eyes grew. The rage. Oh dear.

"Matthew," I said, interrupting him mid-sentence. "My mate is here to take me to lunch, so…"

Matthew stepped back immediately, looking over his shoulder to where Mateo stood just inside the door. The children's librarian sent my mate a head nod that I had to assume held some sort of male mate code in it, because Mateo responded with the same nod.

"Great," Matthew said, putting even more distance between us. "We can chat another time, but thank you for always being willing to help."

"No problem." I was in motion before the words left my mouth, heading straight for my mate. He swooped me up into his arms the second he could, clinging to me as he released a deep but quiet groan. "You okay?"

"Yeah," he said as he scented my neck.

"You looked mad."

"Other men…"

I knew that. But I also knew Matthew. "He's mated."

Mateo placed me back on the floor, still holding on to me. Staring me down in a way that made my knees quake and my insides go liquid. "So are you, young lady."

I died. Right there in the public library, I breathed my last breath as a woman who had never considered having sex in her workplace. This man made me want to be so naughty.

"I am. Pretty sure you confirmed that when you broke my bed."

His wicked smirk returned, his eyes practically twinkling as he said, "But was the night worth the damage?"

To my bed, my thighs, my pussy, my back end. I was an aching mess with nowhere to sleep, and I had never been happier.

"Absolutely."

He dropped lower to place a soft, sweet kiss on my lips before rising back up. "Can I take you to lunch?"

He was my mate, had broken me and my bed, but such a sweet question still made me flush. "Of course."

"Is the diner okay or—"

"There's this new French bistro out by the woods. Lots of vegetarian choices for you and fish for me."

"Sounds perfect." He grabbed my hand and led me out of the library, both of us grinning like maniacs along the way. Being mated soothed something inside me, made the happiness easier to grasp. Made the bad stuff seem so far away. It wasn't, of course. LaPorte, Indiana, wasn't all that far. But somehow, Mateo made all those memories and fears disappear. My big, strong mate would never let anything happen to me. Not even if the "anything" was coming from my own mother.

Thoughts I did not need to have in that moment.

"This place is nice," I said as we were seated on a deck overlooking the woods and, farther out, the mountain. "I'm so glad you were willing to try it."

"Thanks for finding it. The only places I've been passing, other than the hotel restaurant, are the diner and that barbecue place out by the highway."

"I've heard that's good," I said, distracted by the menu. When Mateo didn't answer, I glanced up to find him staring at me with a concerned look. It took me a second to realize what might be wrong. "Oh, right… barbecue. Meat. Specifically, cow meat. So, no. We won't be going there."

He reached across the table and grabbed my hand, giving it a squeeze. "Thank you."

And so went our lunch, both of us happy and chatty. We ate slowly, truly taking advantage of the time together. Neither of us went too deep on our questions, which kept the conversation fun and light. At least, until we were preparing to leave, and I asked him something that made the smile fall right off his handsome face.

"What case brought you to the Cove, anyway? You said a missing persons one, right?"

The words had seemed innocuous enough, the questions ones anyone would have asked. But Mateo went still and silent, face tightening with what looked like anger. The energy around him even shifted into something dark and downright scary.

"Just a case. Come on, princess. Let me get you back to work."

And apparently, that was it. Case closed. His reason for being here was definitely not open for discussion. That fact sent a little ball of worry spinning through my gut. What could the case possibly be that he wouldn't want to talk about? Maybe he *couldn't* talk about it, like it was some sort of official thing and he was bound not to bring it up. Or maybe it was bad. Really bad. Maybe he—

"Hey," he said as he slid into the driver's seat of his car, having already helped me into mine. "Why do you look so anxious?"

I took a deep breath, centering myself in the moment. I was being ridiculous. If Mateo didn't want to tell me about the case he'd been working that brought him to me, there was a reason. A totally logical, likely pretty innocent, reason. One that had nothing to do with me. This was a boundary he'd made clear, and I should respect it.

Physical boundaries, not so much.

I crawled across the console and planted myself in my mate's lap, cuddling close and purring under my breath. His heat, his touch, calmed me immediately. I had never felt as safe as when I was in his thick arms.

"You okay, princess?" he asked, sounding far more nervous than I wanted him to be.

I rubbed my head against his collarbone, scenting him. "Yeah, I just needed a snuggle to calm myself."

He grunted then reached down, sending the seat flying backward. We stopped with a jolt, the steering wheel no longer digging into my hips.

"Better?"

I wiggled over him and stretched, taking full advantage of every inch of space as he stared at me. "Absolutely."

His hands found their way to my waist, his touch strong and solid as he squeezed me. As he moved me over his hard cock a few times. "Naughty girl."

My grin came unbidden. "Maybe. How can I not be? You're just so...*big.*"

He groaned and dropped his head back, rocking up into me a time or two before holding still. Holding me still, too. "I bet you're a tiny thing."

It took me a moment to realize he meant my cat form. That was the only part of me he hadn't seen yet. Without a word, I went ahead and shifted. Popping out of my fallen clothes the second I made it to fuzzy and four-pawed. He picked me up in one hand, lifting me toward his face. I head-butted his chin, purring the entire time. And then I meowed. Loudly.

Mateo laughed. "You are a sassy one, aren't you? You're beautiful, too."

I head-butted him again and reached to place my front paws on his collarbone, kneading his flesh. Purring so loudly that I felt my entire body trembling with the sound.

"Okay, princess. I get it. You're a happy kitty. Now, settle down in my lap and let me drive you to where you can shift without showing off that pretty human body to anyone else." He started the car, keeping his hand on my furry body as I curled up in his lap. "Gotta protect you from everything. Can't have you just naked in my car. At least not with other people around."

Naked in his car and without an audience seemed okay, though. Noted.

Mateo drove us to the motel he had been staying in, cradling me and carrying my clothes into what had to be his room. The space seemed dark and totally out-of-date when we walked in, but it was clean. My mate wasn't a messy man, which was a good thing. He set me and my clothes in the bathroom then closed the door, giving me a privacy to shift and dress that I had neither asked for nor needed. Yet, I appreciated the respect. Shifting could be an odd time for our bodies. One never knew how the bones and skin were going to move when changing forms.

I shifted human then tossed on my clothes, catching a glimpse of myself in his mirror. My face was flushed, my smile wide, and my eyes bright. I looked honestly happy. Unbearably so. That was all because of my new mate and the way he treated me so well. The way he cared for me. He was a perfect mate—attentive and aware of my needs but not overbearing.

"You are one lucky girl," I whispered to my mirror self, my grin widening.

Needing to be with my mate once more, I rushed out of the bedroom. Mateo sat on the edge of the bed, looking downright pensive, which just wouldn't do. I raced at him, jumping into his lap, and knocked him back. We both laughed as I sprawled on top of him, the sound quickly morphing into groans of pleasure as I kissed him good and deep. As I laid my body on top of his and wrapped my arms around his neck. This feeling, this heat, was what I'd needed. What I had craved. I had never felt happier or safer than in that moment.

And then Mateo had to open his mouth. "I believe you need to go back to work."

I huffed. "Spoilsport."

He rolled me under him, eyebrow raised. Settling his hips between my spread legs as if he belonged there. Which he absolutely did.

"I'd be happy to spend the afternoon balls deep in my mate, maybe break another bed. But your bosses may want you to finish your shift."

I sighed and rolled my eyes, purposefully exaggerating the irritated tone in my voice as I said, "Fine. If you'd rather me work than have sex with you."

He growled my name, diving in to kiss and bite my neck. Both of us chuckling as he rolled us back over again. Bliss. My mate and I together was pure bliss. Nothing had ever felt better. Nothing would ever take him away from me. Nothing could ruin this.

"Come on," he said, rising to his feet and pulling me with him. "The sooner you get back, the sooner you can stop working, and then we can get naked together."

"Promise?"

"Absolutely-fucking-lutely." He grabbed my hand and tugged me toward the door. I was still smiling, still sort of laughing under my breath when I saw it. When I spotted the picture that yanked the blissful feeling right out from under me. That sent a shard of icy glass slicing through my gut.

"Mateo?"

He turned, looking confused. At least until I pointed at the picture on top of a stack of papers on his desk. Papers with my real name on them. Papers signed with a scrawl I would recognize anywhere.

"Why do you have a picture of me as a teenager in your room?"

8

MATEO

Pacing in a small motel room was the epitome of ridiculous for a man my size. I walked from one end to the other in a total of two strides, maybe three if I kept my steps small. A quick turn and then I was across the room in two to three more. Ridiculous. And yet, I paced. It was the only thing I could think to do, seeing as how my sweet mate looked to be shaking mad.

I glanced at the end of the bed where she sat stiff as a board, where she glowered at the floor I'd just passed over, and I took a deep breath. This was going to be hard.

"A woman named Lucy Meyers hired me to find you."

Those red lips turned down even farther, that beautiful face filled with an emotion I hadn't thought she was capable of. And she said nothing. Not a word. I had to fill the silence.

"She reached out to me two months ago, claiming you were a runaway and she just wanted to know that you were safe somewhere. I took the job, not having any idea who you were other than the lost child she had made you out to be." I stopped pacing, wary and unsure if I should even bother with the next words, but throwing caution to the wind. "Your mother misses you."

Arabella sat silent, moving only enough to place her hands on the edge of the mattress next to her hips. As if she needed extra support to stay seated. Maybe extra leverage to pop up and attack me. I had absolutely no idea what was going on in that pretty head of hers. At least not until she finally opened her mouth and the most deadpan, emotionless voice came out of her.

"My name in Kinship Cove is Arabella Snow, but my real name is Arabella Gunness. Her name is not Meyers."

My brain took a moment to chug to life, but once it did, the pieces fell together. Gunness and LaPorte, Indiana.

"Are you related to the serial killer Belle Gunness?"

She took a deep breath and nodded. "Yeah. Or at least my mother claimed we were. As if I was supposed to be proud to be the great-granddaughter of a woman who had killed her children, her husbands, and her suitors."

I had to dig through my case memories a little harder than usual to remember all I knew about Belle Gunness, and when I did, I frowned. "I thought she killed all of her kids."

"And died in a fire, right? Except the body in the fire was the wrong height. She didn't die and even went on to have two more children. She killed one but kept the last alive. That's our line. I hated growing up with that name, but my mother loved it. Thought she was some sort of local celebrity because of it."

"That's...sickening."

"No, what's sickening is how my mother took after Belle. How she'd joke about killing me with the neighbors, then put poisons in my food to see how I'd react." Her blue eyes met mine, fiery and truly filled with fury. "I ran away because I was terrified she'd actually kill me one day, on purpose or accidentally."

Every instinct inside me raged right along with her. My mate—my fated partner—could have died before I'd even met her because her mother had some perverted obsession with a possible connection to a serial killer. That was a new one for me, as was the rage boiling up from the depths of my soul.

"She tried to kill you?"

Arabella turned my way, that blank slate of a face finally breaking.

Sadness and anger meshing to pull together a picture of a child who'd dealt with trauma, all grown up into adulthood and still being hurt by the actions of her parent.

"A lot. She tried to kill me a lot. Then laughed about it." She sighed and shook her head, breaking eye contact. "So, you can see why your working for her pulled the rug out from under me."

Oh, I could see it, all right. I was absolutely horrified that I'd allowed such a woman into my life, let alone possibly back into Arabella's. Had I known anything about how horrible Arabella's mother was, I never would have taken the job. But then I wouldn't have met Arabella. My bull didn't like that thought any more than he liked the idea of her being around someone actively trying to do her harm. Neither of us knew what to do, though. How to fix this. My bull wanted me to release him, to let him take over so he could chase the woman down. My man side liked the idea, except it left our mate alone and unguarded. That wasn't happening.

"I'm…" Words were harder than I'd ever thought possible, but I dug deep. Pushed past all the anger and fury that didn't need to be pointed at my sweet princess. "I'm sorry I brought all of this up for you. I'm sorry I wasn't as honest as I should have been right from the start. I didn't realize how hurt this whole thing would make you or the backstory. I honestly just thought I was doing another job to help a grieving mother."

Arabella didn't look up at me, though. She didn't answer either. She sat, eyes staring at the floor, for a long, tense moment. And then she sighed.

"I need to get back to work."

With that, she rose to her feet and headed for the door, and my heart sank straight into my gut.

"Arabe—"

"No." She reached the door, already opening it before I could stop her. "I'm done with this for now. I need to go to work."

I crumpled but followed her out, too afraid of being rebuffed to reach for her hand. Watching her for any sign of my usually happy and sweet mate. Not that I deserved that. This was my fault. Had I told her why I was in Kinship Cove, she could have told me her story on her terms instead of mine. She could have had time to prepare herself. Instead, she had found out in a way that made me look like a liar. I had hurt her with my lack of explanation. I would never forgive myself for that.

The drive to the library was spent in absolute silence—no talking, no radio, no nothing. It was as if we were strangers in the vehicle, uncomfortable sharing space and just waiting out the minutes until we could get away from each other. Still, the drive wasn't nearly long enough. I needed more time with her, needed to figure out how to fix what my silence had broken. I needed to make sure she knew that I would always protect her and would never intentionally lie to her. She needed...

"Just drop me off at the door. You don't need to walk me in or anything."

...me to leave her the hell alone, apparently.

"Arabella, I would like to pick you up after work if you don't mind. So we can talk more."

She shrugged but didn't look at me. "I don't know if I want that right now, but I'll text you."

With that, she rushed out of the car and up the stairs, disappearing into the old, brick building without a single backward glance. My heart shattered right there in my car, my inner bull groaning a mournful sound in my head. My mate had left us without a care, but it was our own fault.

Fuck me, I needed to find a solution for this issue.

As I turned to pull away from the library, I noticed two things almost simultaneously. The first was a woman with dark hair and abnormally red lips standing across the street. Watching the doors. The expression on her face sent ice shooting through my gut, but I had less than a second to take her in before she turned and walked away. Disappearing into the parking lot. The second thing was a man who was most definitely some sort of law enforcement staring off in the direction where the woman had been. He looked familiar—I was pretty sure he'd been hanging around with the main librarian, Arabella's boss, Brittani.

He had that cop stare, that stance that said he was ready for anything. That air about him. Definitely the law and totally noticing the same woman I had. The one who had disappeared.

Fuck, I needed to do a little more digging into Arabella's past, even if she didn't like it. Specifically, stuff regarding her mother. I also needed to track that guy down and have a conversation. I had a gut feeling we could help each other out.

"Hang on, princess. I'll fix this." I pulled away from the library but pulled right into the lot, reaching into my bag to find my mobile hot spot as I cruised slowly past the cars. Searching for the woman. The cop-looking guy met my gaze, and I gave him a nod, heading closer to him. I needed to have a chat with him, and then I could start my digging. Right from that lot. No fucking way was I leaving Arabella unprotected.

9

ARABELLA

Twenty-four hours. That was how long I stayed in my little pity-party bubble. A full day without reaching out to my mate, without seeing him other than from afar—because, of course, the man refused to just…disappear—and without a single ounce of happiness in my world. I knew I was overreacting. Mateo had been doing his job when he'd talked to my mother. He'd had no idea about her history or our past. I knew from experience that my mom could charm the scales off a snake, so why my anger seemed centered around Mateo took a long time for me to work through. When it had finally hit me, waking me from a dead sleep, I had nearly cried with relief.

I was mad at Mateo because I had seen him as flawless, but this mistake on his part—this secret kept from me—had turned him into a creature on the level of the rest of us. Flawed, one who made errors in judgments, human. The man wasn't a prince even if he did like calling me princess. He was simply a man who had found his fated partner in me. He would make mistakes, as would I. There was really nothing wrong in his actions.

I just had to figure out how to tell him that and apologize for needing time to work through my emotions.

"She looks like Snow White!"

221

All that apologizing and explaining would have to wait, though. Today was the story hour at the library, and I would soon be dressed in my bright-red skirt with my hair in waves, looking like a fairy-tale princess ready to meet the youngest Kinship Cove residents. Apparently just the hair and makeup met the requirement when I was standing behind the circulation desk.

"Good morning, children," I said, keeping my voice soft and waving as they passed me. As soon as they had disappeared around the corner, I grabbed the bag with my outfit in it from under the counter and hurried to one of the study rooms to change. I didn't make it without running into the two librarians in the house—Matthew and Brittani.

"Hey, Arabella," Matthew said, greeting me with a smile. "Thanks so much for helping out today."

"It's no problem." I clutched the bag a little tighter. "There are children arriving already."

"And I'm here." Margaret—Matthew's bobcat shifter mate—came racing around the corner, a huge smile on her face. "Hi, babe."

"Hi, darling," Brittani said, rolling her eyes as Margaret and Matthew embraced. "You two are worse than Griff and me."

"No one is worse than Griff and you. Where is the big lug, anyway?"

"He should be here soon."

All the couples, the vibe of the mated ones, tugged at me. Made my stomach sink a little more. I missed Mateo. A lot. And there was nothing more that I wanted to do than to see his face. To talk to him. To snuggle into his arms and feel safe once more.

Just an hour. I could give the library one more hour of my time, then be free to find my mate.

"Well, I should get dressed." I nodded to the collected group. "Good to see you, Margaret."

All three of them froze, staring at me as if I'd said something wrong. It took me a solid five seconds to realize I had called the woman by her name instead of Bob. I never used her name. My brain had apparently been broken by this separation from my mate. It needed to end.

Before they could start asking me what was wrong, I hightailed it across the rest of the library to the back study rooms, shutting myself inside one with a sigh.

"Mateo," I whispered, wishing he could hear me. That he could be there to help calm me down. I grabbed my phone from my bag and held it, clutched it to my chest. I hadn't texted Mateo but once since the hotel. That message had been short and to the point—an ending to his constant messaging. *I need time to process things.* He'd stopped reaching out after that, giving me my time. The time I now regretted.

"You're an idiot, Arabella Snow."

I swiped my phone to life and tapped into my messaging app. Just one note. Just a few words to give myself the illusion that we were still okay.

I miss you.

I bit my lip before hitting send, thinking about erasing it. Thankfully, the grown-up part of me took over and tapped that little send icon before I could erase those three words. She also tucked that phone back into our bag and yanked out my dress for the day. The red dress my mother had made for me. The one that many people saw as me trying to be Snow White even though that princess had never worn red. The one based on something so much worse than a hunted princess.

I donned the red skirt, swaying as I had since I'd been a child and had worn the first of many wide red skirts with dark edges. Skirts that flared when I spun and danced. Skirts that my mother made specifically to remind everyone that we were the Gunness family, descendants of the Lonely Hearts Killer. Children, grandchildren, and great-grandchildren of a woman who had escaped prosecution through fire.

Red for blood, darkened edges for the fire that had set Bella free when she'd faked her own death.

The skirt really had no place around children, but they'd never seen the negativity of it. They only saw a pretty dress on a woman who looked a lot like Snow White, and so my princess persona had been born. Bringing good to something so negative.

But I really needed to burn the skirt at some point and have something more appropriate made if I was going to keep being involved with little kids.

"Deep breath. It's princess time." I closed my eyes and thought about happy things. About my birds at home and the plants that made my space so lush, about the feel of a light drizzle on my face. About the man who had stolen my heart and wrecked my body for even the thought of anyone else. I thought about how much I loved my mate and how I knew he would be there for me now that I was ready to talk to him. I owed him an apology, but I knew he'd show up. We had our happily ever after to get to, after all. "Let's do this."

I walked out of the study room, leaving my bag, my phone, and my other clothes inside, and headed straight for the children's area of the library. I had my smile on, my hands soft, and my pace slow. I worked my hips with every step to make sure my skirt danced around my ankles the way it had been intended to. I was ready to be princess Snow White.

At least until I actually made it to the children's section.

I froze as I entered the open space, hearing the children yell and chatter from their spots on the rug but not truly seeing them. My eyes were locked on the woman across the room. The one glaring at me from the stacks. My mother.

My entire body went ice-cold, my inner cat yowling and scratching to come out so we could escape. So we could hide in her smaller form. I knew better than to shift, though. My mother was also a Siamese cat shifter, and she'd always been faster than I had been. If I shifted and ran, she would likely overtake me. And that was not something these children needed to see.

The children.

"Good morning, young ones," I said, pasting on my brightest smile and doing my best to keep my voice calm even as I fell apart inside. "I heard there might be some storytelling today. Is that right?"

A gaggle of small voices chorused a yes, and I nodded.

"Do you mind if I join you? I do love a good tale."

There was a rash of giggles, and a group of little girls began to move and wave me over. Inviting me into their circle. One brave little girl stood right up amid her friends.

"You can sit with us, Snow White."

I sent her a warm smile and took a grand total of two steps in her direction when my mother decided to do what she did best. Ruin things.

"You idiot children. That woman shouldn't be called Snow White. She should be known as Snow Red, the beautiful daughter bathed in the blood of her great-grandmother's suitors."

I froze, raising my eyes to meet hers. The entire room went silent and still, parents looking worriedly from her to me, children staring with wide eyes and open mouths. My mother began to move around the edge of the circle, stalking me. Hunting me. I mimicked her movements, trying to keep her across from me. Wishing the children would somehow disappear so they wouldn't be caught in the middle of whatever was about to happen. As I came around the side of the circle that left me facing the entrance to the children's section, I spotted my coworkers. I took one second to focus on Brittani, standing off toward the back of the room, looking confused. Griff, her mate, appeared beside her, his sharp eyes capturing every detail, it seemed. I really wished they would step in, somehow convince the parents to leave. Immediately.

But as my mother basically leaped across the circle of youth and raced right up into my face, I knew that wasn't about to happen. They were out of time.

"Arabella," she said, my name sounding oddly like a threat. "You have been a hard one to find."

"Perhaps I didn't want to be found, Mother."

I caught Matthew waving the children from the circle and guiding them to the front of the library, so I planted my feet, making sure my mother's view didn't reveal that. The woman liked an audience for her torture of me. Hopefully, she wouldn't get one.

"Hiring that private investigator was probably my most brilliant idea ever. You know him, right?" She shifted her weight back a little, a cruel smile spreading across her harsh face. "Mateo. I saw you with him the other day. You two looked...cozy."

I held my ground, keeping my head up. "Perhaps you should have said hello then."

Her smile grew. "Oh, dear Arabella. There weren't enough people to put on a show then. Or have you forgotten how much I like to make sure everyone knows what a disappointment you are?"

I shot a glance over her shoulder, making sure Matthew had done his job before letting my own smile loose.

"Looks like you failed at that this time."

My mother spun, her mouth falling open as she took in a mostly empty room. I had a moment of pure joy at my victory over her before she spun back around and a deep fear took over. She looked madder than I'd ever seen her, and that was saying something.

"You little bitch. You don't deserve to be able to hide from the truth. All these years, I've built on the legacy your great-grandmother started, and you throw it away."

"I don't want to be part of a legacy that honors a murderer."

"She was a determined woman with—"

"She was nothing but a killer who wasn't smart enough not to get caught," I said, raising my voice to talk over her. Not caring about the respect she normally demanded. I was done being the quiet daughter.

My mother froze, obviously stunned to have been yelled at. That didn't last nearly long enough, though. Not even enough seconds for me to take a step back, which was my mistake. One second, my mother stood still and staring. In the next, she was in motion. Swinging hard as she growled in her cat's rumble. As she put all her weight into her slap. Her hand landed solidly on my cheek, sending my face sideways, but it wasn't the weight of her hit that hurt. It was the sharp sear of her claws cutting into my flesh.

I wobbled back a step, regaining my footing and bringing my fingers to my cheek. When I pulled them away, they were covered in blood. Red liquid that stained my blouse and fell to the floor, dripping at my feet. I was bleeding right there in the library.

And that was pretty much when all hell broke loose.

MATEO

Kinship Cove was too small, too cute and quaint, to have been prepared for a bull shifter on a mission. I raced through the streets, passing cars in oncoming lanes and running every stop sign and red light I could. I'd spent all afternoon acquiring information about Arabella's mother, the last bit having sent me on this breakneck trek back across town. The woman's cell phone had been pinging against a tower just outside Kinship Cove. For two days.

She'd been stalking Arabella for two solid days, and I hadn't known about it.

I whipped around a corner, tires squealing, and stormed toward the library. "Fucking photo."

Because that had to be what had set the old woman off. She'd seen it —the local reporter had put up a story about the Kinship Cove farmers market and had included the picture he'd taken of the moment Arabella and I had met. That picture had hit the AP wires. She must have seen it somehow. Maybe she checked anything that had the name Arabella in it. Maybe she had just happened across it. I couldn't be sure, but the details didn't matter. She was here, and Arabella was not with me.

"Don't let me down, Griff." Two minutes. I would be at the library in two minutes. Griff was there—a cop with a solid history and knowledge of Arabella's past. I'd filled him in before I'd left the library parking lot. I wouldn't have left her at all, but that phone record had been difficult to get. And costly. I'd needed to move some money around to buy access to it. I'd put my trust in the cop to keep Arabella safe while I was gone, and that had paid off. I'd gotten a text just as I'd looked over the start of the report and seen where she'd been, seen how badly I'd messed up.

Trouble in the library.

I'd known it was Arabella's mother immediately. It'd had to be. I'd rushed out of the diner, where I'd made the handoff, and jumped in my car immediately. Griff was good—a solid cop—but his attention would be focused more on keeping his own mate safe since she was likely also in the building. I couldn't blame him, but that meant my girl needed *me*. Right then.

I screamed to a stop on the sidewalk in front of the library and jumped from my car. Parents with crying children in their arms rushed past me, all looking slightly terrified. I ran faster, absolutely praying to every aspect of fate I'd ever been taught about to let my girl be safe. I would take care of her—just give me the seconds I needed to get there.

It was as I slid through the turn from the entrance hall into the children's library area that I saw it. My mate stood tall and proud, her head up and that luscious black hair cascading down her back. An older woman, one who looked remarkably like my Arabella, stood before her. The two seemed to be speaking calmly even if their postures were filled with anger, and for just a split second, I thought maybe I'd overreacted. But then the old lady raised her hand and slapped my mate across the face. It wasn't the hit itself that enraged my inner beast or the way the red skirt flared when Arabella spun from the blow. My bull wasn't happy but had control of his temper in that moment. It was when he spotted the blood dripping down our mate's cheek that he lost his ever-loving mind. One second, I was fully human and in control. The next...

Well...

Don't mess with the bull—you'll get the horns.

Every ounce of control I'd spent my life building snapped in that instant. The tattered shreds of the clothing I'd been wearing went flying as my bull exploded from my body, and the deep, threatening roar issuing from his chest nearly shook the world around us. Both women turned to stare at us, one looking terrified and the other relieved. *That's right, princess. I'm here.*

I paced forward, not running, keeping my head low and my horns forward. Watching Arabella's mother retreat. That was a smart move on her part. Not smart enough, obviously, but something. That put space between her and my mate.

"She's all yours, Mateo." Griff nodded my way even as he pulled his mate Brittani away from the action. I caught Matthew the librarian and his mate Margaret also heading away from the scene of what was about to be a crime. Good. No one needed to see me lose my cool.

I marched forward, whipping my head back and forth. Making sure old Lucy saw the horns that were coming for her. She saw them, all right. She also apparently had no idea how enraged a bull could become.

"Stop that right now," she said, sounding far more sure of herself than I thought she should be. I huffed and took two more steps forward as she retreated one. "Arabella. Tell your friend to stop this insanity. I am *your mother.*"

I paused for a moment, one leg in the air, and gave Arabella a look. She stared right back at me, slowly slipping deeper into the stacks. Trying to escape. With blood dripping down her cheek and a stained blouse, she looked oddly at peace. Fierce but accepting. Done with this.

"No, Mother. I will not." And then she gave me a single nod.

My attention immediately shifted back to Lucy. I huffed and snorted, pawing at the floor with my head down and my horns up. My mate had given me the okay.

Game on.

11

ARABELLA

The phrase "bull in a china shop" had obviously been coined by someone who had never seen a bull in a library.

"Arabella!" my mother screeched before shifting to her cat form right as Mateo charged for her. She ran into the stacks, giving Mateo something to chase after. And chase he did. Those wooden cases were no match for my big, strong bull shifter mate. They exploded as he slammed his way through them, my mother racing across the tops and jumping from shelf to shelf just a few feet in front of him in her efforts to escape his wrath. The books were not so agile and spry—they flew through the air, becoming projectiles and landing just like bombs in the battle between the cat and the bull. The one I really wanted Mateo to win.

The two disappeared into the back of the library, the sounds of their chase continuing. The crashing, the booming, the bull roars. At least until a weird sort of stillness fell over the space. A quiet I hadn't been prepared for. I listened hard, even leaning toward where the two had rushed off to, wanting so badly to know what was going on but too afraid to risk walking back there. At least, not until I heard what sounded like the groan of a frustrated animal. Or maybe an injured one.

"Mateo." I shifted immediately, letting my clothes fall to the floor and taking to my cat form before running for my mate. I had no idea if he'd be able to tell the two of us apart—my mother and I looked alike in all forms—but I had to get to him. Had to make sure he was okay. I couldn't be bothered by the fact that my mother and I had the same fur color with the same points.

I slid around a corner and came face-to-face with my mate. He had books impaled on his horns, the paper and cardboard no match for their sharp ends but weighing down his head. He struggled with the load, shifting his head back and forth, obviously trying to dislodge the books. I crept closer, knowing I could help if I could just get close enough. If I could just—

There was no disguising the moment he saw me. His enraged huff and bellow had me cowering, and the way he shook his head made me want to run. But I couldn't—my mate needed help. I just had to make sure he figured out the cat coming toward him was me and not my mother. If I could slip close enough, he should have been able to sniff me, but that wasn't possible. Not without endangering myself. I had to do this the hard way.

I stopped in the middle of the aisle, took a seat, and I mewled at him. Sat down right there and stared at him as I called to him again, adding in a purr at the end. He'd met me in my cat form. He'd heard me purr. Hopefully Mateo still had enough control over his bull to make sense of the show I was putting on for him.

My mate was a good man even as a bull. He visibly calmed when I sat down, huffing and sniffing deeper even from down the aisle. He ended up approaching slowly, calmly, his big snout breathing me in with every step. He stopped right before me, towering over me and scenting me. I looked up into his deep brown eyes and did the riskiest thing I'd thought of since running away from home. I lifted a paw and placed it on his wet snout, meowing softly to him. When he made a sound almost like a moan, I took another chance and head-butted him. He breathed out what sounded like a sigh of relief as I began to purr.

That was the moment my mother decided to make her presence known once more. She jumped from the top of a bookcase, landing on me and rolling me away from Mateo. Howling, hissing, slashing at me with her claws. Mateo huffed and started to charge again, but there was nothing he could do. We were too tangled together, too close for such a big beast to come between us. I knew the only way to get out of this was to separate myself from my mother, which meant going on the offensive. Something I had never done.

It's for your mate.

Yes, it was. I had to fight off my mother to help my mate. That thought was one heck of a motivator.

With a yowl that screeched through the air, I clawed at my mother and bit any part I could reach. She jerked as if surprised but didn't let up, coming for me with every swipe possible. It took me three lunges at her to finally bite her ear hard enough for her to retreat even an inch. The second she released me from her claws, I raced for Mateo. He lowered his head, and I jumped on, before he raised it again and hollered his displeasure with the other cat in the aisle. I settled myself atop his skull, right between those book-covered horns, likely looking like some sort of goddess cat with tomes of knowledge floating around her.

If anyone saw this, they wouldn't believe their eyes.

Mateo charged with me riding along, his heavy feet making the shelves shake and the books crash around us. Wearing his crown of books. He chased my mother down the aisle and toward the front door of the library. I worried for a few seconds that she'd escape, run back to Indiana to turn up again in the future. To rattle my life once more just for the fun of it. I should have known Mateo was too smart to let that happen.

My mate bellowed as he galloped, initiating a coordinated event I hadn't seen coming. Obviously, neither had my mother, who raced across the rotunda likely thinking she was going to run right out the front doors. Instead, she fell right into a trap set by Brittani and her mate, Griff. One second, my mother had been running across the floor toward the door to escape, and the next, she'd been lifted into what looked like a fishing net with Griff holding the ropes and wrestling the contained cat to the floor. It was actually somewhat…comical.

And by the looks of my library teammates staring with wide eyes and slack jaws at the sight before them, that wasn't the only funny thing happening. Guess it wasn't every day they got to see a bull in the library with books covering his horns and a cat sitting on top of his head.

"I wasn't expecting this," Margaret said, her voice breaking the heavy silence.

Brittani just shrugged. "That woman messed with the bull. She's lucky she didn't get the horns."

"The books got the horns instead." Margaret stepped closer to Mateo, looking downright fearful. "Do you need some help with that?"

Mateo ducked down, giving his permission, though I kept my eyes on the two women who came to relieve him of his burden. I may have trusted them, but this was my mate they were touching. Each woman moved slowly and carefully, never disturbing my mate. Never taking more liberty than they should have. I appreciated the help they offered him and the respect they showed me in their care.

I still didn't like them touching my mate's horns, though.

"Got her, Mateo," Griff said, holding up the net from across the rotunda and making the women with the gored books in their arms spin around. "I never could stand it when people made money off others' suffering. Usually there was nothing I could do about it, but this time, I've got assault and battery charges to file. Maybe even attempted murder depending on what we find in her possession."

Brittani sighed, glancing around the library and running her fingers over the gored books in her arms. "I know this needed to happen and am thrilled you're safe, Arabella, but I wasn't quite prepared for this mess."

She reached up and tugged a book off Mateo's horn, a little rougher than before. More distracted, it seemed. My cranky mate jerked and grunted, but my boss just shook her head.

"We're going to need to shut down for the week to get everything back to rights." She sighed again and tugged the last book from Mateo's horns before giving me a small smile. "I really am happy you're safe. You've got a brave mate there."

Matthew walked up to us, stopping behind his Margaret, both looking a little shell-shocked. He tossed a couple robes over Mateo's broad back. "There's an empty server room down the hall to the right. Just look for the double doors. I think that'll work to give you both some privacy."

Without a sound, Mateo turned and walked in the direction Matthew had indicated, taking me with him. Thankfully free of the impeding horn decorations. Once we reached the room, he pushed open the doors with his horns, allowing us inside. I jumped off his head as he backed into the doors to close them, putting a little space between us for our shifts. There were no sounds verbalized, no words spoken or communication attempted. There was simply us alone, shifting human at the same time.

We ended up on the floor in front of each other, both of us naked and raw from what we'd just been through. Both of us shaking but not from the cold floor. It was Mateo who found words first.

"Arabella, I am so sorry—"

"I'm the one who should be sorry. I never should have cut you off from me. Of course you weren't trying to hurt me." I sniffed, shaking harder. Needing so much from him. "I've missed you so much. Will you hold me?"

Without a word, he reached and grabbed me, yanking me into his lap and wrapping me up in his arms. Tangling our bodies together as he finally whispered, "Never. I would never hurt you."

I snuggled into him, breathing a sigh of relief even as I collected my words for the hard part. Telling truths you'd kept hidden for years wasn't an easy feat. "She lies and manipulates. She's not some nice old lady missing her daughter."

"I know that now."

"She was so horrible to me."

"I know that too. Griff will help press the charges on her. And if that doesn't work to keep her away from you, I'll take care of it."

"I don't want you exposed to her. She'll twist everything—"

"And I'll untwist it. No one will come between me and my mate. Period." He kissed the top of my head and slipped a robe over my shoulders. "Rest for a bit, my princess. I think we both need a few minutes to calm ourselves."

He was right—we did need some time to just be. To feel the warmth of each other's skin melding together. I stayed wrapped in his arms for as long as I thought was reasonable, breathing him in. Relaxing enough to stop shaking.

Finally, though, I sighed. "I guess we should go out there and help them start to deal with the mess we made."

"No." He tugged my robe around me as I sat up, running a soft finger down the cheek my mother had scratched so viciously. "You've had a horrible day. Not one person out there would blame us for taking the afternoon to go home and recover."

That actually sounded amazing. "You'll stay with me?"

"Every single second."

I nodded, clasping his hand. We rose to our feet, and I grabbed his robe, placing it over his shoulders as he'd done with mine. He tugged the garment closed, keeping his eyes on me. Both of us lost to the other. Needing time alone.

"Let's go," he whispered before dropping down to place a soft kiss on my injured cheek. "That blood is making me anxious."

I reached as if to cover my cheek. "I can wash it—"

"No," he said, gently moving my hand away from the injured skin. "I'll do it. Once we're home and you're safe, I'll take care of you."

He squeezed my hand, and we walked out of the server room in our matching robes, both of us quiet and focused forward. Matthew and Margaret stood in the rotunda of the library with Brittani beside them. There was no sign of Griff, which allowed me to relax just a little. If he was gone, that meant my mother was no longer in the building. Something I hadn't even realized I'd been stressed about.

Mateo's hand tightened around mine as we approached my coworkers. "I'm going to take her home. She needs some time."

It was Brittani who nodded. "Of course. Take as much time as you need, Arabella."

"I'll come in tomorrow," I said, hearing the quiver in my voice as I was sure they did. "To help clean up. I'll be here."

"*We'll* be here," Mateo said, squeezing my hand a little harder. Reassuring me. "It's my mess."

"A worthwhile mess," Margaret said with a nod before looking my way, seeming almost excited. "I can't believe you're related to *the* Belle Gunness. The Lonely Hearts Killer."

I shrugged. "I don't know that I truly am, but that's the legend of my family."

"Just go with it," she said with an almost dismissive wave. "It makes you infinitely cooler in my eyes, even if you do tend to call me Bob."

I laughed, unable not to. "Maybe I'll stop."

"You don't have to." Her smile turned softer, more supportive and concerned. "Rest for a day or two. You need it."

I nodded, giving Mateo's hand another squeeze. He took my cue without issue, walking us toward the front doors without another word. He tugged at his robe the entire way to his car, trying his darnedest to keep the fabric closed around his body. When I was finally in the vehicle, safe in the space with the man I trusted more than any other, I sighed.

"We should stop at the motel to get your clothes."

He threw the vehicle into gear—having never turned it off when he'd arrived, apparently—and glanced my way. "I want you home."

"And I want *you* home. With me. In *our* home."

He looked my way, his forehead furrowed. "Are you sure about that?"

"Yes. So long as you think you can put up with my plants and birds."

He sighed, quiet for a moment as he drove toward the motel. "This may be a reaction to the traumatic event you just lived through."

"It may be, but trauma didn't make me fall in love with you."

He grabbed my thigh, squeezing my flesh with his big hand. "Love you too, princess."

"Then stop arguing with me. We'll collect your things, and you'll move in with me."

He nodded once. "Yes, ma'am."

And with that, he slammed his foot on the gas and took off, racing across town. Apparently anxious to get our life started. To begin our own happily ever after.

To wash away the nastiness of the day and begin again.

EPILOGUE

ARABELLA

Being pregnant with a bull shifter's baby was not my idea of a good time.

"I've got you," Mateo said as he lifted me out of the car and set me on my feet. "Got it?"

"Yeah." I sighed and rubbed my hand over my extended tummy, having never been so uncomfortable in my life. "I need a restroom. Your son is having a blast kicking my bladder."

"I believe that would be your daughter."

Ah, the never-ending argument. "Nope. This child is a total boy. I have no doubt."

Mateo took my hand, raising it to his mouth to place a soft kiss on the back. "We'll see."

I would have argued more—it seemed to be our latest pastime—but I was too tired, and I really did need to use the restroom. The child in my uterus gave my bladder no breaks. I, of course, was thrilled for every movement and sign of life and already loved the little one with all my heart, but I was getting really tired of being beaten up from the inside every day.

Just a couple more weeks.

Mateo escorted me into the French bistro that had become our absolute favorite place to eat then led me to the restroom at the back. Ever the gentleman, he kissed my hand again before letting me go, keeping guard in the hallway. I'd never felt safer than I did with my mate watching over me, even when it seemed ridiculous for him to be doing so.

After I washed my hands, ready to return to my mate and our table, I caught a glimpse of myself in the full-length mirror. I stood up straighter and turned to the side, taking the opportunity to really see myself. I was much bigger than before I had met Mateo—pregnancy and water retention were not friends of mine—but I'd never looked happier, even without a smile. When people told me I was glowing, I believed them because I *felt* as if I glowed. With my mother in jail awaiting trial and a new circle of friends in Kinship Cove, plus the absolute gift of having Mateo in my bed every single night? Of being mated to the kindest, sweetest man on the planet? I had never felt so blessed.

I jerked as another kick rocked me from the inside. My hand immediately fell to my belly, and I rubbed as close to the spot as I could get.

"Easy, young man," I whispered, knowing Mateo would have immediately argued that our child was a girl if he could hear me. "Give your momma an hour to have dinner, then you can go back to roughhousing in there."

Not that he would listen.

With one last sigh and pat to my belly, I hurried out of the restroom. I spotted Mateo at the end of the hallway immediately, my brave mate always keeping an eye out for me. My smile came unbidden, my joy a physical force that had me moving faster so I could touch him once more. I could imagine no stronger love than that between the three of us—me, my mate, and our unborn child. He cared for us, protected us, and spoiled us silly every chance he got. I loved him, pure and simple.

My mate returned my happy expression, his eyes practically twinkling.

"I can't get enough of the way you smile at me when you see me from across the room," he said before placing a hand on my lower back to guide me, bringing his other to my belly for just a moment. "You two okay?"

And there it was—the concern. My heart practically swelled. "I love you, Mateo."

His smile grew, and he leaned down to plant a kiss on my lips. Not a soft or sweet one—no, ma'am. This kiss set my body on fire and made me want to go home so we could be alone. Immediately.

Which was not part of the plan for the evening. Not yet, at least.

Eventually, Mateo broke the kiss, moaning just loud enough for me to hear. "I love you so much, my beautiful mate. Are you ready for dinner, or should I take you home and make you my meal?"

Choices, choices. The baby chose that moment to kick again, reminding me that I needed real food. "Dinner first. Home later."

"Whatever makes you happy." With that, he led me across the room to our usual table. A waiter approached as Mateo helped me into my chair, already bringing sparkling water for the two of us. Once seated, we took a long moment to relax and look out over the mountain views. The restaurant overlooking the Cove may have been the fanciest in town, but this was my favorite. Mateo's too. This had become our spot. A thought Mateo must have been having right along with me.

"I love this place."

I sighed, reaching for his hand. "Me too. We've spent so much time here over the last year."

He nodded, still clinging to my hand. "What are we going to do when our daughter joins the party?"

"I guess we'll have to ask if they have high chairs…for *our son*."

Mateo laughed, the sound big and booming. The argument never stopped, though I supposed it would once the baby arrived. I couldn't wait to meet him—because I was absolutely certain it was a boy inside me—but if by some chance of fate, they ended up being a girl, I'd be just as thrilled. No matter what, I had a man by my side who would love both of us to the ends of the earth.

And apparently a waiter who had overheard us. "Ah, Mr. and Mrs. Torres. Of course we have high chairs. Our head chef is a mother and is fully prepared to welcome the newest Torres member to one of her tables when the time comes."

I laughed at Mateo's surprised face, shrugging when he looked my way. "Guess that takes care of it. We're all set to return here once the baby is born."

My mate's grin reappeared, spreading wide. "I can't wait."

I dropped a hand to my belly, staring into the eyes of the man I loved. The man the fates had chosen for me to be my perfect match. They had been so right.

Happily ever after, indeed.

Stand-alone stories of characters first met in the Feral Breed Motorcycle Club series. Featuring cage fighters, dragon shifters, second chances, and young love.

Claiming His Chance

Claiming His Prize

Claiming His Grace

THE GATHERING TALES

Come and enjoy tales from the biggest shifter event of the year as wolves from around the country fall in lust, in love, and in fate at The Gathering.

The Gathering Tales

THE DEVIL'S DIRES

There's no escaping a Dire Wolf on the hunt…

Savage Surrender

Savage Sanctuary

Savage Seduction

Savage Silence

Savage Sacrifice

Savage Security

Savage Salvation

ABOUT THE AUTHOR

A storyteller from the time she could talk, Ellis grew up among family legends of hauntings, psychics, and love spanning decades. Those stories didn't always have the happiest of endings, so they inspired her to write about real life, real love, and the difficulties therein. From farmers to werewolves, store clerks to witches—if there's love to be found, she'll write about it. Ellis lives in the Chicago area with her two daughters and a German Shepherd that never leaves her side.

When she's not writing paranormal romance, Ellis Leigh can be found writing romantic suspense as Kristin Harte and erotic shorts as London Hale.

Sign up for Ellis Leigh's newsletter for release information, promotions, swag opportunities, and early access to free reads!

www.ellisleigh.com/newsletter.

www.ingramcontent.com/pod-product-compliance
Lightning Source LLC
Chambersburg PA
CBHW060929190726
48286CB00002B/685